MOSCOW
RACETRACK

MOSCOW RACETRACK

ANATOLY GLADILIN

Translated by Robert P. Schoenberg and Janet G. Tucker

OVERLOOK DUCKWORTH
New York • Woodstock • London

This edition first published in the United States in 2007 by
The Overlook Press, Peter Mayer Publishers, Inc.
Woodstock & New York

WOODSTOCK:
One Overlook Drive
Woodstock, NY 12498
www.overlookpress.com
[for individual orders, bulk and special sales, contact our Woodstock office]

NEW YORK:
141 Wooster Street
New York, NY 10012

LONDON:
Gerald Duckworth & Co. Ltd.
90-93 Cowcross Street
London EC1M 6BF

Copyright © 1990 by Ardis Publishers

Library of Congress Cataloging-in- Publication Data

Gladilin, Anatolii Tikhonovich.
[Bolshoi begovoi den. English]
Moscow racetrack / Anatoly Gladilin ; translated by Robert
P. Schoenberg and Janet G. Tucker.
p.cm.
Translation of: Bol'shoi begovoi den'.
I. Title.
PG3481.L24B613 1990   891.73'44—dc   20 90-36728

Book design and typeformatting by Bernard Schleifer
Manufactured in the United States of America
ISBN-10 1-58567-903-8 / ISBN-13 978-1-58567-903-4
10 9 8 7 6 5 4 3 2 1

A novel with Prologue and Epilogue (the trotters' names), private scenes from the life of the Teacher (the principal hero), historical articles by the Teacher, excerpts from "The Rules of the Moscow Racetrack," monologues by people and horses, appearances in the grandstands by leaders of the Party and government, and the aggravation of the international situation and interruption of the action of the novel by outsiders.

INSTEAD OF A PROLOGUE

(Notes on the Program)

1. IDEOLOGUE—bay stallion out of Fickle by Lou Hanover, best time—2:08.5, most recent—2:09.6. At one time fleeced this crew as much as he wanted. Definitely has several seconds in reserve. But after all, the jockey, Petya (navy blue silks with yellow stripes, red sleeves and red helmet) is first cretin at the Central Moscow Racetrack. Well, maybe not the very first—he's neck-and-neck with Anton for the First Cretin Prize. But see, Ideologue is by Lou Hanover, an American! At the derby, almost all the entries are Americans. . . . The All-Union Grand Prix isn't so bad. One hope lies with Mom-Fickle. I'll be damned if I'm going to bet even a ruble on a horse with a name like that. And Mom—Fickle—is suspicious, and there's enough ideologues for me outside the walls of the racetrack. It can't be denied, a new Suslov's been found. So I swear, not a ruble.

2. LIANA—bay mare out of Brass by Apex Hanover, 2:09.4 and most recent performance-2:12.6 in first place.

A finish horse. Mad dash. The jockey, Kolya (black silks, white helmet and stripes on the sleeves), has spared the mare, hasn't been beating the seconds out of her, and he almost beat Othello himself once. Need to start asking and have a look at the warmups. Liana, if she comes in in just one heat, will pull about fifteen rubles in single, but in the long run, way over a hundred. "Dreams, dreams, where is your sweetness?" (A.S. Pushkin, but not about Liana).

3. CHEREPET—bay mare out of Miracle Melody by Progress. 2:10.6 and close to that-2:10.8 in third place.

The jockey, Zhenya (lilac silks-the color of ladies' underwear), almost won last year's derby. You can expect every dirty trick in the book from him. Has he been hiding the mare? All the same, I won't be betting on him.

4. CHUG-A-LUG—bay mare out of Hamletia by Hurricane. 2:10.8.

What kind of scum is this? Where did she come from? From the Kalinin Racetrack. . . . Out-of-towners sometimes bring surprises—in thousand-ruble payoffs. Need to have a look at the warmups. The jockey is Samsonov (pink silks, red helmet). But the Moscow crooks won't let him; they'll ride by on the mare's legs.

5. OTHELLO—chestnut stallion out of Oxana by Lou Hanover. Best and most recent time is 2.09.4. Always comes in first.

The jockey, Mosya (yellow silks and cap), has never done anything special before, but he works well enough with Othello—first class, no dirty tricks. Really, the deal is obvious—put all your money on Othello in single. . . . You'll get two-fifty for each ticket. The silly public (you included) will be looking for a dark horse. It's either Othello without any variations at all, or . . . you'll never guess. Ah, Othello, Othello—you see, I was playing him a year ago, before anybody knew him. He'd come in then pulling thirty rubles in single. And the stallion's a beauty, a chestnut with a white star on his forehead. A fighter. When he runs, it's a sight to behold. Well, promise yourself that you'll only bet on Othello! Is that decided? Okay, let's look around some more.

6. GOUACHE—dark bay mare out of Little Handful by Apex Hanover. 2.09.9.

An out-of-towner from Kharkov. And her time's not bad. Well? But I've seen her in the grave. I'm not even going to look.

7. WHEAT TOP—bay stallion out of Peel by Lou Hanover. 2.08.7 and 2.11. In fourth.

Last time the jockey, Gunta (yellow silks with green stripes, yellow helmet), clearly wasn't pushing. And she was right. She's not fool enough to wear the horse out before the derby. Gunta is my love; I always play her. And Wheat Top II is an excellent stallion. But against Othello? The devil sure does love to play tricks! They always pay Gunta well because she's a dame. No, I've just got to play Wheat Top. It's like this: if Gunta decides to win, my wallet will start weeping, because Gunta will start to get nervous, her hands will shake, the horse'll get revved up and break stride. Gunta wins when she's not risking anything, on the "daring do" principle. Then she rushes headlong, and who's going to hold her back? How do you ride against a dame, how do you set the pace when she doesn't know what'll happen herself? And when

Gunta makes a drive, the male jockeys let it slip right through their fingers. . . . So, I'll be betting some on Wheat Top.

8. PRECIPICE—black stallion out of Opera by Bill Hanover. 2.08.4 (Perm).

The jockey is Lipin—"The Fake"—(black silks, brown sleeves and navy blue helmet). Horrible colors. The name doesn't inspire confidence. And the time, posted in Perm, is more than likely a fake. How can some Precipice, the off-spring of Opera—and the Perm Opera yet—win the derby? That kind of thing just doesn't happen. Then again, anything can happen at the race track.

9. WHITE SAIL—chestnut stallion out of Exchange by Parole. 2.11.

When did he post that time? I don't recall. The jockey, Vanechka (green silks with yellow checks, white helmet), is a well-known crook. He hides them and hides them and then he'll pull any crew. There's something fishy about White Sail. What's the stallion's background? The sire, Parole, was 2.07.9; the grandsire, Ornament, was 2.09.04. The dam, Exchange, nothing special, but she's by Gesture—the Russian recordholder (1:59.6). Hmm, yes, it's a mystery. On one hand, there's not a chance. But once Vanya's entered a horse in the derby, he's probably hoping for something. That guy doesn't ride just for the fun of it. Why should he expose the horse for nothing? What kind of reserve has Sail got? Three seconds? Five? Could he really be up to a 2:06? Then the derby's his.

Let's put it all together. Nine horses. And it looks like you're ready to play four of them. But you see, you've still got to guess the "edge," that is, guess the horse from the previous race.

If Othello comes in—you'll wager more than you'll get. If some dark pestilence like Chug-a-Lug pushes herself—then you're out on your ass.

Maybe you could play them all? The height of stupidity. Just Othello? And Wheat Top? White Sail?

And what if Othello suddenly breaks stride, Gunta gets scared of Wheat Top, Liana slips, White Sail just doesn't get going and Ideologue wins in some simple way, just moving from place to place? And so, once again there's no clearcut plan. However, if the race track wants to use you, it'll use you like a sweetheart.

Tomorrow's the Grand Prix. They've scheduled eighteen heats and races. From one in the afternoon until seven in the evening. You need to get there an hour and a half before the starting time for the warmups. So it's almost an eight-hour workday.

No matter how much you hustle and economize, your capital amounts to eighteen rubles. Not a fat wad. A tenner, a fiver and a brand new three-spot. (I'll hide that in my other pocket—E.R.—emergency ration.) It's a good thing I scraped that eighty kopecks together for admission. Bet a ruble a race? You'll last to the finish, but you'll never guess it exactly right. Hold out for the Grand Prix? Play three heats, six rubles a heat? You won't be able to hold out; you'll take the plunge on the very first race. (You'll say that you're going to get lucky all of a sudden and round out your capital—that's how a losing streak gets started.)

Othello, Wheat Top, Liana, White Sail. Undecided about Ideologue. Cherepet? Damn him! In any case, we'll take a

look at Chug-a-Lug. How about tying them all to the favorite
of the previous race and hedging with a dark one? . . . And
where do you get that much money?

All right, even a short sword is enough for a valiant
knight.

Valiant knight? No, just one of the ten thousand idiots
who'll be shoving his way into the Central Moscow
Racetrack, known to the locals as Fools' Field.

PART ONE

1

PRIVATE LIFE

I WAS JUST ABOUT TO F . . . HER WHEN THE DOORBELL RANG. It could have been anybody: a drinking buddy, the alcoholic neighbor—they might have brought a telegram from the post office—but I sensed right away who'd shown up. And the chick (certainly a cute chick, but no gift from God) buttoned her skirt in a flash and jumped up to the mirror to fix her hair.

The bell again. I inquire through the door and hear Raika's voice. She's flown in on her broom!

I go out to the landing and close the door tight behind me.

There's a slim chance we might get by without a scene. I express interest courteously, but extremely coldly.

"Did something happen?"

"You have a strange way of greeting your guests."

Raika is using the formal word for "you" with me. A week ago, she was in wild hysterics, said it was all over between us—if she saw me on the street, she'd cross to the other side; I wasn't supposed to phone, write or visit—it made her sick to think of all the things that tied us together—she regretted the lost years; said that I was a little coward, a man without honor or conscience, a vile, insignificant character; if I died of anguish and despair without her, it would only be my just desserts, and what's more, she was going to lead a lover to my grave on a summer night, so that right there, on the fresh grass . . . and she was absolutely never ever setting foot in this house again—even if I hanged myself, and from here on in, we're on the formal "you," like outsiders—complete strangers.

Doesn't that sound like it couldn't be clearer? And now she's barged in on me without any warning, not even a phone call; naturally, she's in full parade dress, in war paint (all she needs, pencilled on and running down, plus a kilogram of Polish powder and half a liter of French perfume)—she squints; her nostrils flare.

"Of course, you aren't alone?"

I've been alone every evening. I've waited. I didn't give a damn anymore. Just today I was honestly going over tomorrow's racing form. This chick called. The same one. I had noticed that she'd had her eyes on me. In the end, am I a free man or what? I dashed to the store—a bottle of wine, a bottle of cognac (for the cachet—General Command Reserve) canned fish, cheese, pelmeni, candy—met the chick at the bus stop, brought her here, and I swear to God, all I wanted was to sit quiet and relax.

Then, it's true, I lost my head and brought out the cognac. I've gotten out of the habit of being with somebody new: she's interested in any story I tell her, not like Raika-the-Rat, who tells me, as she twists her lips, that I'm repeating myself. In a word, I've been recalling my youth; I've gotten carried away, and look, the chick is ready—her eyes are shining, a little smile; that means don't waste time, get her over to the sofa. And now. . . .

"A business meeting," I say. "But it would be better if you didn't come in, Raisa. What did you come for? If you need money. . . ."

I didn't have time to figure out how she pushed me aside (an armored personnel carrier, not a woman) and burst into the apartment, but it started:

"You bastard, you've dragged in a whore—she gets a three-ruble note at three train stations—tops! Get out of here!"

I push Raisa aside and make like the twenty-eight Panfilovs ("We'll put up an indestructible wall of defensive steel; we won't let the enemy through") and try to explain intelligently to the chick that this noisy lady is the town madwoman, broken out of the clinic; pay no attention to her least request.

The chick's face was swimming in red blotches. Raiska's makeup was running in black streams. My hands were all scratched bloody.

I relaxed. Brightened up. . . .

I don't know how long I kept up my defenses. Then Raisa announced that she'd run right out into the street and throw herself under a car. And the chick said that she'd had enough—she was leaving. I jumped up to take her to the bus and shouted to Raisa from the doorway to get the hell out and if she didn't clear out quietly, I'd smash her face.

I put the chick on the bus, and she looked at me like an animal. It had all been for nothing and she'd gotten into a mess.

I go back home, mad with rage. Raisa is lying on the sofa. Her eyes are bulging and her lips are black.

She's poisoned herself. An empty packet of sleeping pills is on the floor. A circus—that's what this is! I've already seen this number. One time she swallowed a whole packet of elenium and slept all day. . . .

"Raika," I say, "aren't you ashamed of yourself? Have you no conscience?"

She came to life at once and started to moan. It turns out that she wanted to obligate me. It turns out that she'd remembered what happened last week—how cruel she was to me, how unfair, and how sad my face had been—and now she's decided to come without calling me, a pleasant surprise, an unexpected pleasure—but she saw that carrion and. . . . Of course, now she understood that it would be wildly inconvenient in front of the chick, that the chick was in no way to blame, and she, Raika, was acting like a clod, and so on and so forth, but her mind went blank. . . .

A howl.

I make her drink several glasses of water and then lead her to the bathroom and lock the door. I listen to her as she throws up, then hiccups, then cries, and again. . . .

She comes staggering out, pale, throws me a tragic look. And at that moment, I'm ready to strangle her with my bare hands—for everything—for what she's doing to both of us. And I feel very sorry for her.

I should drive her out into the street, shouldn't I?

I pour her a glass of cognac. She drinks it down, but she won't eat anything.

In a fascist voice I order her to lie down on the sofa immediately and go to sleep. And me? I'll bed down on the floor. It disgusts me to touch her. Yeah, just like that—good night!

Raika's made the sofa, turned out the light and fallen asleep.

I'm sitting in the kitchen, drinking glass after glass, trying to forget today's nightmare. Three o'clock in the morning. Tomorrow, no, today is already the day of the Big Race. I'm going to have a good head. Fresh! The hell with them all! Who's them? Me and Raika. The devil knows what she's doing with herself. Poor girl! But I don't mean Raika, but the one with the unbuttoned skirt. Screw it now, of course. Too bad it didn't work out.

I hear a quiet whisper from the other room. Raika's calling me. I don't have to go to her. Another glass. But what if she's bad off all of a sudden?

I tiptoe carefully into the room and sit on the edge of the bed. I run my palm over Raika's wet face. She takes my hand. I quickly undress.

THE RACES

First Race. Grand Prix for Three-Year-Olds
Two heats to run. Participation in the second heat not mandatory. Winning places will be allocated by speed and a correctly completed heat. A horse that has lined up for the first heat, stopped by the jockey without valid cause or remaining after the flag, will not be allowed to continue in participation for the prizes. Questions of validity of cause are decided by the panel of judges.

—Excerpt from the Rules

Ah, the first race! How revealing!

I'm scratching my head on my way from my place to the race track (I have to transfer twice) and worry: do I bet on the first race or not?

The most logical thing to do is to pass. After all, the next race is the first heat of the All-Union Grand Prix—"the derby" as they call it at the racetrack. I've got five horses to consider there, what with being undecided about that damn Cherepet. I needed to have a look at them, but how could I when I was late for the warm-ups? (In accordance with the theory of universal baseness, last night was so rough that I barely got up.) I'm still in the subway, while at the same time at the racetrack, "the steeds gallop and gallop, while the huts burn and burn." Of course, it's not huts that are burning, but money.

There are eleven horses in the first race. Of course, "Totoshka," as it's toasted, will cost number seven, the big favorite, His Eminence, a bundle. In single, he'll be knocked down to kopecks. There's no sense in playing. (There is if you bet fifty rubles on His Eminence, but they'll pay about a ruble fifty—and here I'm already stirring in twenty-five. But I don't have fifty rubles.) Put down a ten-spot to get a fiver? And what if His Eminence breaks stride or only runs in the second heat? Then my ten-spot will weep and weep burning tears.

No, if you bet, bet on a double. (That is, tie the first race to the second.) But there again, play from His Eminence to several horses, and you won't get your money back. Othello or Ideologue will come in in the second heat and you'll get less than you put down. Go for broke. With a fiver or three! On Othello or Ideologue. Maybe you'll make a ten-spot. But then Wheat Top out of ancient meanness will come in and you'll be tearing your hair out, wailing, "I was the one who said Wheat Top! And besides, Gunta, my favorite jockey. . . ."

Anyway, what a temptation it is to guess the first double! Right away, "Life will get better, life will get happier" (J. V. Stalin).

Decided. Let's risk it.

I get on the trolleybus at Belorusskaya Station. Half the passengers in the car are shuffling programs: they study, they guess, all gr-r-reat scholars. I put a five-kopeck piece into the cash box and tear off a ticket. The first three numbers are eight, three, and four; the second are three, eight, and six. That means somebody just got a lucky ticket! But I was too late. There's no joy in living. . . .

That settles it: I'm passing on the first race.

There are three entrances to the racetrack. One costs twenty kopecks, another costs forty, and the third costs eighty. The eighty-kopeck entrance is solid, with steps and columns.

One of those columns, probably that one, on the far right, was built with money that I personally dropped in the "Fools' Field"—you might say I've contributed to the development of the fatherland's horse breeding. If you added up all the money I've lost in the last ten years, it would be just what the column cost. Well, maybe it would cover a bunch of bricks and plaster, too. Not to worry, the fatherland's horse breeding can rest easy. It won't go to ruin after me. I'll add the remaining bricks.

There are two rows of cars parked on the little square along the columns. There are a lot of them today: damned gypsy cabbies, crooks, store managers, and vegetable center managers have gathered from all over Moscow. It's all right to be jealous; I used to have a Zaporozhets myself. But after all, cars now cost three or four times as much, and where do people get that kind of money? But don't go to the races—save your money. You'll save—screw that! But crooks bet about thirty rubles every race, and it's nothing. That means they're stealing somewhere else. The racetrack has its own crooks, its own mafia. But those guys aren't riding around in cars. Are they embarrassed or . . . ? How do you explain to the Special Department for the Theft of Socialist Property (OBKhSS) what money the Zhiguli was bought on? I should have their worries . . . but I don't—I'm betting with my own hard-earned money. The racetrack is the only institution in Moscow where, according to the principle of "damned capitalism," sometimes you win—more often you lose, but you maintain the illusion that it all depends on you yourself here—that there's room for private initiative. For several hours, you shut out everything in the world, get nervous, take risks, struggle with the superior strength of the racetrack crooks—and not a solitary sign of Soviet power! For that kind of pleasure, you can even spend a ten-ruble note.

On the steps, a lame old man in a baggy jacket is winking merrily at me—he's selling programs. Programs cost ten kopecks at the kiosk, but you have to stand in a long line of people to get them. There's no queue for the old man, but they go for twenty kopecks. Everybody's got his own business. The cashiers who take admission tickets take twenty kopecks for a program, too. But I usually buy from the old man. Better to let him make money than those fat, rude broads. But today I pass the old man by, waving hello with the program that I bought earlier, on Friday. Catching on, he spreads his hands. It's the day of the big race—everybody wants to "study" the program at home without hassle.

I climb the stairs and remember that most often, when I get my program from the old man, I get lucky. Another bad omen? But the hell with them, these bad omens! The mood's pleasant, the weather's excellent, eighteen races ahead, big purses, lots of surprises, which we, of course, will bear in mind and make use of. You might say you have your whole life ahead of you.

I have a hard time forcing my way through to my box. As usual on prize days, there's a big crowd of non-regulars. Racetrack regulars pick their spot just once and never change it. Another omen. My box fifteen, on the extreme left, hangs out over the forty-kopeck grandstand. The place isn't very convenient—when the horses go past us down the home stretch, they've still got thirty meters to go to the finish gate. When they're running neck and neck, it isn't easy for us to tell just who came in first. Usually there's lots of room in the box, but today . . . my buddies are squeezed into a corner, while the box is occupied by the unfamiliar mugs who paid for chairs. (We don't rent chairs—you have to pay forty kopecks for them—an inexcusable luxury.)

My crew is my racetrack friends. Everybody has his own underground nickname: the fat, puffy old man, a chief specialist at some trust or other, is Coryphaeus; the tall, young engineer-mathematician is the Dandy; the taciturn graduate student with the handsome face and the cold eyes is the Professional. They call me the TEACHER, here.

"Hi guys."

"Hi, you're late for work."

"I'm guilty, guys, I overslept. What kind of race is shaping up?"

CORYPHAEUS (condescendingly): "'I knew my sweetie by his walk. . . .' You'll see. Peony's come out—that means it's the sixth."

THE PROFESSIONAL (through his teeth): "A free double's shaped up in the first two. Put a ten-spot down from His Eminence to Othello."

THE DANDY (passionately): "Your His Eminence is going to lose. Patrician stretched out the last quarter—nothing but a blur."

And they all turn back away from me, look at the track and click their stopwatches.

Patrician—that's interesting. I've been following him for some time—a horse with a reserve. Patrician will probably be out of the running. For him, even with the standouts, that is, with Othello and Ideologue, they'll pay a twenty.

I take the Professional by the sleeve: "Does Patrician stand a chance?"

THE PROFESSIONAL (in his previous manner): "Don't waste your money. I flat out can't see Patrician."

But Coryphaeus reports the most sensational bit of news: it turns out that the tax on every ruble will no longer be twenty-five kopecks, as before, but thirty-three. I'll clarify this for the uninitiated: for every ruble put into the totalizator booth, the government takes twenty-five percent for itself, and starting today, thirty-three. Your winnings are diminished accordingly. That's who the big crook is: the Government—it works without a skeleton key. But where else is there to disappear to? There are no private racetracks in the Soviet Union. They don't call the racetrack "the Mint" for nothing: not only are the stud farms on the racetrack's subsidy, but half of Moscow's theaters as well. I want to ask if they've at least raised the grooms' salaries, but I don't have time. The bell sounds. The participants in the first race are on the track. They ride out to the tune of an old guards' march, sad and beautiful. I don't know what they called it before the Revolution, but I've thought up a new name for it: "Farewell, Money." The jockeys are wearing new silks for the festive occasion (or maybe they just washed them) and the horses are assembled military-style, at short rein.

The crowd has rushed to the booths. Coryphaeus is among the first. We stay to watch what we call false starts.

The reason for the false starts is obvious: the jockeys take off down the straightaway or into the quarter turn, readying their horses for the battle. It seems nothing should be simpler than guessing the winner. You take the time shown by each horse over a fixed distance with a stopwatch and compare. The one with the best, according to this idea, should win. However, it does happen that a horse that quickly takes over and leads the race comes to a standstill at the finish line, and anyone who isn't feeling too lazy can get around him. In the second place, the jockeys know full well that the public is nobody's fool, and they try to "hide" their horses.

There's Kochan stretching Ballet out. His time is so-so. About average for him. If Kochan thinks he has a chance, his chums and buddies will wager a lot on Ballet up at some window, while nobody touches Ballet at the rest of the windows (except maybe some drunk or a crazy dame who's a supporter of the Bolshoi Theater, who winds up in the racetrack by chance). What self-respecting gambler would even bet a ruble on Ballet? After all, half the horses in the race have better speed. But if Kochan false starts the hell out of Ballet, they'll note the time in a second (almost everyone has a stopwatch), and Ballet will be knocked down to kopecks, and then Ballet will be worth ten times less in the event of a win. Naturally, that's not good for Kochan.

A jockey's main enemy—not his rival, his main enemy— is the public. THAT is precisely who the jockey tries to deceive in every way. And for that reason, Kochan never exposes his horse in a false start. See, I know him.

Borya is stretching His Eminence out. Borya has nothing to lose, he's a big favorite; His Eminence hasn't lost in six months. And he might not lose today, either.

The Dandy looks dumbfoundedly at his stopwatch. His Eminence's done the straightaway in twenty-one seconds!

"Hm, yeah! His Eminence is all alone. Nobody to run with."

Coryphaeus shows up and shows us a thickish stack of tickets.

They've beaten His Eminence to death; the booths are breaking apart! They're playing him with the first, fifth and seventh.

That is, they're tying him in with three horses from the

following race—Ideologue, Othello, and Wheat Top. This is just what you could have expected. "They bleed the stand-outs white. . . ." Over the loudspeaker, they've announced: "Three minutes remain until totalizator booths are closed." I send the Dandy to the booth to stand in line. We need to hurry. But the jockeys don't hurry. They usually pull the fastest false starts right before the bell, when the booths are already closing. I start getting nervous, glance at my watch. The Professional, unruffled, snarls:

"Polite's not good enough. Hemlock's a stupid fart, Soloist is going to break stride, but Labyrinth looks good, very good —I believe Pasha's come up with something. Maybe we could hedge with a ruble?"

"No," I state categorically. "Never! As a matter of princi-ple, I don't play Pasha."

Labyrinth really does look good. So I check the program: Labyrinth is by Bill Hanover and out of Azure. The famous Scout is out of Azure. Labyrinth's best time is 2:13. His Eminence's is 2:09. Labyrinth probably has a reserve. But see, Pasha's known to everyone at the racetrack by the nickname, Highwayman—not exactly a crook, but a bandit—he steals in broad daylight. On a big favorite, he loses brazenly, and I think the crowd's whistles only give him pleasure. If the horse just isn't good enough, then he does such a terrible false start that the crowd rushes willy-nilly to play him. But in the race, he runs last and chuckles: he says he's got the ninnies wrapped around his finger. The Professional and I've sworn to each other more than once that we won't buy any more of his bandit tricks.

Three minutes to closing, and still no Patrician. He appears at last. He breezes—straightaway: nineteen seconds.

The Professional's eyes stop moving. In an instant, he bolts out of his spot, and I'm hauling myself along with him into the hall with the booths. Thank God, the Dandy is standing right by the window, but we've still got to push through to him.

"Hey, young man, how dare you shove me!"

That's directed at me. I don't answer, but a cultured address like that grates on the elderly *totoshnik,* and I hear a venomous retort behind my back. "Sheesh, what a bimbo! And you can't push him. This is the racetrack. If you don't want to get shoved, go to the drugstore."

The bell!

Are we too late? . . . But the Dandy manages to stick a handful of money into the booth.

"Who?" he asks without looking around.

"Number four, Patrician!" we shout into his ear.

The Professional dictates his combinations to him: four-one, four-five, four-seven. Two tickets each, at six rubles. The Dandy repeats the Professional's wager. I've got half a second to reflect. I slip the Dandy my three-spot.

"Four-five, four-seven, seven-five. . . ."

The Dandy scrapes up the yellow cardboard tickets, and right then, the window closes with a bang. Whew!

We don't hurry back. Five minutes go by while the horses are forming up and line up behind the starting machine.

"I told you right off," the Dandy babbles, "and you started up with His Eminence. . . . It's a good thing we made it. But the Teacher threw out Ideologue for no reason at all. With Patrician, and for Ideologue, they'll pay about forty rubles. Playing seven-five is mindless, a three-spot, maximum. Well, you'll get yours back."

I don't say anything. To get mine back isn't so bad, either.

But you see, even though I swore off betting on Ideologue, I covered seven-five because . . . when they tried Sinyavsky and Daniel, they gave Sinyavsky seven years and Daniel five. On my very first day at the races, I played seven-five, and I guessed it right. (The psychology of gamblers merits a special investigation.)

The starting machine, a Volga pickup, spreads its steel wings, making a barrier all the way across the track with them. Ten horses form the rank, but Patrician takes the rear.

I'm confused: what's he doing that for?

THE PROFESSIONAL: "Patrician's a horse prone to break stride, and he'll break down in the distance."

THE DANDY: "Vitaly's quite the man; he's not crawling in with the pack."

CORYPHAEUS (amazed): "You guys're crazy! Patrician doesn't stand a chance. Vitaly generally comes in twice a year. I'm telling you—His Eminence is all alone."

It's all clear—Coryphaeus played His Eminence. The combination for two, two and a half rubles is his element. The law's not written for fools. More to the point, it's the other way around: it's only written for fools. But we caught a dark horse. Vitaly seldom wins, but if he really goes, it's a sure thing. And then, Patrician has a mad finish. That means it's all okay, said old man Mokay.

"They're off!"

The Volga pickup folds its wings, scoots to the turn, and then drives off the track.

The pack has formed up tight. Polite breaks stride. The Professional was right—there's no way she cuts it. Ballet breaks stride. It serves him right. Labyrinth has taken the lead, well, obviously, in terror.

Patrician's holding back.

Over the loudspeaker, they announce, "First quarter completed in thirty-one seconds." There's a rumbling in the grandstands. A very fast start.

The horses go into the second turn. Labyrinth is all alone in the lead. Several horses are behind him, His Eminence among them. But Labyrinth picks up the pace.

Half the distance has been covered. Second quarter also thirty-one. And Patrician is just barely shuffling along in last place. That's it. The race is over for us.

The racetrack has started to buzz.

"You scum, Vitaly, reptile, trash!" yells the Dandy. "He specialized in cheating!"

"Yeah, a regular no-goer, your Patrician," Coryphaeus laments, and I've been burned like a Swede at Poltava. A twenty—under the dog's tail. His Eminence is a beaten horse. Pashenka's really trained a horse. What was his time? Two point oh four?

"Bandit did a good job," the Professional strains through his teeth. "He really took them to the cleaners. They absolutely didn't touch him at the booths. He'll pull a hundred rubles. I even started to pick him, but then. . . ."

And the Professional looks at me askance with hatred.

Alongside our grandstand, on the steps for the forty kopeck grandstand, a drunk (and where did he manage to get tanked up since this morning?) heartrendingly invokes:

"Bandit-mug, break stride! Bandit-mug, break stride!"

Even the honored guests in our box get out of their seats. Coryphaeus throws the stack of tickets down at his feet. The racetrack shouts and whistles.

But what's there to shout about? Absolutely right. At that

speed, nobody can catch Labyrinth. Bright boy, Pasha. Now His Eminence moves into second place. But no, he won't make it. There's too much of a gap.

Third quarter in thirty-two.

Coryphaeus has cheered up and, just to make sure, pushes the tickets into a pile with his foot.

In the third quarter turn, His Eminence suddenly catches up to Labyrinth.

Home stretch. Pasha whips the steed desperately, but it's already obvious that Labyrinth's reared back. Beneath the racetrack's roar of joy, His Eminence beats Labyrinth by half a length.

I look at my stopwatch. 2:07.1. Excellent time. Coryphaeus hastily picked up his tickets and blew the dust off them.

"What did I say—His Eminence's all alone."

THE DANDY (shattered): "All the same, Vitaly's a bastard. He didn't touch that horse once. He just rode easy all the way to the finish."

THE PROFESSIONAL (authoritatively): "There was nothing he could do. This company's too tough a nut for Patrician. And Pashka didn't get lucky."

And he gave me a conspiratorial wink.

. . . The day is gathering strength. At least we're protected from the sun by the upper grandstands, but down in the "forties," you can't go anywhere. A swarm of folks. Sweaty, steamy faces. The drunk on the stairway has gotten totally carried away. He's hugging somebody, bragging about his win. Guessed His Eminence in single with a fiver. Great joy, he'll get kopecks. But I didn't play with any better reason myself. I'm waiting on a standout with one ticket, once again from the most bet-on favorite. It'd be nice out in the country right now—somewhere by a riverside, lie on the bank and make love to tanned girls. I haven't been to the Silver Pine Forest in a million years, and you know, at one time I wasn't a bad swimmer. Yes, I used to spend my Sundays very differently. First thing in the morning I'd arrive at the Library of History, the research room. . . . It really did happen once upon a time.

Lord, what am I doing here?

2

AN EXCERPT FROM THE TEACHER'S SAMIZDAT ARTICLE, "SO JUST WHO WAS VICTORIOUS AFTER THE REVOLUTION?"

(Part I)

. . . It would be naive and unreasonable to suggest that the founders of Marxism were adroit adventurers who succeeded in wrapping the poor human race around their finger. Marx was the foremost economist of his time, Engels—an excellent political writer. But I'm not going to split hairs here over philosophy and economics. In my opinion, the unsurpassed success of communism can be explained, on the whole, by psychological causes. Young, developing capitalism, in spite of its merits, had a mass of faults, but no one could say exactly how and when they could be eliminated. Meanwhile, the dominant Christian faith promised mankind paradise, but paradise in heaven, and not on earth. "Christ suffered, and He commanded us," they said among the masses. And suddenly Marxism arrives—not some kind of fantastic utopia, but something like a scientific theory that promises paradise not in a thousand years, but in the foreseeable future, not in heaven, but on earth. And every person can hasten the advent of this radiant future through his or her active work.

> Only we, workers of the world,
> A great army of labor,
> Have the right to rule the Earth
> But parasites—never.

Could an honest person really not subscribe to these lines from "The Internationale"? Like everything else, it turns out to be simple: all you need is to fight the "final, decisive battle," and mankind will be happy forever! The happiness of mankind is a great goal, and if, in accordance with Marx, it is near and fully attainable, then it's understandable why people went into this "last battle" and sacrificed their lives. Only after a century has it become patently clear that the last verge to the Marxist final battle is not in sight, and not tens, but tens of millions of human lives have been ruined, but, alas, the radiant dream of mankind hasn't come the least bit closer, but, on the contrary, in countries where Marxism has been victorious, it isn't the heavenly orders that have triumphed by any means.

A government, constructed on a Marxist base—the Soviet Union, land of victorious socialism—has been in existence for almost fifty years. All the remaining socialist countries are copies of this model. There are, of course, some deviations, but the essence is the same, namely: (1.) Instead of flexible capitalism with a capacity for competition, there is unprofitable state capitalism; (2.) A huge, clumsy, voracious ruling

class—the new "nobility"—not hereditary, but bureaucrati-
cally titled, "nomenklatura"; (3.) No personal or social free-
doms and difficult material conditions for the laboring classes, especially in comparison with the capitalist nations of the
West. That is the result. I repeat, all the nations of victorious
socialism resemble each other and exceptions can't be
expected. Does it seem that the facts are obvious? But it's
curious that the contemporary neo-Marxists all the same
dream of constructing a society different from the Soviet one.
It isn't currently fashionable to admire the Soviet Union. It's
fashionable to point out the mistakes, the deviations from
theory, and the numerous breaches of lawfulness. And in
general, they say, the Russians didn't do a good job of creat-
ing a revolution in 1917.

I maintain that not only was the Russian Revolution carried out in accordance with Marxist doctrine, but that its very
nature was, moreover, very successful. The truth is you have
to remember that there were two revolutions in Russia in
'17: the Great February Revolution, which could have
become the main pivotal event in the history of Russia, and
the other, the tragic one in October of the same year. For me,
for example, it's funny to hear stories about what a good and
fine person "Comrade Nicholas II, Emperor of all the
Russians," was. By the way, it's been confirmed that the
French king, Louis XVI, executed at the time of the great
French Revolution, was also, so they say, a very "sincere"
person. Both of them, Nicholas and Louis, were exemplary
family men with many other virtues, but power was contraindicated to both. The Russian saying goes: "In for a kopeck,
in for a ruble." The Supreme Ruler in the government had to
answer for two horrible, mindless wars, the Japanese and the

German, for defeat, for a sea of blood, and for the disinte-
gration of the country. I've no doubt that all of today's so-
called "dissidents" would have supported the February
Revolution without thinking twice. But if we'd been somewhat younger, the same age as our fathers, we'd have just as
blindly and fanatically supported the October one, doubtfully
perhaps in 1918, but for certain in October of 1917. Against the
background of the Russian political figures of that period,
Lenin looked like a tactical genius: at the moment of ruin,
military defeats and endless verbiage, he proposed three
short tempting slogans: "Peace to the People! Bread to the
Workers! Land to the Peasants!" These three slogans were on
the banners of October. How could you and I not have stood
under those banners?

Only time proved the demagoguery of these slogans.
Instead of peace, the bloody Civil War began; instead of
bread, the workers received starvation rations, and the land,
which had really been given to the peasants, was taken away
again in twelve years.

And the Bolsheviks just couldn't make ends meet. And
they didn't even fulfill their promises. But the Bolsheviks
were unusually lucky—lucky in the sense that they had enemies on whom all the blame could be laid. And it's not a question of enemies born of that very Soviet power, that is, the
peasants from whom grain had been collected, the workers
who never got this grain, the soldiers whom they'd forced to
fight again—no, there were primordial enemies: landowners
who didn't wish to part with their land, the old bureaucracy,
the high and middle-ranking officer corps who'd lost their
privileges, big property owners. Back in school, we learned
that "the admiral, the gentleman, and the baron trash came

from sixteen different sides," and that's why it was hard for the Bolsheviks, and "in hunger, cold, and nakedness," the Bolsheviks just barely coped with them. However, in principle, Soviet historiography must not curse these enemies but idolize them—the fact is that only thanks to them was Soviet power victorious, only thanks to them did the masses trust Soviet power—they say that if there hadn't been enemies, the Communists would have fulfilled their promises.

Since then the Soviet government has been searching for enemies and has been searching for them for sixty-five years, because the government of victorious socialism can't exist without enemies. What horror if suddenly, with a wave of the hand, the enemies should vanish! Nothing would remain but to declare solemnly the advent of the long-promised paradise. And where do you get it, this paradise?

***

The October Revolution of 1917, on whose banners was written the most wonderful humanistic slogan, "Peace to the People!" must be considered the beginning of the Civil War in Russia. Not the taking of the Winter Palace and the cruiser Aurora's blank shot, but three years of fratricidal war, which cost the lives of millions of Russian citizens and, finally, consolidated the victory of Soviet power, the victory of the socialist revolution. Could the Bolsheviks have managed without a civil war? No, they couldn't have. And that's not just a historian's subjective opinion. Here's what a more authoritative comrade said at the plenary session of the Central Executive Committee (CEC) in June of 1918: "Just as the working class delivered the lands of the gentry into the hands of the peasantry, so does it now teach the poorer peasants to take from the kulaks (the marauders, the speculators) available food supplies, and turn them into a general food stock. We have no other way! We are told: this is the way of civil war. Soviet rule indeed is organized civil war. Soviet power is not afraid to say this—and call the masses openly to organize civil war against the landowners and the bourgeoisie." These words belong to Comrade Trotsky, who at that time was not yet an oppositionist. His role in the Politburo was enormous, and he held the post of Chairman of the Revolutionary War Council of the Republic. And if the Chairman of the Revolutionary War Council said, "Soviet rule is *organized civil war,*" he obviously had a substantial foundation for it.

But by 1921 the war had ended in the principal territory of the Russian state (with the exception of the Far East). Landowners, the bourgeoisie, and the White officer corps were physically obliterated or banished beyond the borders of the Soviet republic. In theory, they should have established a holiday for workers and peasants, in whose name the Revolution had been carried out—after all, they had won! However, I'm not going to talk right now about the extremely grave economic ruin into which the country fell, of the horrible famine—there's no need to deviate from the theme, and our theme is: the victors and the vanquished. Therefore, allow me to cite one document: "There are no external fronts. The danger of bourgeois overthrow has passed. The acute period of the Civil War has ended, but a grave legacy has remained—overcrowded prisons, where mainly workers and peasants sit, but not the bourgeoisie. . . ."

What kind of devilry is afoot here! The vanquished—the

landowners and bourgeoisie—have been annihilated, ₁
the victors—the workers and peasants—sit in prisons'. ᵤᵤ
that's what the document attests. The inexperienced reader
would be happy not to believe it. Most likely, the inexperienced reader will decide that this utterance belongs to some
spiteful White-Guard or malignant Western critic, in a word,
to the slanderous bourgeois press. I was quoting, however, an
excerpt from a Cheka order from January 8,1921 (the collection: *The History of the Cheka,* published by the State
Publishing House in 1958). I think that, in this case, we must
believe the comrades from the Cheka. For them it was, as
they say, more obvious.

So just who was victorious in the Russian Revolution?

THE RACES

Second Race.
The All-Union Grand Prix

Three heats to run. Participation in the third heat is not
mandatory. Prize positions are allocated by the lowest sum of
position numbers in any two properly completed heats (with
the required occupation of first place in at least one of them for
the winner). In case of equal sums of positions for more than
one horse, prize positions are determined by the lowest sum of
heats recorded.

—Excerpt from the Rules

Nine horses are driven out on parade to the sound of
Dunaevsky's solemn march from the movie *The Circus.* They
are met by fifteen thousand pairs of eyes. Probably not a single artist at a single concert is examined as critically or as
attentively as these nine derby contestants. Fifteen thousand

people judge the horses' every step, trying to guess what speed they can do and what the jockeys themselves are counting on. Fifteen thousand heads are working like computers, choosing the most advantageous combination of money and numbers. Over the loudspeaker, the announcers introduce the contestants for the All-Union Grand Prix:

"Wearing number one, a stallion from the Dubrovsky Stud Farm, Ideologue. Master jockey, Pyotr. . . ."

Want to know what the heroes of the day themselves are thinking about?

PETYA: "What am I thinking about? What's there to think about? Got to ride, not think. I told my old lady to put a ten-spot down on me, but not to waste any more. Moiseika has a strong stallion. Moiseika's a sly Jew; he hangs on right behind my back and shoots past at the finish line. He's set his sights on winning the Grand Prix, the snot-nosed kid, but I've been around the racetrack forty years and haven't once taken this purse. It's tickled my moustache, but hasn't dropped into my mouth. So I'm going to retire with nothing to show for my trouble. But I won't give in to a Jew. I'll take off straight away, just catch me, whistle for me! But I can't do it in the pack; just look, I'm afraid they'll break my little stallion down, the goons. . . . But my hands aren't what they used to be; the years aren't right anymore—last chance to make something of myself. It's just this Othello I'm afraid of. . . . Gunta's a dumb broad, can't build up pace right. . . . Just who does that leave, then? White Sail? You can't fool me, the old man: I've got a hunch Vanya's thought something up. But what's there to think about, what's there to think about? Got to ride, not think. They take it in thirty-two, I'll do it in thirty-one. They in thirty-one—but I've got thirty in reserve. But if they start out with a false pace at thirty-four? But I'll do thirty-one, and in the third quarter, I'll do thirty-two, but then. . . . I'll be weeping and praying—maybe they won't catch up."

IDEOLOGUE: "I'm the strongest, the fastest, the most handsome; I'm terribly ambitious! And this little high-tail Liana is going to stop to look at that chestnut Othello and neigh like a little idiot when she meets him on the track. Of course, when I was winning, she vowed to be faithful to me. I'll tear Othello to pieces. I'll trample him with my hooves; that purse is mine! If only my master wouldn't push me all the way around the track; I just can't do the whole track, all I need is a little breather, but he's going to keep driving and driving me, hitting and hitting me. And then he curses and doesn't give me any sugar. I don't think he's very smart. . . . It's so hard to run when you hear that chestnut's wheezing behind you. He took position smartly! Now let's turn the tables; I'm going to get behind you, save my breath, and then the final sprint is mine. Ah, little Liana, little Liana, all mares are whores!"

"Wearing number two, the mare from the Prilepsky Stud Farm, Liana. Jockey, second class, Nikolai. . . ."

KOLYA: "Poor, pitiful me! Now why don't I get that lucky? That's some little mare I've trained! And she needed it—she was limping with her left hind leg; she'd pulled a ligament. I gave the vet a half liter, I gave him money, but all in vain. Now the foreman is going to eat me alive. He'll say I f . . . up the derby! He, the foreman, is probably jealous that he didn't guess right on Liana; he gave her to me as a no-goer, and I won on her in 2:10. If I took the derby, I'd be made foreman myself. I'd be sent to the thirtieth division—there, it's true, they've got bad goods, but that's okay, I'd make it out in the world somehow. Looks like I'll be hibernating as an assistant forever. They'll lead Liana off to the factory, and what'll I have left? Two and a half mares, only fit for sausage? Well, so I gave her a shot of anesthetic. It's got to hold for half an hour, as long as she isn't limping, she won't feel sorry for herself. They should have started sooner! And if they go at a false pace, if they're watching each other up to the finish, I've got a chance. We'll work it out in the home stretch. If I could take one heat, then stick her with a couple, three shots, I won't let go of that prize even if I have to beat her to death. What a drag it is, being an assistant. . . . Ideologue looks good; Othello's going to piss fire. . . . No, obviously there's no joy in living! . . ."

LIANA: "I'm so sick, oh boy am I sick! They stuck me— stuck me so I could take a step, but I can't feel my leg; it's as if it wasn't alive. The chestnut keeps turning his muzzle to me, he's putting on airs, but not so long ago, he ogled me with lovesick eyes. And the bay's gone absolutely out of his mind—he won't give way. Stallions all have just one thing on their minds . . . but I'm not up to being frisky right now, hobbling on three legs. A young girl's time is short. . . .

"Wearing number three, the mare from the Lokotovsky Stud Farm, Cherepet. Jockey, first class, Yevgeny. . . ."

ZHENYA: "I'm not getting into any swordplay in the first heat, not very likely. But watch the second and third heats—I need points; fourth place would suit me fine. I told the guys to load up Othello; the prize is his and he isn't giving it up to anybody. Othello will set them such a pace that they'll get wasted in the first heat. I'll just hold Cherepushka back for a bit, and then, just before the third heat, when the standouts are getting their pictures taken, I'll send my brother to the booth. There won't be much to pay, but I'll make something. I owe a hundred to the club, give a hundred fifty to Klavka for furniture. Fifty for Nyurka, take care of Masha with a tenner and a bottle. . . . We'll find that edge, we'll guess the edge— I'll put a thirty in for broke. I wonder how much they'll give."

CHEREPET: "I'm easy, I'm obliging, I do what I'm told. I've got a hunch there won't be too much work today, not with my master in this mood. And little Liana—hee hee— she's limping. I've got sharp eyes—you can't hide it. The poor thing was dreaming! She had her nose in the air, said her father was a famous prizewinner, an American! I won't argue; Apex-Hanover is a stud of good color; but the mother, Brass, is a renowned slut. The old mares were telling me that when they led Apex to Brass, he was bucking desperately. And little Liana took after her mother—she whores, too. And who needs her, now that she's lame? Phoo!"

"Wearing number four, the mare from the Prilepsky Stud Farm, Chug-a-Lug, of the Kalinin Racetrack. Jockey, first class, Samsonov. . . ."

SAMSONOV: "They warned me straight off: buddy, you sit tight and don't rock the boat, or we'll accidentally break your carrion's legs. The hay they put down is wet, the bran is low quality, and the carrots were under quota. Moscow shoots from the hip; she doesn't like out-of-towners. Yeah, I could put it to them in the mouth and the nose, and the ear . . . but I don't have the goods. The mare has a 2:09 maximum. Of course, if there's the slightest chance, we won't let ours get by. There's just no need to get into any such conversations with Moscow. They said a Tallnik from Tallin won the derby before last; he did the first quarter in 29, and he lost the whole crew right away. The Muscovites were smelling his tail, just gnashing their teeth with spite. Wait a bit, it'll be a holiday on our street . . . I've got a two-year-old. . . ."

CHUG-A-LUG: "How interesting! What handsome little stallions! So many pleasant acquaintances! I winked to one of them here, and he flung himself at me so that he almost threw his master out of the sulky. . . . I love the temperamental ones. . . . We don't even have anybody to talk to in Kalinin. The mares are little connivers, and the stallions have only one subject, namely, 'Oats're expensive these days.' The provinces are a bore. It's a different life in Moscow: the capital, culture, intelligent conversation. My neighbor with the white mane that's signed up for the Prix Elite whispered in my ear, says he's going to sort them all out in the first heat, and he invited me to the park for a stroll. And why not? He's a stallion in the very prime of life, well kept, courteous, he neighed me a long yarn. . . . Hey, where on earth did ours go?"

"Wearing number five, the stallion from the Pskov Stud Farm, Othello. The jockey, second class, Mosya. . . ."

MOSYA: "Easy, Mosya, easy! Today's your day. You're going to take the purse—and you're going to be promoted to the rank of master jockey by order of the Ministry. The director was hinting about it. You're tied to him by the same thread. When he made me foreman everybody whispered that the division had been entrusted to a boy; he'll pile the work on! But the director is a hammer, he stood his own and told them it was necessary to promote a young person. Stick to your guns, San Sanych, we won't let you down. I've been training Othello for a year, but I haven't gotten near any purses—I was waiting until he built up strength; now it's strictly first place for us. The crooks poked money at me; they said, 'Humor us, let somebody pass, Mosya, you'll bring in a bundle!' But I sent them packing. Any other horse, please, but don't get Othello dirty! They didn't like it—one day they waited me out, beat me up. Okay, who brings up the past. . . . I spent day and night with Othello. I fed him out of my hands; I was afraid of everything: they'll surround a steed, ruin him. And today is my day. Easy, Mosya, easy. The main thing is, don't give in to provocation. If they rush the first quarter in thirty seconds, don't break the stallion; let them eat bread with spoons, and they'll start getting sloppy toward the finish. You've been through all the possibilities: gone from place to place, and rushed at the end, and walked away at the third turn. Little Othello, easy, boy. Don't be nervous!"

OTHELLO: "I hate them all, every last one! How dare they compare themselves with me on the track! No one can get around me, no one can catch up to me. And what's making the time go so slow? I wish the bell would ring sooner! And then, to run, run, to beat the ground with my hooves, leave the ground, fly through the air! And no one alongside, no one close! Because I am Othello—the best in the racetrack. They're all lazy: they don't want to work: they'll show one good quarter, and beyond that, they'll stroll along, tell anecdotes. . . . But I put myself through it every day, cut several laps—to the seventh sweat! The bay walked away from me in the last heat; he thought I couldn't catch him. And I gave it my all and caught up; my heart was jumping out of my chest. And afterwards, when I dragged myself back to the paddock, it seemed to me that all around, both the sky and the grass were a dull red. But it can't be any other way for me; see, all I want is to be first!"

"Wearing number six, the mare from the Prilepsky Stud Farm, Gouache, from the Kharkov Racetrack. The jockey, first class, Madigov. . . ."

MADIGOV: "What a shame GUM is closed today, and TSUM is locked up. Show me a Muscovite, and I'll show you a comedian! Just what do they do with a day of!? Watch TV? That means it's off to GUM first thing, early Monday morning—an overcoat, a jacket, a carpet for my mother-in-law, a belt for my son-in-law, a shirt for my son, and a kerchief for my daughter. They say it's tough with carpets, but one of the stablehands who was hanging around here, sniffed and got wind of something and promised to help. I didn't mark his program for nothing. . . . Don't forget: ten kilos of oranges, smoked sausage, cooked sausage (as much as I can get—they say they only give two kilo jugs to the mug—it's come to that, I swear!). Oh, yeah, three kilos of prunes, too. And if I come across some other goods in short supply, I'll buy those, too. I don't come to Moscow for nothing!"

GOUACHE: "Well, that's the capital's ways for you! For shame! I grew up with Chug-a-lug and Liana—we used to run in the same pasture; we were modest little fillies—shy, you might say. But now they don't exactly hate stallions—they're twisting and twirling their tails! Neither shame nor girlish pride! They'd rather go to restaurants and beat their hooves like our two-legged sisters, not compete for purses! Youth has been destroyed, I swear. . . . I'll give it to them hot for the distance—I won't let any of them by me!"

"Wearing number seven, the stallion from the Yelansky Stud Farm, Wheat Top II. The jockey, second class, Gunta. . . ."

GUNTA: "My hubby's outdone himself—he dragged himself home at six o'clock in the morning. He says he went out on a spree with the gang, says he was taping the Beatles. He doesn't understand, the old dog, that the chicks were sent to him specially. He falls for it, 'Love,' he says, 'La-la

la-la!' and the chicks slip him a program. See, all they need
is information—who in what race, what kind of chance he's
got. But it isn't just information. . . . This black-haired chick
in the glasses is willing to do it in any doorway. . . . My
guy's gotten himself carted off to her place for sure, I know
those tape recordings! To hell with what he was recording
for her—it's just too bad he's already shot his mouth off
about me, says Gunta'll win the prize. I'm sure he even put
money down on me himself. It doesn't look like the winnings will come to the family—he's spending money on that
carrion with the glasses. She took him to the Film Club and
he melted. And why do they let sluts into the Film Club? He
doesn't have time to go to the movies with me—he's taping,
don't you see. . . . Just to spite him, I'm not going after the
purse. Just like that—a dead stop! I can't; I've got to go. And
it'd be a shame to let the derby slip because of that no-good.
He and I lived well in Riga, while I watched his dirty tricks
through my fingers, and he was transferred to Moscow and
made foreman, and it all went to hell! I ask you, where is
justice? I'm at the track from morning till night working the
horses. I run for the veterinarian, swear at the livestock
expert, knock out the feed mix, but my husband shows up
all set to go, he wins—and off to the chicks! . . . If only he'd
act decent. After all, he knows what kind of day this is for
me! He's ruined my mood!"

WHEAT TOP II: "Both the bay and the chestnut are stu-
pid old hacks! 'We've got strength—we don't need brains!'
They're used to hustling from one spot to another, the yokels!
But we'll arrange the race intelligently, in a tactically proper
way. They'll cut their own throats by the third quarter, and
I'll leave them behind with a push. Only my mistress is in

low spirits, and her hands are trembling. . . . Well, Guntochka, don't get discouraged!"

(Wheat Top has started neighing to stir some life into the grandstands.)

"Wearing number eight, the stallion Precipice, from the Lavrovsky Stud Farm and the Perm Racetrack. The jockey, first class, Lipin. . . ."

LIPIN: "I used to tell Valentin: sit tight and don't rock the boat, and most of all—keep your mouth shut at meetings! But what a hothead! And who pulled his tongue? Well, our rations were cut, it's true, and it's a little tighter with carrots and oats. . . . The chief of operations, Shinkarev, explained, 'Objective reasons, either way you look at it,' he said, 'last year the country had a bad harvest, a drought. Now in America, things're good; they don't have natural disasters there. . . .' He explained it clearly, by the book, like he had it written down. But Valentin flew up to the platform, the blessed oaf, to stand up for his rights. He says that's all bull, the stablehands take home bags stuffed full; they fatten their own suckling pigs on state rations, says it's stupid to plead objective reasons when they're always writing about floods and hurricanes in the newspapers in America, only their agriculture doesn't get taken off by cholera, they even sell us grain. . . . Ah, Valka—the guy decided he was smarter than everybody else, that he could do no wrong! In Perm, there really was no salvation from Vitaly's Precipice—he took all the major purses. The guys resented him: there's a bright boy, he's making a 'cherry' of himself! . . . No, Valya, you can't go against the collective! And the comrade from the district committee was at the meeting too—the party group was advised right away: 'That,' he said, 'is that. We can't send a man with that kind of attitude to Moscow.' And Valka was stuck; they handed Precipice over to me. . . . Valka is a militant guy, but I used to tell him: 'Slow but steady wins the race.' And that, comrades, is the way it turned out—he trained the horse, and I'll ride to the purse. A classy little stallion, but he takes after his master completely: malicious, hot, aims to bite. Whoa, brute, and don't you neigh like that! Easy, easy—step by step! . . ."

PRECIPICE: "You're a beast! You planted yourself on my neck, you fathead! He should be riding goats, not trotters! He took the first aid kit they alloted to me for the trip—made off with it for himself! He swapped my new harness for an old one and three half liters! He even reeks of port in the morning! . . . Where is my loving master? He used to scratch behind my ears—bring joy to my heart. But this one brandishes the whip, the turd! Why should I be disfigured for him? . . . I'll make life sweet for him: I'll throw the goat out of the sulky at the first turn! . . ."

"Wearing number nine, the stallion White Sail from the Yelansky Stud Farm. The jockey, first class, is Ivan. . . ."

VANYA: "A crafty guy, Pasha, but he hit a snag. He hid and hid, threw off six seconds and came in second all the same. I, for one, realized a long time ago that Labyrinth was ready. Of course, I didn't say anything to Ilyushka the Vegetable Man. Pasha's secrets don't concern me, but I asked Nyurka to cover Labyrinth with a couple of tickets. There were about four of those tickets in the whole racetrack. I wonder if Pasha was on the level with me. For that kind of stake, they'd be forking over a couple of thousand. (Of course, I was on the level.) No, Pasha, you're wrong. In the first place, to hide your sins from such old friends, in the second, you needed to let the

first heat go by. Nobody was there to pressure His Eminence—
he'd have shown his 2:09 in the second heat, but Borya, who'd
decided no one was going to break his record, would simply
have taken the steed out. That's when, Pasha, you ride like the
wind to your 2:07! Even if His Eminence took part, he would-
n't be up to the second heat—no matter how spirited the little
stallion is, he's winded. What was wrong with you, Pashenka,
couldn't you be patient? You could, but you didn't want to. It
was greed, Pasha, that overcame you. You figured that without
His Eminence, they'd pay Labyrinth off in kopecks. Even if
they didn't pay much, it would all have been yours. And that's
why you're wrong, Pasha, to hide your sins from such old
friends. You've broken Labyrinth down; you've made your
bed, now lie in it. . . ."

WHITE SAIL: "What's the point of running to no end?
Work loves fools. I haven't had a single first place since winter. Aren't I as good as the others? What, I can't? It would be
my pleasure, but my master won't let me. The way it is, he
puts the harness on me, tousles my mane, and whispers, Wait
a bit, little guy, it's not time yet. . . .' But in general, like my
master says, I've seen this whole crew in the grave. . . ."

There's a tight group of men at the barrier across from the
finish pole. They're all roughly the same age, the same
build—Paunch Paunchich, Belly Bellyich, Fat Fattich and
Lard Lardich. And hiding behind their strong backs is the
short, moderately plump Ilyusha the Vegetable Man. These
chums and buddies keep separate, whisper among themselves, laugh back and forth, suck beer from little paper cups,
and it seems as though the passions of the racetrack don't
excite them at all.

Near this group some rumpled characters with bored, indifferent faces circle around—the *totoshniks* (named after the totalizator), long-time drunks who've lost everything down to their last kopeck, who noone's loaned so much as a ruble for a long time. Totoshniks don't risk getting too close to Ilyusha the Vegetable Man's crew. But when it fell to Paunch Paunchich to make his way to the betting window before the first race, the little shrimp was pulling quite a crowd behind him. Actually, Paunch Paunchich had come to the window to look at the odds; he hadn't come to place a bet. Turning sharply, he saw the hot eyes and greedy, open mouths behind him.

"Smell something?" Paunch Paunchich inquired kindly, and with a slight movement of his shoulders, he cut through the crowd and returned to his place.

A thin, lanky totoshnik popped up like out of the ground, trying to squeeze between Lard Lardich and Fat Fattich.

"What people!" the totoshnik bleated humbly, "My respects. . . ."

"Why, it's Yurochka the Gas Man," Ilyusha the Vegetable Man greeted him happily, "What news do you bring?"

"Peacock's all alone in the Elite; Tolya promised he'd go." The gang broke out in restrained smiles, and Ilyusha took a sip of beer and grew even jollier:

"Gentlemen, thank our benefactor, Yurochka the Gas Man, who has brought us Peacock, the biggest standout of them all, at a ruble forty. You'd better tell me. When hasn't Peacock gone for the purse? All of Moscow already knew about Peacock yesterday." And, turning spontaneously to the totoshnik, Ilyusha asked sharply, point-blank, "How much did you lose last night at the Bakunian's?"

Yurochka stammered and answered with a tortured smile. "A bundle and a half . . . they caught me at every trick."

"This with your income? Did you pawn Zoyka's earrings?"

"Zoyka's earrings have been in hock for a long time," Lard Lardich put in. "He's going to steal his mother-in-law's underwear."

"Ilyusha, for Christ's sake," Yurochka bleated on, trying to catch the Vegetable Man's wandering attention. "I'm at my limit. Give me a chance. Whisper me a horse."

A short laugh from the crew and Ilyusha's indignant voice:

"Gentlemen, how about this squareball? I pay the jockeys money, I fix the race, I take the risks, I get burned, but this guy has to have it here and now! I told you not to have anything to do with the Bakunian, didn't I?"

"Ilyushenka, I'm with you all the way! Yurochka the Gas Man screamed in a whisper, desperation on his face. "Remember how I sold you the Bakunian for a dark niner on the sly? I sure helped you strip him naked that time!"

"Ancient history," winced Ilyusha. "How much money have you gotten out of me since then? . . . No, Yurochka, I don't work for free!"

"Save me, Ilyushka," whined Yuri the Gas Man, "put me onto a horse for the derbies! You want, I'll get down on my knees. . . ."

"Great joy! Now let Zoyka come to me and walk like a crab. . . ."

Yurochka's face began to twitch. "You've offended me, Ilya," he said softly.

"Zoya and he will both crawl," thought Ilyusha the Vegetable Man. "The mutt would sell her to that same

Bakunian for a kopeck. . . . However, I've got an idea: today I can use the Gas Man; it's generally against my rules to drive a man to extremes. . . ."

And in a different, condescending voice, Ilyusha peaceably continued:

"Hands up, Zoya, ever done it standing up? . . . Okay, Yurok, it's all just a little joke. Don't bet on the first heat; you'll never guess. Even I won't be playing it. But the miracles will begin in the second heat.

Yurochka the Gas Man half sat and then craned his neck; his eyes began to twinkle.

"Who in the second" he asked, just audibly, using only his lips.

"You can't fool me like that, Yurok," Ilya burst out laughing. "Whisper to you, and the whole racetrack will find out in five minutes."

"No way!"

"That's it. End of conversation," Ilya cut him off, "come up for the fifth race. I'll give you the money, and you'll place bets for me like I tell you, and you can place your own, of course—so be it, a couple of rubles won't kill me. Bet at the forty, so no one can see. Now, get lost. . . ."

And Yurochka didn't have time to bat an eye before he found himself behind the backs of Lard Lardich and Paunch Paunchich.

And Yurochka dashed headlong to the third floor, and he looked down from the balcony at the Vegetable Man's crew. All five of them are standing around, drinking beer, standing there, not scurrying around, and three minutes to closing's been announced over the loudspeaker. That means the Vegetable Man wasn't fooling; he's letting the race go, and the big deal's in the second heat! No, Ilyukha's not fooling, he'd never make it to the booth before the race, and if he goes any earlier, you should see the tail that lines up behind him! He can't make it to the booth in time before the race, with the tail that grows onto him. All the totoshniks want to know what Ilya the Vegetable Man is betting. I'll be repeating Ilya's combination at the forty all right, not with a lousy ruble, but with a ten-spot—that tenner I saved up! . . .

And Yurochka rushed to the second floor and looked down once more from the stairs to make sure: Paunch Paunchich and Lard Lardich were sipping beer, standing there, the damn goons—bloodsuckers! I'll get even with them for Zoyka! . . . But Ilyukha, all the same, is the person who came to my aid—that's to his credit.

Then, as usual, he hung around the betting hall. The people have gone wild, lost their heads. They run up to Yuri and ask:

"Yurok, who in the first heat?"

Yurochka, not a proud man, is willing to do anything for the sake of his chums and buddies. Cautiously, right into their ears, he whispers the right horse. . . .

"Othello can't lose. Drop your britches—bet everything."

"The first heat goes to Ideologue; he's sworn to run in 2:07."

"Wheat Top is going to pull them all. Play him? Well, this kind of crowd isn't stupid, but he'll draw five in single."

"Overall, Othello, but Kolya's sworn that the first heat is his. Liana's been starting the hell out of races. You haven't seen? I have. Risk a couple of rubles, and stake me a ticket."

"Here's the deal: Precipice hasn't lost to anybody in Perm. But who's he had to run against in Perm? Are they going to give it to an out-of-towner? And if Precipice is up to a 2.05? You don't know? But I know. Remember Tallnik. . . ."

"Ideologue and Othello are going to wipe each other out, and at the finish, Zhenya's going to push Cherepet. You don't believe me? As you like. Cover them with a three—easy money."

That's how Yurochka worked. That's why they called him the Gas Man. He told everybody something different. They listened to him and they didn't listen to him. On one hand, Yura delivers rubbish—but on the other hand, you know, he hangs around the stables, and he greets the Bakunian and the Vegetable Man with a handshake. What if he's really gotten wind of something? And people lose their nerve, and they bet in eerie darkness. But then again, Yura has his system: the favorite comes in, Yurka's not to blame, he risked it himself—here's the tickets (picked up in advance from the floor), and if there's a mob scene in the racetrack, and a dark horse pushes in, Yurochka's there on the spot: "Did you play? You did! But where's my cut? Otherwise I'm not coming around anymore." And the winners, high on big money, share the winnings with Yura.

Yura shoved his way into the snack bar, and suddenly he felt the squeeze of an iron hand on his neck. Yura recognized the grip, and without turning around, croaked:

"What's with you, Bakunian?"

"Who did the Vegetable Man pick?" rumbled a quiet bass.

"Let go. Ilyukha's people will see."

"There's nobody here."

The iron grip loosened, and Yura twisted free. Yura was tall, but compared to the Bakunian, he looked like a kid. The Bakunian's black eyes were working their extortion and they were obeyed with trembling knees. (Any second one of Ilya's guys could have come and reported it verbatim.) Yurochka bleated out:

"The Vegetable Man is passing on the first heat, but in the fifth, he's sending me to the booth at the forty."

"Who'd he pick?" repeated the Bakunian.

"He didn't say, I swear to God he didn't say, I swear on the cross," and uttering these words, Yura, as though watching from one side, thought that it was funny to promise and swear on the cross before a Muslim. Instantly calmed by this, he asked:

"Bakunian, knock off half my debt."

The Bakunian put his hand behind his back and shot the Gas Man a nagging, ironic look.

"Could be you're not lying. The Vegetable Man isn't a total idiot, and he isn't going to trust you with a dark horse. Betting through you right at the bell makes sense. So if it works out that way, I'll forgive you half. . . . Go down to the forty, booth 139; Stasik'll meet you."

And once again lifting his mighty palm, the Bakunian gave Yurochka a slight push toward the exit, touched him lightly, even tenderly, but the Gas Man flew out of the snack bar like a bullet.

3

AN EXCERPT FROM THE TEACHER'S SAMIZDAT ARTICLE, "SO JUST WHO WAS VICTORIOUS AFTER THE REVOLUTION?"

(Part II)

ALLOW ME TO STATE A PARADOXICAL THOUGHT: THERE ARE NO winners in socialist revolutions. It was not without reason that Vergniaud, one of the heroes of the French Revolution, used to say, "The Revolution is like Saturn: it devours its own children." In the case of the French Revolution, it has been proven that all of her leaders perished in her fire, and the active revolutionaries, the Montagnards and Jacobins, found their deaths at the war fronts or under the blade of the guillotine. Even Soviet historiography agrees that it wasn't the revolutionaries who profited by the fruits of the Great French Revolution, but the bourgeoisie.

Just what happened in Russia? It's well known that the February Revolution of 1917 (I emphasize, in my view, the great and pivotal event in our history), was accomplished

entirely by the Petersburg proletariat. The Petersburg proletariat was the most active, best organized, and most revolu-
tionarily prepared part of the Russian working class. It had a
good deal of experience in political, trade-union, and strike-
related struggles. I am convinced that Soviet power wouldn't
have succeeded in obliterating the basic rights of the workers, wouldn't have enslaved them or have converted the trade
unions into an appendage of the police apparatus if the
Petersburg proletariat had preserved their former contingent.
But let us leaf through the pages of the Civil War. The headlines in Soviet newspapers: "Detachments of Petersburg
workers against the forces of Kolchak," "Detachments of
Petersburg workers against the bands of the Ataman Dutov,"
"Petersburg's proletariat hold off the attack of Denikin's
armies. . . ." It sounds beautiful, of course, but let's consider
the meaning of these reports. Workers against professional
soldiers! Yes, they, of course, defended the republic, beat
back the enemy's onslaught. But at what cost? It cost them
their lives! One of the regrettable results of the Revolution is
the fact that the avant-garde of the Russian working class perished almost entirely at the fronts of the Civil War.

Further, we know that professional social revolutionaries, who had a lot of experience with revolutionary work and
a solid socio-theoretical knowledge, joined the Russian
Revolution. The Revolution enticed the youth as well, the
most ideologically and politically active part, young men and
women ready to sacrifice their lives for the sake of a fanati-
cal belief in Marxist teaching, which promised to bring happiness and justice to the people in the immediate future. It
was these young people who shut down the district committee and went off to the front. It was they who fought at the

very vanguard and didn't sit it out in installations in the rear. And naturally this flower of the revolutionary movement to all intents and purposes was almost completely destroyed in the Civil War.

And still it is necessary to point out one extremely important circumstance: the most active supporters of the "White Idea," the defenders of the Constituent Assembly, adherents of constitutional democracy, didn't sit it out in the bars of Odessa or in the rears of the White Armies either. They did battle with the Bolshevik evil at the fronts and bore the heaviest losses.

A sad, tragic outcome for the country. The flower of the nation, people sincerely believing in their ideas, ready not just for words, but to defend their convictions in practice, had mutually slaughtered each other. Out of a million active functionaries capable of constructing a new government, only hundreds survived. But the "ideological Whites" set out for emigration and disappeared from the horizon of the country's social thought. The "ideological Reds" who had survived, thanks to their very ideology and their adherence to ideals, turned up before long on the left or right opposition and were annihilated by the Stalinist party apparatus, while the individuals who by some miracle survived all the "purges" and the year 1937 were put to use in a practical way in local work and didn't play any kind of role.

And so, it turned out that there were no victors in the Russian Revolution. But just who profited from the fruits of this Revolution, which segment of the population gained from it? If the bourgeoisie gained in the great French Revolution, then the Russian Revolution advanced the petty bourgeoisie to the proscenium. Yes, yes, that same slumbering self-interested petty bourgeoisie, whom all the progressive Russian writers, beginning with Chekhov and ending with Gorky, were ridiculing as far back as the beginning of our century. I'll be more specific: what I mean by "petty bourgeoisie" in this instance is not a social order, but the people whose vital credo has been recorded in *The Great Soviet Encyclopedia*—and I quote: "In the figurative sense, those people are called the petty bourgeoisie whose views or behavior are marked by egotism and individualism, money-grubbing, an apolitical attitude, and an absence of principles and ideals." That is, the petty bourgeoisie is egotistical, apolitical and lacking in ideology; they waited it out in a quiet plant for the storms of the Civil War to blow over, and crawled out whole and unscathed to the outside to serve Soviet power—it didn't matter what kind, what mattered was power, so one could chop off a somewhat larger piece of the government pie for oneself.

I'm not going to quote now the Russian classical writers who broke a lot of pens in their time on the mug of this petty bourgeoisie, albeit without any injury to the latter, for the petty bourgeoisie has one enviable quality: no one could ever make them change their minds about anything. And the convictions, that is, the essence of petty-bourgeois ideology, are simple and reliable: they give—you take, they hit—you run, it's no concern of mine, not caught—not a thief, charity begins at home. This guileless wisdom always helped the petty bourgeoisie step out of the water dry. Humane problems, problems peculiar to all mankind, never disturbed the petty bourgeoisie, and sacrifice and heroism were contraindicated by their very nature. The Revolution, of course, frightened the petty bourgeoisie at first, but then attracted it with its

concept of "grand larceny." However, having gotten its bear-
ings, the petty bourgeoisie soon realized that Soviet rule wasn't
as terrible as it had been painted. You only needed to master
the new rules of the game. Instead of church—go to meetings,
instead of psalms—sing revolutionary songs, instead of the
white tsar—glorify the red; at first "Karla Marla" and later the
wise and great leader of all times and peoples, the genius of
humanity, the best friend of Soviet athletes. . . . In the depths
of its soul, power commanded the respect of the petty bourgeoisie; it loved order, and when the militiaman with the red
star replaced the police officer's figure in the long overcoat,
so dear to its heart, the petty bourgeoisie rejoiced: everything
had come full circle. But not completely. If the petty bourgeoisie's range had been limited earlier to the rank of police
officer on duty, then it could now fight its way to power, moreover, to such heights of power that it made his head spin.
However, I repeat, all you had to do was adhere to the new
rules of the game. And the game was worth the candle. And
the petty bourgeoisie took a briefcase and went to serve the
Soviets. The Sov-petty-bourgeoisie came crawling out of all
the cracks. To the old, tested, wise sayings of their fathers
and forefathers, the petty bourgeoisie added new, Soviet ones:
"Let the authorities do the thinking—they get the big pay,"
and "Let the bear work—he has four paws." "The egotism,
money-grubbing, and apolitical attitude," so aptly noted by
The Soviet Encyclopedia on the nature of the petty bourgeoisie, greatly assisted its career and prosperity. These valuable
qualities allowed the petty bourgeoisie to stay on its feet during the sharp turns of Soviet history, which cost those people
who were even a little bit ideological and true to their convictions their heads. The petty bourgeoisie was absolutely

indifferent as to whom was attacked at meetings—Trotskyites, Bukharinites, Zinovievites, the kulak's henchmen, cosmopolitans, "killer doctors"—so long as they weren't touched. The year 1937 completely razed the new cadres, advanced by the youth and the enthusiasts of the first Five-Year Plans (and there were such people). "And it serves them right!" the petty bourgeoisie affirmed, "there's no point in thrusting yourself forward or imagining that you're smarter than others. In this regard, it's interesting to take a look at the biographies of all the current leaders of the Soviet government. There is one constant, present in all their careers: up to the year 1937, they're rank-and-file engineers, teachers at technical colleges, provincial agronomists, at best, low-level party apparatchiks. The year 1937 saw an abrupt leap! Secretaries of regional executive committees, secretaries of town executive committees, directors of large industrial complexes. In my opinion, it was precisely the year 1937 that summed up the Russian Revolution: the people who came to power had displayed a talent for blind obedience and had demonstrated their terrifying lack of principle. The petty bourgeoisie stood at the helm of power. One could make the case that the Revolution had come to an end.

But the petty bourgeoisie prevailed not only because of its apolitical nature and craving to snatch a piece of the pie at any cost. Soviet power had one feature that made it very attractive for the petty bourgeoisie, and perhaps more attractive than any other power. The Soviet system annihilated everybody who was talented, vividly individual, and freethinking. The idea of universal equality, carried to the point of absurdity, corresponded to petty bourgeois ideology, for the petty bourgeoisie had always, in all times, wanted to live "like all people do" and for everything to be "like other people's." For the petty bourgeoisie with its bestial hatred for everything exceptional, Soviet power was simply a gift.

Where and when could we still find a system in which, as a rule, dullness and mediocrity would be victorious? "As a rule" is not a stipulation, but conformity with a law. Naturally, exceptions occur as well, especially in such an enormous country as Russia. But look: in our country, as a rule, the most mediocre and obedient writers, artists, musicians, people in the arts, historians, sociologists, journalists thrive. . . . It is dangerous to be original, to be yourself. Be like everybody else!—and your career is guaranteed. Talented, original engineers don't become directors: just who would entrust a plant or an undertaking to an "uncontrollable person?" Even among scientists, outstanding figures have appeared only in spheres connected with military industry. It is here, as the saying goes, that "it was propped up," and the powers reluctantly had to tolerate Tupolev and Kurchatov, Sakharov and Kapitsa, Korolev and Landau. However, when there was a chance to annihilate somebody, then they annihilated the likes of Vavilov, and promoted the likes of Lysenko.

And what about the rulers themselves? Members of the Politburo, secretaries of the Central Committee, members of the Central Committee, ministers, secretaries of regional committees? Peer attentively into their faces. Isn't it true that for "proletarians who have nothing to lose," they're too well fed? But to hell with it, with that so-called "outward appearance." The trouble lies elsewhere: these people, on whom the fate of our country depends, and perhaps the fate of the whole world as well, are not only incapable of having any ideas of their own, but also even any kind of useless, albeit original, little thoughts! The Soviet hierarchy, the Soviet petty bourgeoisie won't tolerate independence, even in trivial details. Moreover, these people can't say even a word without a scrap of paper! All the solemn speeches, all the political appearances, even toasts at receptions "to the leadership" are written and approved by workers of the apparatus.

And this isn't even a question of ideology. No one has believed in it for a long time, above all the ruling state machinery. The stuffy atmosphere of drabness and the mustiness of the petty bourgeoisie has shrouded the whole country. It's difficult, almost impossible, for a normal person to breathe. But in this atmosphere the petty bourgeois is like a fish in water; he's used to it, it's his "life-force." Let me remind you that before the Revolution, the ruling class—the nobility—numbered about three-hundred thousand persons. By the most modest calculations, the present ruling class—the power-holding Soviet petty bourgeoisie—is composed of more than five million persons. And the petty bourgeoisie holds on tenaciously to its privileges, to its piece of the pie. That is, to its posts and appointments, personal dachas, cars, special distributors, to the very possibility of suppressing whatever does not resemble his petty bourgeois frame of mind. And the petty bourgeois won't easily give up these blessings of his, which he received thanks to Soviet power. . . .

THE RACES

And there's another jam at the booths. I got in line just as the derbyists rode out on parade. I looked quickly—all the horses seem to have four legs and no one is obviously lame, but there's no time to watch the warm-ups, because there

wouldn't be time to place a bet. The line is moving slowly;
they're lining up in droves. Just how should I play? Got to
decide right away. There're two standouts in the next race—
Careful and Faithful. Pasha, who already lost on Labyrinth, is
on Careful, and Kolya, who's on Faithful, by my reckoning
ought to win on Liana. If Liana's first, then Kolya'll hang on
to his double or die trying—to come in on Faithful too, that
is. So, I'll put a ruble down on that combination. But after all,
it's stupid to guess Liana and let the winnings go by if Careful
comes in. Anyhow, you've sworn not to play Pasha! I won't
play him already, but how did he train Labyrinth? From the
point of view of names, Liana and Careful don't go together
well. Othello and Faithful are much better. Faithful
Othello—that makes sense. But there's no way you can put
Careful Othello together. (He strangled Desdemona—a
strange kind of caring.) Faithful Wheat Top? How can a
Wheat Top be faithful? But Careful Wheat Top is pure abra-
cadabra. Okay, two more rubles—from Othello and Wheat
Top to Faithful. Faithful Precipice? The very names guaran-
tee a loss: that's out. Harmonious: Faithful Ideologue and
Thoughtful Ideologue ("Winter is gone; Summer has come.
Thanks to the party for this.") Well, show some character:
Ideologue—not a ruble! I've got three combinations—maybe
that'll do it?

Well, how's that for arrogance, for impudence—he cut in
line, and I've been stuck here for an hour! Why'd they let him
in? Hey, cashier, don't give him anything! But he's betting
fifty rubles! Just where does a crook get that kind of money?
I'm a crook myself? You're a fool! All right, guys, let's push
him! There, that fixes that; that's one pushed out . . . now this
one's betting twenty rubles! You can choke on your rubles! . . .

No, you can see we won't make it—won't make it to turn our hard-earned legal rubles into government revenue. . . . Hey, lady, where you going? To hell with her; we're not standing here for milk; she'll manage. It's time for the bell, and they're closing the booth in my face. No, it looks like I'm going to make it. There's one man in front of me. The man slowly pulls out a ten-spot and, without batting an eye places it from Ideologue to Careful, then gets another tenner and he repeats the combination. Twenty rubles for broke without flinching! It means he's got good information. Now I'm at the window and I'm getting shoved from all sides.

I have a hard time making my way from the cashier and only now do I realize what I've done—in my hands is a packet of tickets—from Wheat Top and Othello I've played a ruble apiece to Faithful; from Liana—to the two standouts; from Ideologue, two tickets each to Faithful and Careful. Altogether, I've bet eight rubles! At that rate in a couple of races I'll be left without a kopeck . . . That's called, "I gave in to provocation." And what do I want with Ideologue? However, the guy in front of me kept placing his bets pretty confidently. There must be something behind that.

"Hello. . . ."

"Good day. . . ."

"Excuse me, please, but you're a cultured man. . . ."

. . . Not the usual greeting at the races. I wonder what this old fox wants with me anyway?

"I don't wish to trouble you, but could you please give me a clue. . . ."

It's all clear, he's just following suit. It seems they already consider me a professional; they're asking for advice.

"Sorry, but nobody knows anything in this heat. They're

mainly hitting on Othello and Ideologue, playing the dark horse. . . ."

The old man knits his brow: "You've misunderstood me. You're a teacher, and they say, a good teacher. . . ."

. . . I can feel myself blushing. It's a bad business. Fame, of course, is a pleasant thing, but one fine day at my school they're going to get wind of the fact that I play the horses and someone will remark at the next teacher's meeting: "Yes, dear comrades, what kind of example is our historian setting for the future generation?"

The old guy generously doesn't notice my embarrassment:

". . . So here, clue me in, in *Evening's* latest crossword, there's a Turgenev play, a long word, second letter *a*. . . . Did Turgenev really write plays?"

"Yes, he wrote *A Month in the Country*. . . ."

The old guy, dejectedly:

"Quite right, but I need one word, a long word, second letter *a*. . . ."

"Parasite."

"That's it. Thanks, you saved my life."

Whew!

I go back to the box. Our guys have already taken their places. They're looking like demons and not saying anything. Obviously, everybody's bet a lot; they're engrossed in the race.

"Well, guys, who do you want me to root for?"

"What, did you bet, too? A dark horse, most likely. . . ."

I, in turn, assume a demonic look, too. It would be embarrassing to admit that I discovered nothing supernatural and bet mostly on the biggest standouts.

And they're off with a dash, a whirl, a leap, and a gallop!

. . . Ideologue paced off two quarters—no one alongside—
and ran easily through the third quarter, and nobody could
catch up because they were boxed in behind the leader.
Wheat Top got a toehold on the sulky behind Othello, and
they dogged each other, while Ideologue was in the home
stretch, and right now, of course, Petya can't be caught, and
Petya easily comes in first and makes his bow to the esteemed
public, while Petya's wife waves a book of tickets from the
grandstands—she bet a tenner on His Eminence; they'll give
her seven rubles per, and that's bread on the table.

. . . and they came out all proper and regular, and Kolya
on Liana did a great job of setting the pace, while Petya and
Moysika kept an eye on each other; they turned the third
quarter in thirty-five, but Wheat Top and Gunta, in general
didn't find their stride, so while Ideologue and Othello were
watching each other, Kolya flashed by from the outside on
Liana like a whirlwind; Moysika and Petya go to the whip
and weep and moan, but Liana is already first at the finish,
and the loudspeaker announces an administrative order:
"Jockey Kolya is promoted to first class and is designated captain of the thirtieth division." It's just a shame he didn't wager
a ruble on himself, but money can't buy happiness. . . .

. . . and they were rushing like madmen, first quarter—
29, second quarter—29, but Zhenya's riding easy; he's holding Cherepet back as he hums along. But at the third quarter,
Zhenya sees that everyone's reared up, reared up to the barrier. But Zhenya goes by easy, so easily; why not win if
there's a chance. You don't ride in a derby every day.

. . . and here in the third quarter, everyone reared up
except Cherepet, who ambled by and went alone to the finish line; Zhenya was checking the little mare; he'd decided

that was that. Here's where Samsonov rushed Chug-a-Lug and won by half a head right at the pole. Half a head—but that's enough; the main thing is to keep a head on your shoulders. And there's a groan from the grandstands; orderlies flash by in white smocks and carry the crooks, who bet hundreds of rubles on the favorites, out on stretchers. Moscow, of course, shoots from the hip, but we aren't wooden dummies in Kalinin, either.

　. . . when they gave the start, Mosya closed his eyes, and when he opened them, Othello was first at the finish. He'd lost them all in the distance.

　. . . while Magidov lost properly on Gouache. He stopped after the first quarter, a carpet was loaded into his sulky, and things got more cheerful right away. He built up the pace, but then he couldn't build it up when they were giving away smoked sausage at the second quarter. At the third quarter turn, he got East German scarves, Polish shirts, Romanian overcoats, and some other items in short supply. Now they were holding all the horses back because they were weighing out oranges and there wasn't a line, but Magidov shunned the oranges—he'd have time tomorrow at GUM. After all, oranges are just an amusement; got to win the All-Union Grand Prix.

　. . . just as they've come out of the second turn, Gunta sees her husband standing by the track, pale, lips trembling, asking—imploring—"Don't let me down, honey, I bet the last of the money on you," but next to him, next to the damn dog, is his bespectacled, black-haired whore with her uncombed hair; she turns her back. "And I don't give a damn about you!" says Gunta. Her husband makes his play: "We'll buy a Rubin TV set with the winnings and start living quietly, as a family," while the bespectacled snake lifts her skirt and sneers. "I don't believe you!" says Gunta. Her husband says in a sobbing voice, "Guntochka, one last chance, I swear, absolutely no chicks. And with the change left over from the television, we'll go to the movies in the evening." "Okay!" says Gunta, and she lets the bespectacled carrion have it across the backside with the whip! She gives a yell and runs off, but can you really run from Gunta? Gunta's after her, and with the whip, with the whip! The bespectacled one's vanished as though the earth had swallowed her, but Gunta looks at her stopwatch—it turns out she's turned the quarter in twenty-nine! Well, the rest was going according to scientific principle: nobody was getting around Wheat Top in the home stretch.

. . . It's like this: once the collective, together with the comrade from the district committee, had entrusted Lipin with an important mission. Lipin wouldn't let them down. It's like this: a high-calorie feeding was distributed to each horse yesterday—three eggs and three bottles of Borzhom water to each of them. More than likely, of course, the others scarcely thought about it: they chased vodka with the Borzhom water and fixed themselves an omelette with the three eggs. But Lipin is a responsible man; he knows when he can steal and when he can't. He mixed the eggs with the bran, and he didn't spare the salt—"Eat, Little Precipice, enjoy." And he fed all the Borzhom water to the stallion; let him walk, if it feels good. Well, of course the stallion understood his concern; he walked from place to place; it doesn't mean anything that Valka trained him in Perm.

. . . well, the first heat was remarkable for Vanya! You'll never see anything like it in your worst dreams. It started with Petya's error when he ran the hell out of Ideologue at the start. The stallion was making a cut and rode off the track, but as he was going off the track, Othello ran into him—and right then he broke his stride! Naturally, Vanya could sympathize with the guys: look what rotten luck they had, but all because they did it wrong: you can't just come roaring out of the gate—and he rode along easy, without any regrets. What's there to be nervous about when there're still six horses ahead? But look there—Precipice is galloping; he's galloping and galloping; Lipin, the Perm salt-ears, can't hold him back. And Precipice's cited for breaking stride! But Lipin has fouled twice, because he cut into Wheat Top and broke Gunta's sulky. Gunta drove off and then Vanya got the idea that what was cooking was starting to stink. Sure, there were still four horses ahead, but they were no match for White Sail. Time had come to pull up and ride with the pack, to hide behind Gouache. But the grandstands are already whistling—there's already a racket in the grandstands. They ran and ran, and then suddenly Magidov had a detached harness, and Gouache hurried off to the stables at a gallop! True, Mosya rode past on the outside, and although he led the race it doesn't count because Othello broke his stride. But the hands of the guys who were telepathically sending messages to Vanya have started to shake with fear: they didn't know—they never guessed—that they'd win the first heat. Cherepet jostled Zhenya out of the sulky. It's a good thing Vanya checked his stallion, or he'd have accidentally run him over. Now all hopes are on Liana and Chug-a-Lug. Home stretch. Well, guys, don't pass out! No, such things don't even happen in dreams: a wheel's falling off under Samsonov, and Liana's gone lame and is limping. . . . Vanya's holding his stallion back with all his might, but he won't listen; he's tearing down to the finish. The grandstands are whistling, straining; the grandstands are howling like wolves. The home stretch— and nowhere for Vanya to hide. Liana has really reared up; she's thrown a shoe. And now Vanya's the only one and it's ten meters to the finish pole. What's that poor crumb Vanya to do? See, he can't come in in the first heat: Ilyusha the Vegetable Man would kill him. And he'd have a right to. Once Vanya's taken the money, Vanya has to fulfill the agreement. And that's how the agreement went—only in the second heat. Vanya didn't even bet a ruble on himself in this race, and only a fool rides for nothing. What rotten luck! Where is there to hide? Five meters to the pole. And Vanya mentally crosses himself and steels himself—well, here goes! He whipped Sail, pulled the reins, and started bellowing in a wild voice, showing off a valiant send—the stallion spooked and went by the post at a gallop. That's the way. Now let the money be returned to the public. Vanya's both innocent before the public and clean before Ilyusha the Vegetable Man. But we'll check it out in the second heat. . . .

CORYPHAEUS: "Whoa, what's this? Start being held up? The driver's jumped out of the Volga pickup and opened the hood. Well, that's business as usual; something always breaks down before the large purses. The racetrack brings in millions, but they can't keep a starting machine in working order! In past derbies, the starting board wouldn't work, and they'd make the announcement over the loudspeaker. Technology is on the verge of the fantastic. . . . Yeah, in bygone derbies, I'd play Peacock, but when Little Huguenot came in, they paid ten-to-one. There won't be any jam-up this time.

Othello should win. Or Ideologue. Or Wheat Top. In any
case, I played all three. To the Professional, of course, that
kind of play is laughable. He only bets on one horse. But the
Teacher and the Dandy more than likely loaded up a dark
horse. Hey, boys, you make fun of an old man, but I've been
at the races forty years, and I know: you have to believe in the
booth; the one who's the favorite at the booth is the one that
wins. Jockeys have plenty of buddies, and they invariably tell
them who they think stands a chance. The buddies have their
friends; the friends have acquaintances with whom they
trade information. . . . Look, half the racetrack's already gotten wind of what's what. And all this information is reflect-
ed in the booths' registers. Hence the moral: 'The booth is
always right.' In my time, boys, I've tested every variant of
play. I've gone with a 'fan,' thrown out both 'two-by-two' and
the favorites, and hunted around for a dark horse. In '51, on
the ninth of July, my shining hour came: I guessed Guardia
with Orion, and they paid. . . . No boys, you laugh at the old
man—say, 'He strains himself for kopecks . . . ,' well, for one
ticket, as I now recall—I got 8,132 rubles, and that's in new
money! The only ticket like that in the whole racetrack—
three-seven—was mine! With a sum like that, boys, I could
have bought three Victories, built a dacha. True, they weren't
setting up cooperative houses then; I would have gotten into
a cooperative. After all, I've been pining away in my one-
room communal apartment all my life. But there weren't any
cooperatives then; that, most likely, is what decided it. Well,
boys, what would you have done in my place? Put the money
into savings? Started buying diamond rings? Gone to a Black
Sea resort? But boys, you don't know the old man very well
at all. And back then, in '51, I was still—oh-ho! I used to wear a

suit of English wool, and Marya Yakovlevna, my wife, didn't resent me; we'd eat at the Metropole once a week. And besides, guys, I had a mistress—the director's secretary, Annechka. On the whole, I was right in my prime, boys. And it seemed to me that life still lay ahead, and boy-oh-boy, it was a long way to retirement. . . . In a word, I got my winnings (I left the cashiers a hundred—and I will never forget the look on their faces, boys. . . . For two years after that they let me come up to the booth without standing in line), called my friends, who were sitting in this box right where you are—Ivan Ivanych (deceased), Mikhail Mikhailych (deceased), Mosya Naumych (laid up in the Botkinskaya Hospital with a stroke), Kirill Trofimych (it's been a long time since he had anything to do with the races!), and I invited the neighboring box, and more people that I knew came running, and some young chicks came out of nowhere! Those that came running were making a fuss; they were sucking up, but I was giving the orders. Taxis for everybody! They came in a flash. To the river station at Khimki! We got there, boys, and I reserved a whole steamboat—an excursion steamer that conducted four-hour tours up and down the canal. But there was more: there was a sumptuous feast in the steamboat's saloon. The bar-maids caught on; they gave us first-class service. There was a bottle of champagne in every cabin, so if anybody wanted to be with a lady, as you please, it's all at your service. . . . A redhead was close by me in a whirl, a smart one—she might have been a waitress, or just hanging around, but to tell the truth, I don't recall if I was able to avail myself. That was when I was solemnly declared to be the Coryphaeus! It's no joke, guessing Guardia with Orion! I had to work up the nerve for that one, boys! Yes, boys, we went on a great spree—drank only KS cognac; they served us caviar, sturgeon, fried chicken (there wasn't any shortage of that back then), dancing on the deck. The whole boat drank a toast to my honor—they were kissing the captain! . . . But now, boys, rack your brains: at any point in my life could I, a simple Soviet worker, have afforded the like, if it hadn't been for the races? . . . Oh, yea-a-ah . . . I came to in the morning in the apartment of a person I'd never seen before and never met again; I took out my wallet with a weak hand, and there were exactly seventy rubles. (Seven in new money.) My comrades had shown me their sincerity, left me the hair of the dog. And my unfamiliar bosom buddy and I dragged ourselves off to drink some beer. In the evening, of course, I had a special conversation with Marya Yakovlevna, my wife, but Annechka wasn't the least bit offended; on the contrary, she began to respect me. And believe this, boys: that eight thousand didn't bother me a bit. I'll remember that sweet day to my death. After all, I felt human for the first time in my life. . . . Well, what's this, have they fixed the machine? They're off! Come on, Ideologue, push it! Ideologue's all alone! Othello's all alone! As a last resort, Wheat Top! Boys, I forgot to tell you the most important thing: since that bright day, I've lost so much money in search of dark horses that I've been convinced by my own experience that in the majority of cases, the one that they're playing at the booth comes in. The booth knows everything. . . .

Nothing special happened in the first heat. They formed up tight from the start. Precipice went into a gallop right away and beat Wheat Top out, but Gunta, it's true, was holding the stallion back. Ideologue started out in the lead, thirty-one in the first quarter, thirty-one in the second. . . . By then it was already clear that none of the out-of-towners could cut it for a fast ride. Othello was holding sedately back behind Ideologue; in the third quarter, Petya, who'd apparently realized that there wasn't a chance, checked the stallion. Or maybe Ideologue just got winded. Or maybe Petya was just being "sophisticated." Wheat Top, after being beaten out, took no more part in the battle, while Liana tried to come out third and broke into a gallop. At the home stretch Mosya set an easy gait and Othello won the heat in record time—2:06.3.

The racetrack went wild. All the totoshniks raced in three or five tickets, while the smart people had as many as thirty. Me, it turned out that I had just one winning ticket— seven-five. And in the next race Kolya brought Faithful in with no trouble, while Pasha came in last on Careful.

The results: from Othello to His Eminence, they paid three rubles, ten kopecks, from Othello to Faithful, two rubles, ninety kopecks. I bet eleven rubles and got back . . . six. And I suffered greatly!

They announced over the loudspeaker that in the second heat of the Grand Prix for three-year-olds, His Eminence, Ballet and Labyrinth were being withdrawn, and from the second heat of the Grand All-Union, Precipice and Liana. So why had I thrown away two rubles on Liana?

"Well, guys, what'll we do?" the Professional cheerily inquired. (He had gone for broke on Othello, so things are Okay with him.)

"Personally, I'm not even betting a kopeck on Patrician," the Dandy declared. "I'm not falling for Vitaly's tricks anymore."

We hastily considered the situation: two heats are coming up: one right after the other. We've seen the horses. Clearly,

Othello isn't letting anybody get by in the second heat of the Grand All-Union. No one's going to better Othello's time. True, Wheat Top's not out of the running. After all, he got thrown off kilter. Okay, we'll cover Wheat Top with one ticket, but when we go for broke, we'll play Othello. But who from? Let's have a look right now. Patrician—to hell with him! Not a kopeck or a ruble on him! Do we swear? We swear! Polite? Doesn't impress me. Guys, Soloist is stretching out! Boy, look at him go! There's no doubt about it, Soloist is all alone! Even I've marked five rubles for this one. Four tickets to Othello and one to Wheat Top. Cowards don't play cards (or for that matter, the horses).

The Dandy ran to the booth and returned with pleasant news: they're hardly touching Soloist, but they're hitting hard on assorted trash, mainly the out-of-towners. That means Soloist is dark enough that they'll be paying a minimum of ten for him, even to Othello. I've got four tickets and Wheat Top for insurance. This is the life, guys!

Coryphaeus appeared and I could tell by his lascivious eyes that he'd come up with something sly. We took Coryphaeus aside. He hemmed and hawed, but then showed us five tickets—from Soloist to Othello.

"It's bad," the Professional grew morose, "if Coryphaeus is betting on Soloist—there's no way Soloist will make it, I guarantee it!"

We take it as an omen: Coryphaeus only guesses the biggest favorites. If he picks out one that's a bit darker, then something is definitely going to happen—either a break into a gallop or a broken harness.

Coryphaeus, of course, is offended. "Hey, guys, you don't appreciate the old man, but in '51. . . ." Okay, enough already.

We've heard that ancient story before and it's not all that believable! Let's cut the talk! Pay attention, you guys, the race is about to start!

Well, well, Soloist, come on, baby, let's go! So, all set, guys? Soloist really took the lead: 31.5 and he's going, going . . . and nobody's near him. Nice work, Professional, you spotted the horse. And you say Soloist was barely touched? There wasn't even a line for him at two windows? And the second quarter—thirty-two, while the rest are way back. "Way, way back in the drifting mists. . . ." But what kind of chestnut scum is that breaking out? He's catching up to Soloist, passing him like he was standing still. . . . Guys, it's Patrician! What a creep! What a beast! Soloist is beginning to fade; he's fallen back to third place. And Patrician's going faster and faster. . . .

On the steps of the forty-kopeck grandstands a drunk, the same one who managed to lap his share up since morning, is wailing: "Break stride, Vitaly—you mug! Break stride, Vitaly—you mug!"

That's it, right, break stride. Which way? It's all over. Patrician's gone past the finish pole. But what's the stop-watch say? 2:07.5. He didn't better His Eminence's time—he took second place overall, but see, if Vitaly'd run in the first heat, who knows, Patrician could have gotten around His Eminence.

The Professional tosses his tickets in a frenzy and curses in a fierce voice: "Really, that scum Vitaly and his carrion! In the first heat we'd have made millions on him—well, not millions, but hundreds, but now he hasn't won the purse and he's ruined us."

By the way, I've got two rubles saved in reserve from my

basic capital. But there's thirteen races still ahead. You can dodge as much as you want. I've got to stand in line for half an hour to get my lousy winnings from the first race; the lines at the window are huge. . . .

Ah, damned poverty!

4

PRIVATE LIFE

In the morning Mama called and said she felt bad. Then my sister called and said that Mama was resting quietly; she'd fallen asleep, and said we weren't to hurry, but to come all the same. When I got there, there was an ambulance parked at the entrance. There's a doctor in the room. Mama's wearing an oxygen mask.

"It's for you to decide," said the doctor. "She needs to go to the hospital. I'm afraid we'll never make it. . . ."

But Mama heard these words and requested: "To the hospital!"

The hospital was three blocks away. The ambulance was rattling over potholes. I sat by the stretcher, squeezing my mother's hot hand. We made it.

At the hospital they immediately hooked up Mama to some device called an IV. The ambulance doctor kept repeating, "Granny's very bad." (For some reason, he kept calling my mama "Granny.") However, the doctors at the hospital were very reassuring—nothing terrible, they said, the crisis is past—go back home—if you want to visit the patient, come back tomorrow, during regular visiting hours.

We returned to Mama's apartment. There were telephone conversations with my brother. My brother is a busy man. Pressing work, small children. We agreed there was no big rush, but he'd go straight to the hospital in a couple of hours.

My sister was pacing back and forth in the room like a pendulum. She said, "We'd better go to the hospital." We got there. They don't allow you upstairs. Unauthorized. The cloakroom attendant was implacable, like the custodian of a secret factory. My sister left her coat with me and went up the stairs. The cloakroom attendant howled after her. Then I tossed the coat and took off running up the stairs. My sister was on a landing, howling with all her might. I leaned out into the corridor. At the other end, right there on the floor . . . Some women in white smocks were bent over her. Suddenly these women straightened up all together as though on command and backed away. And she was left lying on the floor on a narrow stretcher. A bed on wheels materialized from somewhere. They picked her up from the floor, laid her on the bed, and silently covered her with a blanket. They carted her off to the side.

Flanking me, the white smocks formed a sort of wall. I said: "You can see I'm calm. There won't be a scene. Lift up the blanket."

They still hadn't had time to close her eyes. Her eyes were black; the stamp of horror was on them. And there were drops on her cheeks. But my mama's face was astonishingly alive. . . .

I stayed in the hospital waiting room and waited for my brother. I saw him coming through the glass door, and he also

saw through that door that I was coming to meet him. And he
understood everything.

My brother and I got to the district registration office less
that half an hour before closing time. There was no one at the
registration window, but the registration clerk yelled:

"You made it; you didn't gather any dust. But couldn't
you have made it just a little bit later?"

My brother gnashed his teeth and sidled up to the window. I felt like he was going to fling a chair at the dear girl at
any moment and spoke up as calmly as possible:

"You see, we're not here to register a marriage. Someone
has died. . . ."

"All right," muttered the girl, "I see. Give me the papers.
But next time. . . ."

That's exactly what she said: "Next time. . . ."

A poster graced the hall: "Welcome!"

My mama received a special pension. After the death of
a special pensioner, family members have the right to receive
the pension for two more months.

I pushed the papers through the savings bank window.

The inspector put her glasses on and threw her hands up
in the air: "Just like it was all arranged for you!"

I could guess what it was that disgusted the woman.
Mama had received her usual pension payment on
November 20th. And she died on the 22nd. If she had died
on the 19th, then her November payment would have been
considered part of those two. Really, they arranged it clev-
erly! They receive a payment and die right then, and the
state still has to pay another two months. However, the
inspector refrained from further remarks. Nothing to be

done about it. Once you've been outwitted, you've got to
pay. The law's the law.

My mama was seventy-eight years old when she died.
She worked as a doctor all her life. But they didn't give her
the special pension for that. She'd joined the party in 1919.

When an old party member dies, it's customary to make
an announcement in the paper. They only accept this
announcement with the district party visa. Several little old
men pensioners from the party organization attached to the
housing services office (ZhEK) that Mama was with in her last
years voluntarily offered to take the trouble. And the little old
men honestly ran up and down the district committee stairs,
waited in reception rooms, and really did get the visa. But
then there was a ring and a devastated voice on the receiver:

"We got the visa, and the district committee's supposed
to pay for the announcement in the paper, but. . . ," the
receiver was sobbing audibly, "they say that the district committee doesn't have any money now. They'll have the money
at the end of the week, but . . . what can we do now?"

I ask them not to worry. Thanks, comrades! We'll pay for
it ourselves. My brother takes off for the newspaper; he'll fix
everything. . . .

Mama was in the party for fifty years, but the district
committee doesn't have the money to announce the death of
an old Bolshevik. It's a good thing Mama will never find out
about this.

My brother goes to the newspaper. And the phone rings
again. My brother's done-in voice:

"I don't have enough money for the announcement. I
just didn't know it was so expensive. The cashier's window

is closing, and they don't believe in credit. . . ."

This way the announcement is going to appear after the funeral. And then I recall that I have the ability, so to speak, to shed the skin of a simple Soviet. I'm acquainted with this newspaper's editor-in-chief's daughter. She was once a student in my class. I dial the number. Confusedly, I explain what the problem is and promise that of course I'll pay him when I see him. . . . I'm interrupted in mid-sentence. . . .

"Where's your brother? In the corridor of the editorial office?"

Later, my brother recounted that five minutes after our conversation, the editor-in-chief's secretary came hustling out to him, lamenting, waving the money the chief had given her personally.

In short, in the end everything was done the way Mama probably would have wanted. The retirees from her ZhEK organization brought a wreath they'd pitched in for, and they organized right there in the apartment a sort of political meeting, made speeches—they acquitted themselves well. I wasn't listening. I was sitting in the other room with my friends. And I caught myself thinking, "I think Mama would be pleased to know that lots of people came to honor her memory. . . ."

And I still remember that I kept fussing around the whole time, busying myself with trivial things and smoothing things over. I could have managed quite well without this, but you know, it's somehow easier when you make like you're attending to business. Anyway, somebody had to be "attending to business." Why not me?

In the morning, I got on the bus at Vagankovsky Cemetery and went to the morgue on the other side of town. The bus

driver was like a representative of the government, while I
was a typical citizen he could fleece three times over.
Somehow nothing that had been paid for earlier counted. I
accepted these terms. The driver sat in his friend's bus for a
while, like he was helping him. Another ten-spot. I agreed to
this, too. A colleague of mine from school, a physics teacher,
was waiting for me at the morgue. The four of us (a funeral
procession of two teachers and two gravediggers) dragged the
coffin to the bus. . . .

The new crematorium now "serving" Muscovites is located
ten kilometers beyond the ring road. We went clear across
town again, and the streets with their thin gruel of snow and
filth boiled under the wheels of roaring industry. Our bus
wove daringly between huge trailers and dump trucks—we
were going like there was a fire somewhere.

The new crematorium is a modern factory, an assembly-
line production. We stood at the tail end of the line. And now
the driver said he couldn't wait because he was supposed to
pick up his kids at the kindergarten. No doubt, that's a good
reason, but why didn't he tell me this beforehand, when I
submitted my order at the office? A naive question. I paid
him. And the satisfied driver decided to help me out. He
brought the driver of another bus, obviously a fly-by-night. A
predatory, calculating look. Okay, so be it. The fly-by-night
will take us back to town, but . . . it's an astronomical sum.
I've no choice. A lot of old men have shown up to bury my
mama. How can we drag them to town from out here, trans-
ferring three times on the subway? I need a bus. I agree.

The conveyer line moves along unhurriedly. The fly-by-
night approaches again. A violet flame is burning in his eyes. He
understands that he can keep fleecing me. He threatens to drive

off in five minutes, or. . . . Okay, I agree, I dig into my pockets and count out the money. Then, ten minutes later, it's the same thing all over again. It's like a game—the stakes keep going up. And he came up to me like that three more times. . . .

The service of the world's first workers' and peasants' government was baring its fangs.

It's a good thing, I thought, that my mama will never find out about this.

THE RACES

Yurochka the Gas Man corkscrewed himself in between Belly Bellyich and Fat Fatych and noticed right off that the beer bottles and glasses had vanished from the barrier. Ilyusha the Vegetable Man was biting his lip and looking at the track. Yurochka followed that gaze. White Sail was breezing. The stallion placed his hooves sharply, like a ballerina on pointe.

"Who's the booth playing?" asked Ilyusha the Vegetable Man, and there was no trace of the former joking and rakishness in his voice.

"They're only hitting Othello; he's only worth a three."

"Are they touching Ideologue?"

"A little," Yurochka answered readily, and he felt a slight disappointment. In the second heat, Ideologue, of course, would be good for five rubles in single, but could these really be the miracles Ilyusha promised?

Wheat Top breezed. Gunta leaned back, pulling on the reins, restraining the stallion with all her might.

"How much will they give for that one?" The Vegetable Man shot a predatory look at Wheat Top.

"Around ten to fifteen rubles, no less. After all, he didn't show anything in the first heat."

The Vegetable Man took three tenners and looked condescendingly at Yurochka.

"You're going to put a ten-spot from Wheat Top to five, seven, and eight. Run to the forty."

Yurochka dumbfoundedly shifted his eyes from the Vegetable Man to Lard Lardych. Lard Lardych's face was imposing and impenetrable.

And Yurochka the Gas Man took off; he took off ahead of his own joyful scream; buttonholing between people, shouldering, oozing, flying and crawling through, he took off at a bold stride for booth 139. And at the entranceway, a little man with a moustache and a seven-peaked cap hooked on, repeating Yurochka's intricate buttonholes.

The Bakunian was watching attentively down from the balcony at Ilyusha the Vegetable Man's crew. He saw how quickly Yurochka the Gas Man galloped off to the forty. The loudspeaker noted that three minutes remained until the booths were closed. And then the foursome of Ilyusha's crew fanned out into the depths of the grandstands. They moved powerfully and purposefully, cutting the crowd like icebreakers cutting through thin floes of ice.

The little man with the moustache in the seven-peaked cap came running up to the Bakunian, panting as heavily as a hound. The Bakunian impatiently ripped a hefty pack of tickets from his hand, shuffled them, and knit his brow.

"The Vegetable Man's loading up Wheat Top? Just how much did the Gas Man bet?"

"Thirteen tickets per, three ways," reported the moustache, puffing like a steamer.

"Thanks, Stasik," the Bakunian rumbled affectionately, stashed the tickets, kneaded a cigarette and lit a match. His movements were demonstrably slow, but as he brought the match up to the cigarette, the Bakunian's thoughts flashed quick and sharp:

Thirteen per. The Gas Man added a three of his own. That means with a tenner. And we repeated with twenty rubles. The Vegetable Man is all sewed up. Now I understand— Gunta was simply holding Wheat Top back in the first heat. That's what it looks like. But a ten-spot isn't the bet for Ilyukha. Ilyukha doesn't dabble. So what do we have? He's loading three of them up. Five and eight are the favorites. Seven is a dark horse. For now, that's very valuable information. Paunchich and Bellyich are going to make the main bet. Who from?"

The Bakunian threw away his cigarette and, with an ease unexpected of such a massive man, with elegance, started to glide down the stairs.

Paunch Paunchich pushed through to the booth. A character with a jacket over his naked body silently ceded his place in line to Paunch Paunchich. They were calling after him in outrage. The totoshniks knew that if Ilyusha the Vegetable Man's man walked up to the booth just under the bell, the rest wouldn't make it. But they were making noise more for the sake of propriety. Everybody was curious to see Paunch Paunchich's bet, and then all of a sudden, luck takes a turn for the better, and you can play a ruble with a cashier you know.

Paunch Paunchich put three rubles on Wheat Top, three rubles on Ideologue, three rubles on Othello, then rummaged in his pockets at length, extracted a fiver, bought a ticket from

Gouache, from Cherepet, and again three rubles from Wheat Top.

"Ilyukha's looking for dark horses," someone sang merrily behind Paunch Paunchich's back.

The bell sounded, and simultaneously Paunch Paunchich adroitly threw a crisp, green piece of paper into the window—a fifty-ruble note.

"Fifteen tickets each from number six to numbers five, seven, and eight."

"Ilyusha's loading White Sail up!" the line gasped.

Like Alexander Matrosov, who closed off a gunport with his body, Paunch Paunchich leaned in the window, and with a satisfied grin, followed the nimble fingers of the cashier as they feverishly filled out the sixth line of the registers with a dark blue pencil. The cashier counted out the tickets and covered them with a fiver in change. But what's this? The cashier's opened a new line for number six, and she swiftly writes out some new tickets: 6-5, 6-7, and again 6-7, 6-8. Paunch Paunchich collected his tickets, but who are these for? Maybe the cashier's made a mistake. But no, she matter-of-factly tosses them over to the right, into the hands of a young honey sitting at the pay window. "It's an outrage, selling after the bell!" Paunch Paunchich wanted to roar, but having glanced to the left, to the pay side of the booth, he was met by the triumphant gaze of the Bakunian.

*   *   *

I couldn't think of anything interesting to do with the remaining two rubles. I connected Othello and Wheat Top with number five, Little Huguenot, the big favorite. Of course, they'll give something from Wheat Top, but frankly, there's no hope for Wheat Top. For Othello with Little Huguenot, they'll pay the same two rubles. The question arises, what were we struggling for?

I hung around at the cashier's window until the beginning of the fifth race. Have to get suffocated again to get my six rubles legal winnings. . . . Well, yeah, my present stake isn't a wager, but a capitulation. Anyway, it serves me right: I shouldn't have gotten burned on Ideologue; after all, I'd sworn not to touch him with so much as a ruble. Hence the lesson: don't give in to provocation; play your play. And how many lessons like this has the racetrack taught me? A full university course's worth, although evidently I'm a mediocre student.

I went back to the box. The guys were somber. What kind of merriment could there be when they've let Patrician get by them, and there're no bright ideas at all for the next races? Or should we switch to playing the sorry favorites?

Coryphaeus's come squeezing through sideways. He has that old storyteller's look again. But enough keeping it secret; out with it. . . .

"Boys, I've been to the forty; down below, the crooks are loading Wheat Top up, and I covered him with a fiver."

The Professional winced: "I was counting on Wheat Top, too. But once Coryphaeus has bet on him it's death, guys; pitch your tickets."

Coryphaeus, of course, took offense: "Hey, boys, you don't appreciate the old man, but in fifty, I. . . ." Enough, we're up to here with that story! Pay attention, you guys, the start!

They're off, they're off to a good start. Don't break stride,

Wheat Top. Come on, baby! There you go, just don't let 'em get too far! . . . Of course, as usual, Ideologue's stampeded out in front, but he doesn't scare us. . . .

But what's this? For some reason White Sail's turned out to be first. Quarter completed in 31.5. He's widened the gap at the back stretch. Second quarter—30.5. The racetrack's gotten quiet. White Sail is scooting along like a machine. Ideologue and Othello are bursting for strength, but there's no question of there being enough! And Wheat Top is in the pack; he just plain didn't pace himself. . . .

The familiar voice of the drunk cuts through the silence: "Break stride, Vanka, you mug! Break stride, Vanka, you mug!"

And all at once, the grandstands explode. It's a mob scene at the racetrack, a mob scene: millions are riding! The Dandy is yelling into my ear: "What kind of time are they running?" Thirty-one in the third quarter. They're running at 2:04. Maybe White Sail'll rear up at the finish?"

"No," yells the Professional, "White Sail isn't going to rear up!"

Coryphaeus sighed and smacked his tickets on the floor. The horses went into the home stretch.

CORYPHAEUS: "So, I lost, I'm not sorry. It's a real derby, a pleasure to watch. There'll be a new record in the Moscow Racetrack. Vanya's a fine fellow, trained the stallion well, and wowed the crowd! Can Othello really have lost? Can Ideologue have lost? But 2:04—they're not up to it. Vanya'll make master—it's long overdue. Oh, what a race, what a race! These aren't the same disgraceful derbies as when Tulumbash came in first. That was shameful: he came in in 2:10 and took the purse. The two-year-olds run faster in other countries. But see, the management most likely wanted in on the glory for success in the nation's horsebreeding. And they sat down in the mud. And who presided over that? Semyon Mikhailich and Leonid Ilich!

The Story of How Tulumbash Won the Derby in 2.10.
(Historical Information by the Teacher)
But First, about Marshal Budyonny.

Semyon Mikhailovich Budyonny, a descendant of poor non-Cossacks, was drawn to horses from his earliest years. While still serving in a dragoons regiment, he was sent to the St. Petersburg Cavalry School for Horsemen. He dreamed of staying at the school as a trainer. Alas, the authorities judged otherwise and ordered him to return to his regiment. Semyon Mikhailovich harbored a grudge against the officers, although he didn't leave the army; he received the rank of senior sergeant and continued to serve as an enlisted man.

In September 1914, Budyonny distinguished himself in battle near Bzheziny and was awarded the St. George's Cross, fourth class. Soon the division was transferred to the Turkish front, where Budyonny carried out the duties of a platoon leader. A bold, skillful swordsman, he earned three more crosses and became a full holder of the St. George's medal. On the German front Budyonny, no doubt, would have been made an officer, but military affairs with Turkey developed slowly and lazily.

Nineteen-seventeen came. The whirlwind of revolution began to sweep through Russia—divisions disbanded, soldiers scattered to their homes, but non-commissioned officer

Budyonny sensed that he wasn't through fighting.

And then 1918 arrived—a glorious time for those who stayed firm in the saddle. General Krasnov raised the banner of the White Revolt on the Don. The Civil War began. Red Cossacks were organizing partisan detachments.

One blizzardy February night Budyonny's detachment, consisting of twenty-four men in all, carried out a daring raid on the large Cossack village of Platov, massacred a Kalmyk convoy, and liberated some Red Guard prisoners. The prisoners and part of the villagers enlisted with Budyonny. By morning, the detachment had 520 fighters.

After they attached themselves to the retreating tenth army, Semyon Mikhailovich took part personally in the breaking of young horses and the training of young soldiers. He would laugh at those recruits who mainly relied on the rifle in cavalry attacks and didn't know how to use a sabre. On the Salsky steppes, spirited control and good swordplay decided the outcome of battles. Semyon Mikhailovich rose fast in the world; only one thing irked him: serving under the command of regular officer Dumenko. Dumenko was the regimental commander, Budyonny—his exec. Dumenko was brigade commander, Budyonny—again his executive officer. Dumenko was division commander, Budyonny—his chief of staff. (And later on, Semyon Mikhailovich would be irritated by the presence of regulars in the Red Army: General Kamenev, Colonels Yegorov, Mironov, and Shorin, Lieutenant Tukhachevsky. He hated with a special ferocity one individual who planted military specialists everywhere—Revolutionary War Council Chairman Trotsky. However, Klim Voroshilov, "the first red officer," commanding the tenth army, noticed Budyonny. The Lugansky metalworker Voroshilov and Sergeant

Budyonny found a common language. Thanks to their combined efforts, Divcom Dumenko vanished "into non-existence,"
and Budyonny obtained some operational scope.

Budyonny's cavalry division functioned with great success in the defense of Tsaritsyn. Budyonny ordered all the
cavalry's front strength to form a spearhead. The command
hesitated. But in the summer of 1919, a successful dash by
General Mamontov's White Guard Corps along the Reds' rear
confirmed that Budyonny was correct.

Budyonny was appointed commandant of the First
Cavalry Corps. Now just one minor detail remained—to liq-
uidate a rival, Second Corps commander Mironov. Before
pursuing Mamontov, Budyonny arrested Mironov on the
ostensible charge of treason. Only Trotsky's personal inter-
vention saved Mironov from being shot, but the deed was
done. Parts of the Second Corps joined Budyonny and went
to Voronezh. After a victory at Kastorna, Budyonny came to
command the First Cavalry.

The legendary march of the First Cavalry on Lvov made
all Europe quiver. Semyon Mikhailovich was convinced that
he would surely have taken Lvov and would have thorough-
ly beaten the Polish company had it not been for mistakes by
Yegorov and Tukhachevsky, the commanders at the front,
and Kamenev, the commander-in-chief.

We're red cavalry men, and of our glories
Shall the epic bards weave stories. . . .

For some reason, the epic bards are silent about Divcom
Dumenko and Second Cavalry Arcom Mironov, who,
together with Budyonny, stormed Perekop. In twenty years,

as if by command, the "epic bards" will forget almost all of the heroes of the Civil War who didn't die on time. . . .

The war years stopped thundering, and the army gradually rearmed and changed its tactics, while Budyonny, as of old, was confident in his adherence to cavalry pressure and frenzied swordplay.

"Senya, you ought to study something," Frunze told him in a fit of rage.

And Semyon Mikhailovich studied hard—the game of billiards.

The war years did stop thundering, but revolutionary struggle flared up in the country. Wartime People's Commissar Frunze was "knifed" on the operating table, and former chairman of the Revolutionary War Council Trotsky was expelled abroad. "First red officer" Klim Voroshilov, who had the valuable knack of telling which way the wind blew in upper party spheres, took their places. True, former military specialists still occupied certain positions, and Tukhachevsky and Yegorov became, along with Voroshilov, Budyonny, and Blucher, the first red marshals. But 1937 was still on the horizon. Tukhachevsky and Yegorov, who didn't fully investigate the situation, went on and on about the necessity of the technical rearmament of the army, tank maneuvers, and landing operations, and irritated the Leader and Teacher with their erudition. Blucher also ran afoul—he forgot that the Inspiration and Organizer of our Victories was always Stalin. Semyon Mikhailovich stood to advantage against the background of these thinkers because of his fundamental principle, which was "Let's have at them with sabres." For this very reason, the "first red officer" protected Budyonny.

Budyonny's glory as a commander grew by leaps and bounds in peacetime.

Beginning in 1936, the Red Army courageously and victoriously joined battle with those who comprised its high command. As if by the wave of a magic wand, renowned heroes vanished without a trace—Tukhachevsky, Blucher, Yegorov, Yakir, Uborevich, commandants, commcorps, commdivs. Not once did the brave swordsman Semyon Mikhailovich intercede for anyone. He didn't even intercede for his own wife, who was arrested as a foreign spy. The legendary sabre was rusting away in its scabbard.

However, fate saw fit to come after even Budyonny himself. Possibly the young lieutenants, tired out from nightly visits, fouled up the details, or something like that, but late in the night a cavalcade of cars drove up to the dacha, to Bakovka. Then and there, the holder of St. George's cross showed his courage: a Maxim machine gun, stowed in the attic by Semyon Mikhailovich's solicitous orderly, greeted the unexpected guests. The NKVD platoon threw themselves on the ground. The bullets pinned down anyone who tried to crawl away. Semyon Mikhailovich desperately held the defenses and called the Kremlin. Stalin picked up the phone.

"Comrade Stalin, enemies of the people are surrounding me! I'm defending myself with a Maxim.

"Where'd the machine gun come from?" the receiver inquired with interest.

"I kept it from the Civil War, as a souvenir. . . ."

The receiver coughed uncertainly, and the telephone fell silent until morning. In the morning, Stalin himself called.

"Semyon Mikhailovich, we've figured it out here—

there's been a mistake. Take down the defenses and turn in the machine gun."

Apparently, the "first red officer" had come to the rescue again.

In the summer of '41 Marshal Budyonny commanded the forces of the southwestern sector. Kiev was surrendered under his direct command. The armies fell into a gigantic cauldron. The Germans took half a million prisoners. The famous marshal was safely evacuated by airplane. The next year, Budyonny "ruined" the northern Caucasus sector and was no longer permitted to go to the front. And so he remained chief inspector of the Soviet Army Cavalry for life, thanks to the fact that the cavalry almost never took part in battle, and in the years that followed, the stock of horses in the army was kept to a minimum. (Just how many fighting hobbyhorses, old nags included, are left for sanitary purposes? A thousand, five hundred? We shall be silent, so as not to divulge a state secret.) In the corridors of the Ministry of Defense, young general staffers would laugh up their sleeves when they caught sight of the owner of the legendary moustaches. On the other hand, at the Central Moscow Racetrack a traditional purse was established in honor of Marshal of the Soviet Union, S. M. Budyonny.

On big Racetrack holidays, the marshal would appear in the government box. Totoshka would greet him with joyous applause. (Devastating articles on the racetrack were appearing periodically in the newspapers; satirists suggested banning the totalizator; Budyonny's attendance instilled hope in the hearts of the frightened regulars: "as long as Semyon Mikhailovich is alive," the old timers would say, "they'll never close the racetrack.") The marshal, moved, would greet

the crowd, while the crooks rushed to the booths to bet on
Kochan. Why Kochan in particular? Rumor had it that
Semyon Mikhailich was partial to this jockey. And maybe a
fatal coincidence was to blame, however, it was noted that if
Budyonny was in the booth when there was a purse Kochan's
horse was running for, the miracles would begin—the
favorites would go into a gallop and break stride, and Kochan
would take first place.

. . . . That particular day the totoshniks had been agitated
since morning. The middle boxes in the eighty-kopeck grandstands were cordoned off, and in them sat bored, anonymous
young men in identical sports jackets with bulging pockets.
Down below, in front of the judges and the government
boxes, there were a lot of rookies hanging around, as though
picked for basketball height, not one of them with any trace
of a racing sheet in his hand, and the sight was such that the
cautious crook quickly preferred to migrate to the forty.

They were waiting for Semyon Mikhailovich. There he
appeared at the government heights, and behind him. . . . But
this can't be! It's him—Leonid Ilich Brezhnev, himself! Demo-
cratically, he simply decided to drop in at races, decided to
rub shoulders with the people for a while. . . . Naturally, the
appearance of Himself commanded wild applause, but when
Leonid Ilich, after bowing theatrically to the crowd, kissed
Semyon Mikhailovich three times on the cheek, in accordance
with Russian tradition, the grandstands started weeping.

Alas, even the Lofty Presence didn't distract Totoshka's
attention for long. Soon base, habitual interests occupied
their minds again, the more so since they had to rack their
brains over them. This time the derby was being run on a
new system: the eight best horses were determined from two

semifinal races (four from each race), and the victor of the
final got the main purse. The angle here consisted in the fact
that it wasn't absolutely necessary to occupy first place in the
semifinals—the important thing was to fall into the final four.
That is, the favorite could quietly come in second or third
and save his strength for the deciding race.

The ironclad favorites were Prologue and Direction
Finder. Both stallions had fought each other desperately all
winter and spring with alternating success, leaving no chance
at all to their other competitors. By the luck of the draw, the
favorites were sent to different semifinals, and at first glance,
picking the winners presented no complications at all: "Drop
your britches and put all your dough from Direction Finder
to Prologue. . . ." But the much experienced Totoshka sensed
that the jockeys would want to start working in the semifinals, bearing in mind that there was nothing worth taking
risks for—they'd let by a dark horse into first place and the
payoff would jump up sharply.

Tulumbash was warming up on the track, a handsome
black stud of mediocre blood, and true, one day he'd turned
up third after Prologue and Direction Finder. Tulumbash was
running with a guide rein. Having come out onto the home
stretch, the jockey sent him all out.

Semyon Mikhailovich valiantly twirled a moustache,
and with an unwavering hand, he pointed out Tulumbash:

"There's the one that'll win the derby!"

Leonid Ilich nodded politely, paying tribute to the old
cavalryman's sharp eye.

The face of the racetrack director went deathly pale.

"Comrade Marshal," he ingratiatingly whispered behind
Budyonny's back, "you're a stupendous connoisseur of horses,

but it sometimes happens that conditioning beats class. Of course, you're absolutely right to point out that Tulumbash is classier, but unfortunately, Prologue and Direction Finder are in better condition."

The marshal's neck started to flood with color, and the racetrack director quickly recalled the violent temper of his former cavalry commander.

"Nevertheless, you've got a marvelous sense," the director hastily added whispering, almost sobbing.

Thereupon, the director abandoned the government box for ten minutes. All the jockeys taking part in the All- Union Grand Prix were urgently called to stable five. The director spoke with each of them briefly and in special confidence. The racetrack wolves, who'd seen a lot in their day, hemmed dumbfoundedly and confusedly scratched their heads. The Master, best jockey in the racetrack, a touchy, capricious man, was coming out on Direction Finder, but with him the conversation was simple—in a week, the Master was due to go to France, so let him think it over; he's no child. The Master didn't answer at all; he spat and went out onto the track. That left only Andryukha. The director understood that Andryukha, having just gotten a section, would sooner die than lose on Prologue. It was pointless to try to persuade him. "Andryukha's ready to sell out his motherland for the sake of the derby," the director thought maliciously, but he gave the jockey a friendly pat on the shoulder and didn't say a word.

In the first semifinal, Direction Finder plunged into a gallop out of the gate and left the track. A wild dark horse came in—an out-of-towner from Ramensky.

In the second semifinal, Prologue came in second—

Andryukha wasn't pushing himself—he was sparing the horse.

A fantastic sum of winnings lit up on the board.

"That kind of money for one ruble?" Leonid Ilich was shocked. "That's more than my salary. . . ."

And Leonid Ilich got kind of thoughtful.

The final race began. Tulumbash led from the start. Faithful to his tactics, Andryukha was calmly holding back—Prologue usually intensified the pace suddenly at the third quarter and go out into the lead, and at the finish line, not even Direction Finder could take him. In the absence of his main rival (Direction Finder, having committed that silly break of stride didn't qualify for the final), Andryukha wasn't afraid of anybody—there was nobody to ride with! At the end of the second quarter, Andryukha wanted to send the stallion, but to his horror he discovered that he'd been taken dead into a box—the two horses ahead were going at a false pace, and three' others suddenly came pushing up with Prologue on the inside.

"Sanya, Petya, let me pass," Andryukha begged.

A strange deafness came over the jockeys. They didn't hear Andryukha—they didn't let Andryukha pass.

Prologue almost had to be stopped, and, having waited out the daylight, to go to the outside. Prologue flew into the home stretch like a bird. However, there was no chance at all of catching Tulumbash. The clock gave the winner's time at 2.10. The racetrack was howling.

"It rained last night, the track's sloppy, that's why they came in slow," the director mumbled, averting his eyes. But nobody was listening to him.

There was an amicable bustling in the box. Leonid Ilich

was hurrying off to his dacha for dinner; he thanked the management for the pleasant time and shook their hands.

Semyon Mikhailovich, the dashing cavalryman, decided that it had been a nothing derby—if that dickhead Sashka couldn't produce the genuine article, he'd have to be thrown out of the directors; however, what a trifle that was compared to the fact that he, Budyonny, was invited to dinner at Ilich's. It means the new leadership, unlike that boor Nikita, appreciates the old guard! Oh, hot We're showing ourselves again! ". . . Cross my heart, Grechko'll come running to me tomorrow at the reception, he's probably 'forgotten' my number, but no-the new minister's a stern man; he won't come running, but he'll definitely call."

*   *   *

The horses came out the home stretch.

Vanya glanced at the stopwatch he was holding together with the reins in his left hand: "Hook done in eleven; we're going for 2.04. Hang on, little man, hang on, you gotta put out, put out a little more, let 'em break their legs, the carrion —let it tear 'em up, let 'em swell up! . . . Hang on, little man, hang on!"

Petya kept repeating just one thing: "Oh, Lord, oh, Lord. . . ." He understood that Vanya'd shut everybody down, and he was just hoping for second place. And all of a sudden, a miracle happened: Ideologue shook his head, shook his tail, came to life, and started catching Sail.

"Save us, little brother!" Mosya bit his lip bloody, picked up the reins, and sent the stallion flying.

Even though they were going at a terrific pace, it seemed

to Vanya that everything had come to a standstill; it jelled, and just alongside, quietly, slowly, inevitably, Ideologue moved ahead.

The finish pole was in arm's reach. Ideologue was beating Sail by a head; Petya had already sung his praises to the Lord, but the roar of the grandstands, resounding behind him, like a squall, caused Petya to glance to his right.

Othello was passing on the outside at an incredible stride, spitting wisps of pink foam.

Mosya's yellow silks flashed first across the finish line.

The stopwatches showed 2:03.6.

Ilyusha the Vegetable Man was gulping air like a fish on the bank, tearing up tickets in a fit of rage.

EXCERPT FROM THE RULES:

   Tickets that are ripped, torn, or stuck together are considered invalid and are not honored in payment of any money *whatsoever.*

   Statements concerning lost tickets are not accepted.

   Payments of winnings are made only to the bearer of the totalizator ticket to whom the winnings belong. No claims of any kind by third parties to a share of the given winnings *will be accepted.*

5

OUTSIDE INTERFERENCE

AT THIRTY MINUTES AFTER TWELVE A BLACK VOLGA WITH AN antenna on the roof and two yellow headlights leapt out from a certain back road of the Rublyovsky highway, cut off from the whole world by dense forest and explicit road signs ("Entrance Prohibited"), and after roaring through the turn and abruptly attaining maximum speed, shot off in the direction of Moscow. The armed guards on duty at every kilometer of this government route, armed guards accustomed to the many members of the high command, armed guards who usually glowered lazily at passing Chaikas and only saluted armored ZIL's, snapped to instant attention at the sight of the Volga with the familiar markings and watched the car pass with vigilant gazes.

At one o'clock in the afternoon, the Volga with the yellow headlights braked smoothly alongside the columns of the Moscow Racetrack. The operative who had been sitting next

to the chauffeur got out of the car and obligingly opened the
rear door. A man in a gray suit, middle-aged, of medium
height and average weight, with a face that expressed nothing, absolutely nothing, unhurriedly but briskly climbed the
stairs. The operative hurried ahead of him, energetically
shouldering aside the crowd that was in the way.

The appearance of the gray suit set off the alarm in the
government box. The Deputy Minister of Agriculture, considered to day's most important and honored guest, dropped his
binoculars. A couple of words were quickly whispered to the
racetrack director, who at first didn't understand what was
up, and he nearly had heart failure. "Really?! What an honor!
But why didn't he let us know in advance? And what if
Himself suddenly appears?" A few minutes passed in weari-
some expectation. The man in the gray suit sat down in a
thoughtfully offered chair in the first row and delicately kept
quiet. And then it was surmised that a surprise visit by
Himself was not forthcoming, and this was just a private
visit—after all, doesn't a leading comrade have a right to
relax on Sunday?

Some Borzhom mineral water and little caviar sandwiches from the snack bar were hastily offered. The man in the
gray suit nodded benevolently, but he didn't react to the
sandwiches; he continued to watch the events on the racetrack with avid interest. The deputy minister cast his eyes
eloquently toward the racetrack director—they said, "Don't
be a nuisance; don't bother the leadership." The box calmed
down.

Strictly speaking, the man in the gray suit couldn't be
counted among the leadership. According to hierarchical
nomenclature, even the deputy minister was his superior.

Could a chief of a Union ministry really be compared to an assistant—in essence a rank-and-file office worker? However, the assistant worked in Himself's office, and that changed matters radically; in official newspaper accounts, the name of Himself's assistant came right after the secretaries of the Central Committee.

It seemed that the modest but powerful assistant was utterly captivated by the derby—he even saw fit to applaud Othello's victory in the second heat along with everyone else. But that was just the way it seemed. The man in the gray suit was contemplating different problems; other "races," hidden from the view of outsiders, were what excited him.

"Ten thousand idiots," the relaxing comrade was thinking, as he gazed down from above on the human sea of heads. "Some horses that aren't much to look at, some pointless prizes, some sorry winnings. . . . And this is how the people live? And no one suspects that at our place, in the Big House, our own deciding 'race' is secretly being made ready. . . . Who'll come in first? That's the question I rack my brains over at night. It's a pretty serious game. The favorite is my chief. In principle, he shouldn't lose. Almost everyone is betting on him, and I among them. However, in accordance with race-track regulations, on the favorite even a win is no big deal. Of course, I'll remain in my place—that's not bad at all. But what if I take a risk? Bet on a 'dark horse?' On the economist Stepanych or on 'Iron Shurik?' A sudden twist of fate! I come out in the first rank! But do dark horses stand a chance? The risk is enormous—I lose everything, and irrevocably. All the same, experience teaches that when the Boss goes over, his assistants aren't treated too nicely. Please, God, don't let my chief have a stroke—they'll drive me out of their sight as well, throw me onto the devil's horns as some kind of amb: to Zambia. True, while the chief's in good shape, m) guaranteed. Well, all right, another ten years, maximum—and that's it! There's no prospects. The chief is supported by the Politburo, the Central Committee and the regional committee secretaries. But the moderates are sympathetic to 'Iron Shurik.' The political machine wants to tighten the screws: 'That's enough display of liberalism!' And they'll listen to Stepanych—he'll propose internal monetary reform instead of foreign credit. Why humble ourselves before the West when we can simply take the money from the people? That's how it looks on the surface. But how many underwater currents are there? Yes, I almost forgot Ideologue. Our own Ideologue also aspires to be first, after all. Oh, he'll aspire, all right, he'll aspire, but he hasn't got a chance. Not in that class. Let's throw Ideologue out. (By the way, the situation on the track is really graphic, too: the favorite is too tough a nut for Ideologue.) Stepanych? But if there's no favorite, 'Iron Shurik' will get around him. What trump cards does Shurik have against the chief? First, his youth; second, the support of the political machine; third, the failure of peaceful coex . . . , coex . . . , to hell with it, coexistence; fourth, the impossibility of accepting foreign credit because of one-sided political conditions. Bet on Shurik? Oh, how tempting! You want to, and you hesitate, and Mama won't allow it. . . . And Mama won't allow it because the devil isn't as terrible as he's made out to be! Let's weigh the pros and cons. Here we're expecting a visit by the American president. In principle, in the international 'race' before us, the American is the favorite. He's smarter, more charming and more energetic, and the potential of America is beyond comparison to ours. '(To use racetrack terminology,

he's got better speed.) But after all, a race is tactics. And the
American's tactics depend on parties, on elections, on
Congress, on the newspapers. Ours is free to choose any tac-
tic—he's as free as the Lord God. The American is past master of words—he pours it out like a nightingale. But how will
he explain himself in Congress? Those guys don't sit there
like wooden dummies. But ours just says the word, and it's
the law of the land. Maybe if you really examine it, then
despite the seeming superiority of the American, he's doomed
to lose all the same. (To be sure, that's the American's nature:
despite his intellect, flexibility, perspicacity and resourceful-
ness, he's been raised from childhood so that once he's given
his word, he's got to make good on it.) Of course, he has his
misgivings; he says, couldn't they be deceiving us? But he
won't be able to verify it completely. That's where ours will
get around the American—on the inside. For us the only laws
that exist are those that are advantageous at any given
moment. We accept them ourselves—we reject them ourselves. We regard all treaties and agreements, starting with the
celebrated Brest Peace Accord, as sham paper: to win time, to
gather our strength, and then the paper is brushed aside. . . .
And the people always support us, and the newspapers come
out with arshin-high headlines: 'Such is the Will of the Soviet
People,' 'At the Request of the Sormovsky Workers.' And let
the leaders in Washington, Paris, and London, chatterboxes,
gasbags, orators, the favorites of the crowd scratch their asses
in confusion: 'How can this be? Wasn't there a treaty?' (As
they say in the racetrack, 'How could he break into a gallop?'
That's it exactly: 'If a weenie gets shoved in your face, bite it
off!) Because our goal is the victory of world communism,
understand? And the bourgeoisie and the exploiters are our

class enemies; what could we have to say to each other? Up against the wall with them! And we'll put them there when we can. But meanwhile, we're diplomats, meanwhile, we're for peaceful coex. . . . We've been maneuvering back since NEP; the nepman patched our holes, fed us, gave us shoes— but all the same, cast the nepman down under your heel! No, we began maneuvering earlier, in October 1917, when we swiped agrarian reform from the leftist SR's and gave the land to the peasants. We gave them the land, but when grain became plentiful—we took it away. What the hell kind of private ownership was that? That'll do—we were only joking! And whoever's against collective farms is a kulak! We wrap everybody around our little finger. Iran, Turkey, Germany, France, England, Poland, Finland, Japan, the USA. True, a couple of times we got stuck—by Hitler and Mao Tse Tung; we intended to trick them, too, but they were bright boys; they beat us to it. By the way, even our allies of today—Arab nationalists, black progressives—aren't all that promising. . . . We finalize agreements with them, but they're like wolves, always looking into the forest to see who'll pay more. Regular bandits. And just who taught them that? And so, let's sum it up. Judging by everything, we'll gallop round the Americans again. That means I need to bet on the chief. Leave well enough alone. But won't internal problems bring us down? Nonsense! Almost fifty years of Soviet power, and every year, troubles with agriculture. We've gotten used to it. . . . Russia is a wealthy country: the petroleum and gas reserves are good for a hundred years. The capitalists will drop their britches and salute us for petroleum and gas. We won't die of hunger; we'll hibernate. But then, you see, in another five or ten years, we'll put the system right, and then maybe we'll start feeding ourselves. No, the chief is really a bright guy; his aim is true. The main thing is to get by for now, to get money, money, money! In the government, money comes in bulk; if there isn't enough, we print it. But our money isn't worth anything. They say for money, for rubles, you can't buy a decent pair of pants in the shops these days. Currency is the devil's own need. Got to get it any way we can! A chicken pecks by the grain. Is the racetrack the national mint? Phooey! Now, if it were in dollars or francs. . . . But dollars and francs are only found at foreign racetracks."

The leading comrade in the gray suit suddenly, as though awakening, was pleased to turn his attention to his neighbors in the box. Questions occurred to the comrade. First, do we take part in international horse competitions? Second, what kind of success have we had there?

Chairs for the racetrack director and the deputy minister were hastily set next to the chair of the leading comrade. The neighbors moved over to the other corner of the box, all the more since one of them, the head livestock technician, was having trouble stifling his laughter—"international horse competition" struck him funny.

The director and the deputy minister made a thorough report on the reinforcement of politico-educational work at the Moscow Racetrack; about the pace of socialist competition between training divisions; about the great success of our athletes at equestrian competitions in Poland, Hungary, and Czechoslovakia. (The management pronounced the word "equestrian" fleetingly, so as not to underscore the leading comrade's error.)

"But what currency do they pay the winnings in?" inquired the leading comrade.

They explained it to him: "In local currency—in zlotys, forints, and kroner."

"Aha," said the leading comrade, "And have our horses run in France or America?"

The management politely explained (true, with less enthusiasm), that Soviet trotters and thoroughbred horses had appeared more than once at the racetracks of capitalist countries, but, alas, they'd beaten us mercilessly.

"Why?" The leading comrade was dumbfounded.

The deputy minister began to discuss in detail the difficulties of the postwar era, while the director complained that currency funds had been cut, and, for that reason, we couldn't even begin to buy classy breeding stock from abroad —and without classy breeding stock, if the goods aren't right—we can't pull down the big international purses. The deputy minister interrupted the director, clarifying that several years ago, three American trotters had been purchased. To which the director replied that it was said the results of that might be seen in ten years or so.

"Currency, again!" the leading comrade snarled gloomily through his teeth. And having thought a bit, he asked, "But are there any big winnings at your track?"

"Of course it happens," said the director, "although we try. . . ."

The director stopped short. He was no judge of whether big winnings were good for the racetrack or not. He didn't even understand the connection between big winnings and the leading comrade's gloomy exclamation, "Currency, again!" There was a connection. The leading comrade had come upon an ingenious idea: if it's so hard to breed horses capable of winning the big international purses in hard currency, then it would be much easier and less trouble to find people capable of guessing these winnings. However, finding people is the problem of the proper authorities. And so, we'll have to toss the idea their way. However, he didn't consider it necessary to share his thoughts with the racetrack management.

"If there're any big winnings today, report them," he tossed out tersely.

THE RACES

How quickly things happen at the racetrack! They hadn't had time to announce the victors of the derby over the loudspeaker and hadn't had time to fawn over Othello's high-class and combatant qualities, and the participants of the first semifinals were already riding out on parade. The sixth race is in fifteen minutes, and there are eight horses in it. They have to run with the second semifinal in a double. There're eight there, too. Who to choose? We didn't get a good look at the warm-ups; we were jostling at the booths. Just what's to be done now? Bet blind, relying on our knowledge of the horses? In principle, number five, Little Huguenot, should win the first semifinal, and number six, Peacock, should win the second. But after all, the story of Prologue and Direction Finder could repeat itself: the Prix Elite is played by the same rules, and in the semifinals the favorites don't necessarily have to come in first. Might as well make a guess based on your coffee grounds. . . . All that remains is to appeal to the jockeys' honesty. Say, guys, don't you have a conscience?— the public trusts you, and they're taking their hard-earned savings to the booth: don't let them down, citizens. But in the first place, the favorite can lose the semifinal for purely tactical reasons, and any people's court would acquit the jockey, while in the second place. . . .

While in the second place, the Bakunian, famous in the racetrack, who at one time was his own man in the stables, used to say, "If you formed a rank of all the foremen, their assistants, the jockeys, the riders—in short, of everyone who took part in the races, and if you had the chance to walk down along this formation and peer attentively into the faces of the honored laborers of the racetrack, you'd never put so much as a kopeck on another single jockey!"

"Whom can you love, whom can you trust?" (Alexander Pushkin, apparently about the Central Moscow Racetrack.)

From Othello, I'm waiting for Little Huguenot, the biggest standout, with a ruble. My capital—six rubles. Thirteen races ahead. The age-old problem: to play or not to play?

Number seven, Danube, is stretching out. Boy, look at him stretch! Orange, the out-of-towner from Ramensky, is so-so, nothing special. Peony, the light gray stallion, is the winner of the Orlov Grand Prix, but can the Orlovian really compete with trotters of American blood? Moreover, Peony doesn't look bad at all. Peony's a fighter. Believe in him? But just where is my dear Little Huguenot? She's hiding, the bitch, on the back stretch. Oh, yeah, dirty business there. Little Huguenot, if she goes, usually turns around at the finish pole.

I look at the Professional, questioning. The Professional abruptly tosses me "Peony and Danube."

Could be—looks that way. At the booth, just as it was conjectured; they're making Little Huguenot with Peacock pay through the nose. About eight lines are filled with one combination: 5/6. The professional assigns two rubles to 8/6 and a ruble to 7/6.

"Peacock won't lose," warns the Professional.

Really does look that way, but they've been hitting on him awfully bad. And is there a second horse in the seventh race? Then it dawns on me: number three, Lot, is from the very same stable as Peacock. On Peacock is the foreman; on Lot—his assistant. Two variants: either the assistant won't dare to go against the foreman, or, conversely, the foreman will let the assistant by him.

I bet from eight and seven (from Peony and Danube) to six and three—8/6, 7/6,8/3, 7/3—and from Little Huguenot—only to Lot—5/3, letting the most probable combination—5/6—go by. All totaled, I've got one ruble left for future exploits. C'est la vie!

It's announced over the loudspeaker that by the sum of two heats, Othello has won the All-Union Grand Prix. The rest of the places will be allotted after the third heat. And all the horses except White Sail and Cherepet are being struck from the third heat (the eighth race).

It's still a long way to the eighth race, although the announcement is intriguing: White Sail, it's understood, will be fighting for second place in the purse. To do that, he's got to beat Ideologue's time posted in the first heat, because the regulation reads, "Prize positions are determined by the lowest sum of times in heats counted." Ideologue's sum of positions is four (two and two), and White Sail is going to have four as well (third place in the second heat and first in the third). Of course, he'll win the third heat. However, two questions naturally arise: (1.) "Why did Petya take Ideologue out? (Is he completely unafraid of White Sail?") (2.) "What is Cherepet doing here?"

Enigmas, enigmas. . . .

In the box it's become clear that the Dandy loaded Little Huguenot up all the way, and Coryphaeus—Little Huguenot and Danube (he peeked at the crooks' bet again). I solemnly suggest that everybody throwaway their tickets on Danube. Coryphaeus declares angrily that from now on, he won't say hello to me any more.

There's the bell! They're off

Danube takes the lead. Little Huguenot settles solidly into third and doesn't even dream of doing better. And Peony is holding on to second. Danube is running at 2.05, but with a finishing sprint, Peony gets around him.

Coryphaeus curses the crooks, and the Professional carelessly holds up the ticket from Peony to the astounded public. I say that I played Peony to Lot; the Professional knits his brow.

Wasted money!

*   *   *

ILYUSHA THE VEGETABLE MAN: "By the way, the fifth and sixth races cost me five hundred rubles. Of course, money can't buy happiness, but I'm not really such a millionaire that I can afford to toss it to the wind. The bet on Danube was risky, but, in gambler's terms, correct. Boroda was riding Danube. He beat all he could out of Danube. It didn't do him any good, nor me either. I also covered myself with Peony. But Peony is considerably cheaper, and with Peacock, he'll be basically worth kopecks. White Sail—that's where I hit a sure one. I didn't feed Vanya for three months for nothing. There should have been a miracle, and a well prepared miracle at that. Might that not be my mistake? Vanya's used to being the victor when I take out his competitors. Right when the swordplay started at the finish, he couldn't take it. It's time Mosya got down to serious business; he's grown up, and he's turned out to have golden hands. I'll have to start all over again; I'll have to pay again. They're all so sure that I'm rolling in money. And they all ask, 'Gimme, gimme. . . .' And I pay the director of the district office, the head bookkeeper, the OBKhSS inspector, the two goods managers from the central board, the forwarding clerks of the Kursk and Kiev stations, loaders, inter-city transport refrigerator truck drivers. Give to all of them. Where do I get it? What have I got, a printing press?! Sure, I steal, but I think I'm an honest man. Let's assume I didn't steal—how would you want me to live? The warehouse is huge, but the location is remote. It's already been twelve years since repairs have been made. Don't you see, there's no money. They economize rubles and lose thousands. If you figure out how much produce we throw out, gone to rot in the cellars, the kind of round figure it comes to, they could have long ago put up a skyscraper in my old ruin's place. But the office construction repair fund would fit in a pigeon's beak; to improve that (the fund, naturally—not the pigeon's beak) in light of the balance of trade would be a jurisdictional affair. The inspector general would take a breath and sign the report, affixing fifty thousand of the damages. Reclassification? The very nature of our work! Everybody's used to reclassification—they feed on it. And then, construction is a long and troublesome venture, and gratuities and bonuses are relied on for the economics of the annual fund. I need to get the roof patched quickly, to cement the floor. I invite workers over from neighboring construction sites and pay them out of my own pocket. It would take several months for certification through official channels, and no one knows when they'd start work. If there's a flood in the basement, the loss is a hundred fifty thousand. I payout of my pocket, but my pocket isn't bottomless. I let day-old produce pass for fresh to cover expenses. If you want to live, learn to duck. The people at the warehouse are complete criminals and alcoholics (a normal person won't mess around in that filth). How do you make them work? Put up posters: 'Let's give our own Moscow more fruit and vegetables?' They'll wipe themselves with those posters. Push them and they'll run in all directions. And look through your fingers at how they take things out of the warehouse. There's one principle: if you want to live yourself, let others live, too. True, they drive students out to us in the fall. They sort out the tomatoes, put them in the cellar, and in a month, instead of goods, there's rot. It grieves the soul. The stores don't have their own warehouses; they get it piecemeal. And when the goods are in condition, we have to push them on the sly—the people get their vitamins, anyway. I need money, a lot of money—you go around like a louse in a frying pan, and all to no end: you barely make ends meet. Of course, the races are a gold mine, but there isn't enough cash flow. After all, if you look at it logically, with a broad scope, if you hold all the stables in your hand, then you can make a little pile every race. For the sake of decency, let the favorites by a couple of times, but close down the rest. Rule out the slightest chance. A brief talk with the jockeys. Not sure of your horse—get back. You reckon your competitor stands a chance—don't hide—confess it honestly; I'll take out a rival. If I had an extra twenty thousand, I'd teach the racetrack a lesson. Maybe I could join forces with the Bakunian? He doesn't have enough capital, either. What's more, he's gotten used to small-time, independent action. He goes after kopecks—he'll ruin the business. You can't trust anyone for sure, since even the jockeys are unreliable: they're afraid of each other, afraid of the OBKhSS, afraid of the management. But the main thing is, they'll sell you for half a liter—you come to an understanding with a guy, you slip him a thirty, everything's all proper. He goes, but someone brings him half a liter on the track, and for a bottle of red wine, the horse drags in second on his own. . . . How many times have I encountered something like that?! . . . You can't work with people like that.

"My Paunchiches have gone completely sour. . . . Gentlemen, it's too soon to despair! Let's look at what shines ahead for us. From Peony to Peacock—kopecks, from Peacock to White Sail—it's really not worth getting your hands dirty; the ninth race, I don't know; we'll pass. The tenth race is the final of the Prix Elite. There, gentlemen, is the one we need to be racking our brains over. If we could just come up with something effective and simple. At the races, gentlemen, they don't pay money for nothing, but after all, the public's a fool. . . . Eureka! What's this 'Eureka?' Gentlemen, raise your cultural level and don't get drunk in the Aragvi. Eureka, in ancient Latin, or in ancient Greek, signifies that Ilyusha's come up with an interesting idea."

The Bakunian was worrying on the balcony. He'd thrown away a hundred rubles on the last two races, and his only comfort was that the Vegetable Man had thrown away even more. Like Ilyusha, the Bakunian understood that the bet from Peony to Peacock was miserly. True, Peony had unexpectedly pulled four and a half in single, but in double, they'd give seven to one. You won't get rich. However, in contrast to Ilyusha, the Bakunian's businesslike nature demanded instant decisions. Try to find a horse against Peacock? Irrational. Peacock can't lose. Let's be more specific: he couldn't exactly lose if Danube had come in in the previous race. At one time, Boroda worked in Tolya's stable, and Tolya would unfailingly load up from Danube. Now the situation's changed. Peony's an out-of-towner and his master isn't "connected" to the Muscovites. That means Tolya won't necessarily be first in the semifinal. Who might Tolya let by? Maybe Guipure, Lot, Surgut, or Carat. The only way Peacock can lose to the rest of the horses is with a fatal break of stride. Tolya won't allow a break of stride. . . . Bet these four to White Sail? You'd barely get your own back. They've come up with a race for me, too: two horses in all, and besides, White Sail's time is 2:04. Cherepet's is 2:10.8. White Sail needs third place in the main purse, and it goes without saying that he'll be running all-out. For Sail, in single, they'll give ruble for ruble; once again, there's no point. . . . Just a minute, simple arithmetic: let's check the results of the two heats—three plus one, three plus two—by the sum of places, nobody's going to catch White Sail. That means it isn't necessary for him to come in first. Genius! That smart ass, Vanya, may have a fourth-grade education, but he knows how to count to five! Stake your head on it: there're only two horses in the race, but Cherepet will bring a solid payoff.

The Bakunian snapped his fingers, and faithful Stasik appeared in a flash.

"Can Peacock lose?" asked the Dandy.

"No, he can't," said the Professional.

"But in the lower booths, they're starting to hit Guipure and Lot," said Coryphaeus. "People aren't fools, and they don't throw their money away just like that, now do they?"

"Well, how can he lose?" The Professional was indignant. "Take a look at the stallion—a beauty, long stride. . . . Compared to him, the other horses look like they're mincing along."

"But he could break into a gallop," Coryphaeus noted.

"Why should he gallop?" the Professional was indignant.

"Hey, boys," sighed Coryphaeus, "every time I hear the words, 'How could he break into a gallop?' I remember an old story. But don't worry, it's not about '51. There was this master, Petrov. He was before your time. A good jockey, but, it goes without saying, like all of them, he'd soiled himself in Totoshka. I used to visit him at his place and he'd pass on a tip. One time he says to me, 'On Friday, I'm going to be riding Habitus, and I can't lose.' Naturally, I loaded Habitus up. Habitus is first at the break and all of a sudden, within twenty paces of the finish line, when nobody's been bothering him, the stallion breaks into a gallop! Petrov rode Habitus several times after that and each time the same thing happened. The stallion starts to gallop at the very same spot! Nobody can understand what the deal is, while Petrov is cursing Habitus a blue streak. . . . By and by, Petrov told me about a curious event that took place in the summer on tour in Kharkov. The local crooks there bet among themselves over which horse would come in last. They narrowed it down to major pairs, and they tried to fix it accordingly. So Petrov was given money so he'd definitely come in last. And Petrov was on Habitus. The race began. All of them are fighting it out, while Petrov calmly drags along in the rear. He stays out of it, humming along as he rides. In the third quarter he notices that a

certain little local mare has fallen back, moreover quite successfully, behind Habitus, and she's clearly going to lose to
Habitus by half a length. Petrov said he thought it was just by
chance, but held his stallion back anyway. And the little
mare came to a standstill right there. Petrov looked around,
looked into the jockey's eyes, (an Armenian was riding the
little mare), and he figured it out: a competitive outfit, another
mafia, was paying the Armenian. They came out of the final
turn while the rest of the horses crossed the finish line.
Petrov—it's not for nothing that he's a master—pulled the
reins, lay on Habitus, and didn't let him go, but it turned out
that the Armenian knew what was what, too, and he was
walking the mare. The crowd was hooting; the crowd was
wise to the game. But Petrov absolutely had to lose to the
Armenian; jokes were a bad idea with the Kharkov crooks;
they'll beat you half to death. Petrov gave the stallion a jerk,
so that he'd break stride, but Habitus, the dirty scab, didn't
break stride. . . . Thirty meters to the finish. It was necessary
to fake a drive, if only for the sake of decency. Petrov made a
face that said he was resigned to defeat, as if to say, okay—so
be it, the Armenian had fooled him. He drives Habitus and
tears away from the mare, but twenty paces from the pole, he
bears hard left—and Habitus, at full stride, goes muzzle-first
into the acacia bushes! Of course, the stallion stopped like he
was rooted to the spot, while the Armenian, weeping and
sobbing, went on to the finish. . . . 'At the time, I reasoned,'
Petrov boasted to me, 'that the local management would forgive an out-of-towner a dodge like that. They'd have punished one of their own—transferred him to the stables for
half a year. And in Moscow, it would have gone badly for me,
but it was tolerated in Kharkov. There was no other way

out—my bones would've been broken that evening, and my money taken, too. . . .' And all the same, Petrov sincerely wondered why Habitus galloped the last twenty meters to the finish line every time! Yes, guys, a horse remembers everything. . . . That's why I laugh when our old-timers get indignant: "How could he break into a gallop, how could he break into a gallop!"

*   *   *

I didn't take part in that conversation. I didn't care whether Peacock came in or not. Peacock wouldn't save me, but I'd sunk my last ruble on Guipure, having tied him to White Sail.

Peacock broke stride after the start. True, Tolya quickly positioned the stallion, but in the long run, apparently fearing a new fight, guided him cautiously and came in third. The whole way, first place was being decided between Lot and Guipure, and Lot won by half a length.

I couldn't believe my eyes when the winnings lit up on the board: in single, Lot was worth six rubles. Clearly, in the seventh race, the mob had seriously latched on to him and loaded him up to Sail. But in the sixth race, from Peony, the crooks weren't touching Lot. Against all odds, I received seventy-six rubles for the eight-three ticket.

Now J. Pierpont Morgan and Rockefeller couldn't hold a candle to me.

Common sense urged me to hide the money deep in my pocket and flee the races at once. But can you really leave, when there're twelve interesting races ahead?

"The Teacher got lucky!" said the Professional. "Nobody but him could have guessed such an insane combination."

And he asked to borrow a ten.

"An open combination," the Dandy authoritatively announced. Think it'd be bad to put a fiver up for broke?"

And he asked to borrow the fiver.

Coryphaeus said he'd played Lot to White Sail; they'd be paying nine rubles. But for the time being, he asked to borrow three.

I left two rubles at the booth, even though the cashier whimpered desperately and kept trying to hold onto six.

In the tenth race, I chose the jet black mare, Palmetta and loaded her up from White Sail. That was the most popular combination, but I decided there was a rationale behind going for broke. Five brand new tenners were crinkling pleasantly in my wallet. I felt like a big man.

Two horses in the eighth race. White Sail was lazily leading the race. It was obvious that Vanya wasn't trying to beat Ideologue's time. So what? That's the master's business. But Sail couldn't lose, no way.

They ran in 2.10. Cherepet sat it out behind White Sail's back, and shot out at the finish.

"Just what Vanya needs," gloated the Dandy. "He wanted to economize on seconds and it made me sick. Even though I drowned on Sail, I'm satisfied."

"No, boys, this time it was all honest," said Coryphaeus. "White Sail laid himself out in the second heat, while Cherepet was saving his strength. Nice job, Zhenya!"

The Professional gritted his teeth.

"An honest race? This is what they call being robbed in broad daylight! They took the money and there was no one to complain to. Just look at the payoff."

In reality, the payoff turned out to be modest. Apparently they played big with Cherepet somewhere.

Nothing supernatural happened in the ninth race. They started the race in a close pack and nobody hustled Palmetta. Anyway, Palmetta, accordingly, was worth about thirty rubles in single. I was waiting for Palmetta, with a little fiver riding on Little Huguenot and Peacock each. A most primitive wager, but there were no bright ideas looming. The eleventh race wasn't entirely clear—nobody could figure out whether to pull for Little Huguenot or Peacock—a fanciful pursuit.

Little Huguenot shot out of the gate and quickly got her stride.

"I think there's something wrong with Peacock," said the Professional. "I'm going to put something down on Little Huguenot in single."

In single, they pay kopecks. I'll do without. The Professional runs to the booth, but I've decided to pass on that deal.

* * *

Like all mathematicians, the Dandy reasoned in a strictly logical way. No matter what they say, it's impossible to win in the Central Moscow Racetrack. You know the horse's strength, but you don't know the jockey's intentions. You know the jockey's intentions, but he's overestimated his mare's chances. And then the jockey himself isn't certain until the finish: suddenly right before the start, he's offered thirty to "take it on himself." Just who's going to turn down sure money? And then, the crooks run the jockeys, and there are a lot of crooks and they compete with each other. The bottom line is that a simple gambler doesn't stand a chance. Yet at the same time, according to gaming theory, he does stand some kind of chance. According to this theory, everyone has to get lucky sometime. The main thing is to sit tight and continue to believe, to continue your play. And the Dandy believes. He believed that he'd win on his birthday, on his wife's birthday, on his wedding anniversary, on the fifth anniversary of his thesis defense, on the anniversary of his graduation from school, on the anniversary of the day he slept with Ella, the famous Moscow model, on Victory Day, on May Day, and also on March 8th, Women's Solidarity Day, because the Dandy's been lucky with women. Today was also a portentous date: exactly three years ago he came to the racetrack for the first time. Three years—a symbolic number! True, fate seldom makes presents, and not necessarily on the appointed day. However, holidays have brought Dandy more prospects—otherwise, what's the sense of a theory of play? Naturally, the Dandy hadn't shared his calculations with anyone in the box. They'd have burst out laughing, while the Professional would have simply stopped talking to him. But everybody has his own method. Two years ago, also at the Derby, the Dandy guessed a big double. Two anniversaries coincided today. Three plus two is five. Five is a good number. There's a chance. That means we need to put a fiver (borrowed from the Teacher) down for broke, but from whom to whom? From Little Huguenot—wearing number two (she can't lose) to number three in the next race, since nobody understands anything about that race. Combination two-three. And suddenly it dawns on the Dandy that his apartment number is twenty-three. . . . The finger of God? The racetrack and ZhEK should do so well with their combined strength as to get this combination.

All the same, you've got to give the Dandy his due: it took a lot of courage to put his last five rubles down for broke without a bit of insurance. You can't borrow money a second time at the racetrack. And to find yourself without money at the peak of the Grand Prix is a bit like discovering two fresh babes when you've got the clap. You want to do it to the point of distraction, but it just can't be. The comparison to babes pleased the Dandy. Have to tell the Teacher—he always likes witticisms. By the way, about the Teacher. Most likely, he's squandered it all searching the darkness. No one to borrow from. Maybe I should hold back a ruble? The line was getting down to the booth; he had to decide. Two-three, two-three, what else are these numbers tied to? Aha, on March 23rd he parted with Lida with whom he'd been having an affair for half a year. Or rather, Lida had let him go, since she had traded him for her bachelor pilot. It was precisely on March 23rd, on a Friday. He remembers how badly torn up he was at the Youth Cafe. And so, exactly two years from the day of major winnings, exactly three years at the races, apartment number twenty-three, and the date twenty-three—the break with Lida: the racetrack, ZhEK, and Lida, where could you get a greater coincidence. Save, me, brothers! Save me, theory of play!

"Two-three," the Dandy said into the booth window, he picked up the five cardboard tickets with shaking hands.

The Professional returned after the bell highly disturbed.

"You guys, they're really paying through the nose for Little Huguenot in double—for five lines, but in single, there's no play."

We were amazed. "But that can't be! So did you get through?"

"That's just it—I couldn't," grieved the Professional. "Some fat cretin stood at the window for half an hour and played rubbishy nonsense by the ruble. The line was really outraged—shouting! The fool almost got strangled. . . . Well, what do we do!? There's a total of three single-play booths at the racetrack. When the window closed, I noticed that the lines for Little Huguenot were barely started. Wonderful!"

"Don't cry," the Dandy soothed the Professional. "You can be sure that they were beating Little Huguenot to death in ten lines in the other singles windows. No great loss."

Later on, it turned out that Little Huguenot wasn't touched at the other booths. Ilyusha the Vegetable Man's people had planted themselves firmly in front of the windows and bet liberally on all the other horses except Little Huguenot.

*   *   *

Ilyusha the Vegetable Man approached Genochka the bookmaker. Genochka pricked up his ears. He took large bets, no less than ten rubles on one combination. The Vegetable Man was a client, but you had to be on the alert with him. Ilyusha just didn't bet like that. "If he suggests a dark horse," Genochka decided to himself, "I won't take it, or else I'll double it at the booth."

"How's life, Genochka?" Ilyusha showed his interest.

"What life?" the bookie made a wry face. "I had to pay Pal Palych thirty rubles."

The Vegetable Man nodded understandingly. Pal Palych, the local OBKhSS man, regularly took payoffs from Genochka.

"I got taken to the cleaners, too," Ilyusha the Vegetable Man confided. "White Sail let me down."

"I'd be in good shape," thought Genochka, "if I'd taken a bet on Sail from the Vegetable Man. Ilyusha is hoping in vain to foist his dark horse off on me. Screw him! Let him go to the window."

"Genochka," the Vegetable Man continued, "I don't think Peacock is up to speed. Will you take a hundred from me on Little Huguenot in single?"

Genochka brightened. A hundred rubles on a standout— always a pleasure! If Little Huguenot does come in, they'll be paying about eighty rubles maximum for her. No great risk. Peacock's break of stride in the semifinals had frightened the public. But Peacock still hadn't had his final say. The final of the Prix Elite! Peacock will go pell-mell, and. . . . A hundred rubles—pure profit!

6

PRIVATE LIFE

USUALLY, WHEN I GO TO THE STORE IN THE AFTERNOON, A couple of characters come running joyfully up to me. Both wink conspiratorially; one raises his arms like he's ready to hug me, and the other points to me. I walk by the wine counter with a stern, arrogant face, leaving the two chumps in complete confusion and bewilderment. They just can't understand why I refuse to go in on a bottle with the two of them. Am I avoiding their company? Don't I drink? Then why the hell did I shove my way into the store? Is it really a man's business to stand in line for butter and sausage? Really, it's kind of awkward for me to disappoint the expectations of people who're in a sociable mood. And besides, I think it must be written across my ugly mug: "Here I am, the third, all ready, come running to get a hair of the dog." And that's how it is every time. . . .

But one day I wound up in an unfamiliar section of Moscow (a comrade gave me the keys to his apartment for the day, and I had to help Raika after a complicated operation— in a word, it's a long story), and I was forced to look for the "third" myself.

I bought groceries for lunch and supper, and then, when there were two rubles and some change left in my pocket, I recalled that we needed vodka for the compress.

It was 3:30 and there wasn't anybody in the wine department. The off season. There weren't any quarter liters to be seen on the counter. I asked the bored saleslady to pour me some. She looked me over with a professional glance and probably decided that it was better not to get involved with a stranger in a leather jacket: what if he's an auditor or from the OBKhSS?

"We don't serve liquor here!" the saleslady snarled maliciously, and she turned away.

I looked around. Not far off a tall, stoutish guy was hanging around and squinted bashfully in my direction. We were drawn to each other as if by a mysterious magnet.

"Well," I said, "want to split one?"

The guy got embarrassed.

"I don't have enough to split one. Payday's not 'til Tuesday," and then he hesitatingly suggested, "maybe we could wait for a third?"

"Let's give it a try." I graciously agreed and made my way toward the dairy section.

Having exchanged my empty kefir bottles, I returned to the wine counter. A little man of ill-favored appearance was fidgeting around my companion.

"Well, well," I said, "our third's shown up."

"You don't mean it!" the lug clasped his hands together, leapt away from us and moreover looked at us with a glance of such esteem we could have been persons of royal blood.

"He doesn't have any money," my companion drawled dejectedly.

We stood like that for about five minutes. My colleague got really morose. He was probably afraid I'd leave.

"Listen," I said, "I've got two forty. Chip in a ruble forty and pour yourself a third."

"Right," the guy livened up, "just a third, and not a gram more. Like at the drugstore."

The saleslady followed us attentively with an impervious, armored face (I know a face can't be armored, but it gave the impression of armor that had been beaten on for a long time—that's where "armored" comes from), put the bottle on the counter with a thud and maliciously remarked:

"We won't sell glassware for a pour."

Apparently, she wanted us to beg her. Or else it was just offensive in general that we'd worked it out so quickly.

"No problem," said the notably happier guy, "there's a glass in the garden."

His apathy and uncertainty had lifted. He started energetically and purposefully moving toward the exit.

There was no one in the sickly little garden across from the store. My companion was rummaging around in the bushes. Caught up in his enthusiasm, I was looking over the nearby trees, too.

Some thick, empty branches with no bark were polished as though glasses twirled in them day and night. But now there wasn't a glass to be seen. There was a thick layer of dust on the leaves.

"The old man said that there was a glass here," the guy relayed as he dove into the next bush.

"Maybe the old timer was joking?"

"You don't joke about things like that!" the guy replied sternly.

I realized that there are certain sacred things, which I didn't know about, that are not subject to doubt. The open alcoholics club for the entire microdistrict clearly met here. Only at night. Right now, in broad daylight, two guys rummaging around in the dusty bushes must have made a comic sight.

Finally my companion ended his search. "Let's go to the carryout," he said in a directive tone.

"Well, now," I thought, "we have to drag ourselves over to the cafe, grovel to the cashier, panic at the sight of the woman bussing the tables . . . What a pain! I've gotten myself into a real mess."

However, it all turned out to be astonishingly simple. We didn't have to go up to the second floor of the carryout. My comrade exchanged a couple of words with the cloakroom attendant, jingled some copper, left a couple of coins on the table by the mirror, and promptly brought back a glass. And here we are in the washroom, and I'm splashing it out of the bottle with a generous, inexperienced hand.

"What're you doing?" the guy was alarmed. "You're pouring too much! Take it easy!"

But I filled it up. My companion drained it in a gulp.

"Ugh. That's better! Thanks, you saved my life!"

"Don't mention it," I mumbled, screwing the cork back in, intending to take off on the double. And again, I'd broken the ritual. You couldn't just leave, just like that. Etiquette required a friendly conversation.

"Yeah," the guy went on, generously and magnanimously, not noticing my haste. "I cried all last night like a little kid."

"What's this all about?" I was astounded and made ready to listen.

"Ah, my damned students! Boy, do they make me sick! They're killing me. I'm an instructor at PTU. So these fatheads locked the current down direct, without a transformer. It really ticked me off (naturally, he used a different verb). Probably about four hundred volts. I barely survived. I'm all right now." My companion's eyes softened at once. "What if I went and called in sick? I've been depressed all morning."

"You'd probably have to go to the clinic first," I was doubtful.

"But that's my problem," my companion went slack, "I can't now. My breath stinks like Gorynych the Snake's."

He pulled out some change and started counting the silver.

"You ought to get a bite to eat," I advised him. "You need some spare change? Look, it'll take. . . ."

"Who, me? Never in my life! I can think better with a little beer. Put 'er there!"

He stuck out his hand and we parted best friends. He went back into the store, where some hard freebooters were waiting for him, while I, having snatched up my grocery bag, turned to my dull and uninteresting obligations.

THE RACES

Master Jockey Anatoly Petrovich, who the totoshniks called Tolya for short, was one of the most honest people in the racetrack (if the concept of honesty can be applied to this institution at all). Of course, as it happens, even he was famous for crooked races. Anyway, how are you supposed to live, dear comrades, on a base pay of a hundred and fifty rubles? Well, prizes brought in an average of another fifty rubles. And that's it! Two hundred clams for the best foreman in the best training division! A drunken loader in a furniture store makes more! So where's justice, citizens? And Anatoly Petrovich didn't drink and he stuck it out every day from six in the morning until night. True, he had excellent "goods," that is, he was getting horses from the Smolensk Stud Farm, renowned for its trotters. But getting the goods is only half of it. It's important not to overdo the training, not to whip the horse to death, but to bring it gradually into condition. Anatoly Petrovich had struggled for three years with Peacock. He picked out the promising trotter as a two-year-old, but spared him and let the Grand Prix for three-year-olds go by. Everyone took notice of the four-year-old Peacock. And how! A long-legged beauty with a wide gait. The crooks were offering incredible money, just let us know, Tolya, when you're going to bring the stallion out. But even in the derby, Anatoly Petrovich didn't strain Peacock, didn't force him. He ran third. He felt the stallion was still a little green. But to make up for that, later Peacock was without equal. Peacock would lead the race easily and freely from the start to the finish line. Last year, Peacock took the biggest purses for the senior classification of horses. Just this winter Peacock let the Winter Grand Prix go to Little Huguenot, the devil's own mare that Mashka trained on the sly to his, Anatoly Petrovich's, misfortune. Theoretically, Little Huguenot was weaker than Peacock, but furious and persistent, just like her mistress, Mashka Polzunova. And Anatoly Petrovich realised that if it worked out so Peacock could tear off right away, then Little Huguenot would be smelling the stallion's tail. Then let them send her off to the meat packers for sausage. But if Little Huguenot puts up a fight, and it gets down to real butchery head to head, Peacock won't hold out—he doesn't have the character; he's gotten used to easy victories.

He absolutely had to win the prize. It wasn't a question of money, though there were ten thousand points pinned on first place. Every point was eight kopecks. All told, eight hundred rubles. That seems like a good, solid sum. But shell out the stud farm's share, shell out to the racetrack, hand the rest out to the whole training division—to the jockeys and the grooms. A hundred rubles'll be left for Anatoly Petrovich. That's why money can't buy happiness. It's a question of prestige. Well, even the guys from the stable expect something: they didn't have extra fifties lying around.

Little Huguenot got a good number—two, near the inside. But Anatoly Petrovich's assistant on Lot was supposed to hermetically seal her in. Meanwhile, Peacock shoots down from the field, takes the inside, and then, as the song goes, "Write us, girls, at our new addresses!"

They came out of the gate at a dash, and Anatoly Petrovich saw that Lot was pushing Little Huguenot, hanging on with a death grip. Anatoly Petrovich started slipping to the inside, but what scum is this in the way? It's Vanya, who's built up full speed on that cripple; he's going to parry Peacock back outside. Can Vanya really have fixed up this couch like White Sail? No, that fool Vanya, his stallion's broken into a gallop—a fatal gallop. (Vanya, by the way, was no fool. Ilyusha the Vegetable Man had sent him a messenger with orders—beat Peacock at any cost. Vanya didn't beat Peacock, but he did slow his pace.) But then . . . what then, oh esteemed management? Little Huguenot walked away with it; she lost Lot in the second quarter. Anatoly Petrovich drove up to but couldn't take the mare. Coming into the home stretch, Anatoly Petrovich, employing a device of the old masters, of the honorable Semichev, peace to his ashes, pulled Peacock to within half a length. Still not quite there, a neck remained, but the stallion started getting nervous. Use the whip, get a sharp thrust? Maybe one of the young jockeys would've decided to do just that, but Anatoly Petrovich didn't dare. What if Peacock breaks into a gallop? Spare yourself a disgrace like that! And even though it's only second place, five thousand points in the pocket is bread on the table.

Little Huguenot won by half a head. From the grandstands they were shouting, "Tolya's a crook!" which really wasn't the point at all.

*   *   *

As always after the bell, the Bakunian took a walk along the booths. The register for singles piqued his interest. An empty line on Little Huguenot! The Bakunian placed twenty rubles through a cashier he knew, just to be sure.

Peacock faltered at the start, and Little Huguenot went out ahead. For horses of the same class, the odds turned out too high. The Prix Elite belonged to Little Huguenot. They lit the winnings up on the board. The racetrack met it with laughter. It can't be, the judges got the numbers mixed up! In double from Palmetta to Little Huguenot is two eighty. That's normal. Nobody expected any more. But in single, Little Huguenot is twenty-two rubles! The board's broken! Two twenty is top ruble for Little Huguenot.

The numbers on the board, however, didn't change. The crowd started getting worried. And the rumor soon spread that Ilyusha the Vegetable Man had stripped Gena the bookie.

EXCERPT FROM THE RULES:
> *Parimutuel booths are operated in the racetrack. Play out-side the totalizator booths is categorically forbidden. Offenders will be held strictly responsible.*

* * *

"Mind you, Taras," they used to say to him at the stud farm, "a jockey's time, like a young girl's, is short, and the racing season in Moscow is shorter still." From this moral admonition, it followed: "Succeed, my son—make money; it isn't for nothing we're setting you up in the capital!" Of course it isn't. You're going to have to bring presents for the grooms, the trainers, the production manager, the veterinarian, or else they'll send someone else next year. It's easy to say, "Succeed in making money," but how? For the Moscow jockeys, there're races year 'round; they rake the money in with shovels. But for us racers, there's only five months: from May to October. The foreman's taken all the top goods for himself. Taras has four little mares, four poor things for a guy who isn't even considered a jockey (there is no other athletic category), and who's designated on the program as "rider T. Tarasyuk, green silks, red helmet and sleeves."

Taras Tarasyuk took to his work with spirit at first. Once he came in first, two second places, one third. But then the good fortune of the rider in the green silks and red helmet and sleeves came to an end. They took his little mares off to the next group, to the stronger horses, and Taras was reduced to the usual dusteaters. True, after the first victory they began to respect Taras at the track. They'd give him twenty when they fixed a race, which means he wouldn't go. Taras took the money eagerly; he reasoned things looked brighter that way.

But then the crooks figured out that Taras' little mares didn't have any reserve—and they stopped coming up to him.

Like today. The race was decided without Taras. They let Scout and Saishen by, took out Thoughtful and Little Lip, and handed Uncle Seryozha a tenner for insurance, but they didn't even bring Taras a glass of port.

"Uncle Seryozha, it isn't fair," grumbled Taras. "Tell the guys that they ought to throw down at least a five."

"But what can I do about it?" sighed Uncle Seryozha, jockey first class, and he lasciviously looked askance. "Talk to Snake himself; he's the boss these days."

Snake, Master Jockey Zmiev-Snakitch, greeted Taras rudely. Snake reeked of brandy from ten paces away. Evidently, the master jockey had acquired it only this morning.

"Don't mess with me, pal," Snake said as he interrupted Taras's call for fairness and brotherhood, "I'm not the Gosznak factory; I don't print tenners. I'll tell you straight, like before the comrade's court: my Scout is ready for a 2.25. And what's your Deep got? Will she finish in under two and a half minutes?"

"Deep's got balls," Taras mournfully squeaked, but Snake burst out laughing.

"Fuck your mare with the balls, and you'll be in deep shit."

Snake had offended Taras and had offended him deeply. And Taras started thinking about pulling the plug on Snake's music today, I mean, teaching the master not to make fun of a young rider next time.

They took the start, but already by the first turn, Taras realized that Snake, the little creep, had it all figured out like clockwork. Scout and Saishen tore away by two poles, while the remaining jockeys brought their horses to an easy gait—why try—the race is already decided.

Master Jockey Zmiev-Snakitch looked around. Somewhere way back there, the pack was dragging along, and between them, between the leaders and the pack, only Taras was hanging on like a fly on shit. "The mutt's running third!" Snake grinned; he started holding his stallion back. And Saishen cut his stride as well. The race is won—we can slow down for a couple of seconds. If Zmiev-Snakitch hadn't been "courting" half a liter since morning, he'd have looked around one more time. But Snake was riding easy, figuring out his winnings—say, how much they'd give from Little Huguenot to Saishen or to Scout, and whose nose it would be better to stick out at the finish. And when he heard Deep's hoofbeats behind him, it was too late.

True, both Saishen and Scout were stronger than Deep. In a proper race Deep wouldn't 'have even come close. However, the masters flubbed it; they held their stallions back, and the mare turned out to have a speedy move.

* . * . *

The Dandy, who was gnashing his teeth, observed with sorrow how confidently Scout and Saishen were hustling along. "Ah, our life is ruined! No, I can state with full authority that there is no joy in living. That's enough, it's time to break with the racetrack. It's a diversion for idiots. I'll never set foot in here again. The ball is over!"

And now, out of the turn into the home stretch, out of a cloud of dust, some dirty scab came along the inside, shot like a bullet by the favorites and picked up the pace to the finish. "What the hell . . . ," the dandy had time to think, "a jockey in green with red sleeves. . . ." And suddenly the Dandy started yelling in a shrill, piercing voice and didn't stop yelling until number three crossed the finish line.

And then the Dandy calmed down, cleared his throat, mopped his sweaty brow, and having shown the Professional the tickets with the combination two-three, noted casually:

"The five for broke came through. Can it really be so bad?"

The Professional nodded encouragingly.

*   *   *

The Grands Prix were over, and the crowd in the grandstands had noticeably thinned out. The usual races were left and the Bakunian was pondering whether he should plunge into them, or. . . . In accordance with that idea, the jockeys'd try to doctor up the doubles themselves, now, and they'd send their messengers to the booths. The messengers could be intercepted—the question lay elsewhere—how reliable is this information? There's always a risk in races fixed off-handedly. In the first place, the jockeys always tend to exaggerate their horses' strengths. In the second place, you might get deliberate misinformation. In principle, the Bakunian didn't trust jockeys. The Bakunian's claim, that, say, if you stood all the jockeys out in a row and walked along this row and looked into their faces, any sane man would take to his heels and flee the races, wasn't going around the racetrack for nothing.

Once, when he was still working as a cameraman in a popular film studio, the Bakunian had shot some footage of Soviet stud farms. And it was through this deal that he got to

know all the foremen in the CMH (Central Moscow
Racetrack). Besides that, Bakunian had close-ups of the jockeys at home in a special collection. He would show them to
his friends and always asked the same question: "Would you
loan these people three rubles?"

The exhibition of the portraits always had exceptional success, and usually his friends would answer that they wouldn't
trust them with three kopecks, let alone three rubles.

However, not too long ago, another, more impressive collection "got past" the Bakunian. His compatriots, who'd come
to Moscow from the republic, had brought an album of photographs on which there were printed such roguish snouts,
such suspicious, nose-turning faces, that Bakunian thought
for a minute: "They're either jockeys from the Baku Racetrack,
or, more likely, pictures of second-hand store managers and
bosses from some underground businesses." The Bakunian
gave his opinion, and his compatriots smiled with restraint
and then let out the secret: collected in the album were
photographs (not done officially, of course, but at friendly
blowouts) of the chief inspectors of the procurator's office of
Azerbaijan, of the People's Judges, and of prominent officials
of the republic's Ministry of Internal Affairs.

The Bakunian appraised how wickedly they'd tricked
him and noted philosophically, "That's the world we live in,
and there's no way out."

The Bakunian was a gambler by nature, and he took an
interest in cards, billiards, and assorted types of gaming with
equal enthusiasm. But, unlike the majority of gamblers, the
Bakunian could stop at any given moment. Right here and
now the Bakunian decided the day hadn't turned out badly:
he'd recouped his losses on Cherepet, Little Huguenot had

brought a clear profit, and the most logical thing was to hang it up for today.

On the other hand, it would be depressing to mope around the racetrack with nothing to do. And the Bakunian slowly descended from the second level of the grandstands to the barrier, by the finish, where Ilyusha the Vegetable Man's crew had carted itself.

The Bakunian was met cautiously, but respectfully, with a full salute of the nations, as befits a large ship. As etiquette demanded, the Bakunian drained a large mug of beer at one gulp.

"Well, Ilyusha," said the Bakunian, wiping his moustache, "you almost sank me on White Sail."

"Don't talk about it," Ilyusha peaceably answered. "I plunged in up to the ears, myself. It's a good thing Genochka the Bookie turned up and made me a present of a little something. They say he's been crying in the toilet at the eighty since one o'clock."

"The way you put it together with Little Huguenot in single was brilliant," the Bakunian admitted.

Ilyusha the Vegetable Man's cheeks blushed with a girlish hue. It isn't every day you get compliments from the Bakunian himself, much less in front of all the honest folks.

"And where did you make your stand?" asked Paunchich.

"Guess."

The crew knit its brow. Ilyusha the Vegetable Man figured it out first: "There was a disproportionately low payoff for Cherepet. Your touch?"

The Bakunian bowed, giving Ilyusha's perspicacity its due. Now everyone's bread had been buttered.

"What's the outlook for the rest of the races?" asked the Bakunian.

"Lousy races," answered Ilyush. "Nobody expects to see anything interesting."

"What say we make a bet on what the biggest payoffs'll be," the Bakunian proposed.

"More than five hundred?" Ilyusha considered the variants for several seconds. "It's a go; we'll lay it on the table. Small fry are racing. They won't top five hundred."

They shook hands.

Now the Bakunian was in business.

Totoshka, which had been holding its breath, witnessed this "summit meeting" scene and decided that the Bakunian and the Vegetable Man were probably undertaking some unthinkable double. "Keep your eyes on the skies, guys!"

7

PRIVATE LIFE

"RAIKA," I SAID, "YOU'VE BAWLED, PESTERED ME, AND BORED me all to hell, so let's get married."

"You've got a strange way of proposing to a girl!"

That formal "you" again! She's gotten all huffed up again! She suddenly has these lapses where she clean loses her sense of humor. But I just couldn't tie on a tie, buy a rose and crow about love like in a nineteenth-century novel.

By the way, I had the most serious intentions. After Mama's death, I felt an acute loneliness. I'd get a little worried about my health at night. I'd wake up, listen to the beat of my heart, count my pulse and be frightened by headaches. Generally speaking, a schoolteacher needs some kind of stability in his life: the students you become attached to take off in all directions after the tenth grade like birds out of a cage. Nobody even wants to remember a cage. And they only say hello to me if they wander into the the racetrack by chance, and then not to pay their respects, but to find out who's coming in in the next race. Maybe I'm laying it on thick, but it's all because I've become a bore; there's just one thing for a bore to do—get married. And marry Raika. In the first place, she's a person with a passion for cleanliness; she tidies up an apartment so everything shines. In the second place, when I'm hurting, she never leaves me—you won't find a better nurse. And she can make any medicine in short supply appear right out of thin air. In the third place, I'm used to her. "At night," as Comrade Mayakovsky wrote, "you like to hide your sound in something soft and female." But that's not quite accurate. At my age you simply like to hide at night. And then we get along that way. She knows how and what to hold on to. And in the fourth place, she's significantly younger than me.

"Raika," I said, "let's tear off a piece."

We live together for a day and the sink, washbasin, and pots and pans in my apartment glisten with the blue light of polar radiance.

We live together a second day. The borshch smells wonderful as it cooks on the stove.

We live together a third day. My ironed shirts crackle like brand-new five-ruble bills.

On the fourth day, the reproaches start: she says I'm an intelligent man, but I don't know how to talk with a girl about literature and art.

And I, by the way, coming home from school for the fourth evening in a row, am reading the compositions of three tenth grade classes and correcting them. Ninety-two compositions on the theme, "The Krasnodonets Heroes—A Model for the Emulation of Soviet Youth." According to A. Fadeev's book, *Young Guard*. I wasn't the one who thought up this theme: it was handed down by directive of the Regional Section of the People's Education.

I've been teaching literature for fifteen years. Fifteen years I've been trying to teach my boneheads to love Pushkin, Tolstoy, Gogol, and Mayakovsky. I even find a lot that's interesting in Gorky, because the "stormy petrel of the revolution" invented, if you'll excuse me, not only the image of Danko, but also wrote the curious little book *Klim Samgin,* which I highly recommend that everyone reread. Well, okay. Anyway, for fifteen years the Regional Section has demanded a composition on the theme of the Krasnodonets heroes, and only the title of the themes is altered: "Komsomol Young Guards—The Party's Faithful Helpers" and "Oleg Koshevoy—Patriot of our Country. . . ."

And I can't—I don't have the right—to explain to the students that there never would have been any *Young Guard* if Oleg Koshevoy's mother hadn't been living first with the German officer and then with Comrade Fadeev.

Ninety-two compositions! And you want me to be able to converse with a lady about literature and art at a time like this?

On the fifth day came the scene. It turns out that I look at Raika without love—I don't pay her any attention—there's no sensitivity in me, no understanding, and I need a maid, not a girlfriend.

On the following day, having returned the compositions to my classes (I wound up giving out three "A's"), I made a beeline to my own Moscow Racetrack. In the fourth race, the dark gray stallion Yawn, out of Patch by Flint, brings me thirty-five rubles. The Professional and the Dandy come out successfully in the last double. In short, at nine in the evening, we spill into the Aragvi. I've earned the right to forget the heroic Krasnodonets heroes and get my nerves back into shape, haven't I?

But like an honest man, burdened all the more, in a sense,

with family obligations, I consider it my duty to call home from the restaurant, that is, call Raika, and invite her to dinner. I am sent "far, far away where the mists drift." I am called a scoundrel and an egoist who doesn't think of others, by the way, as others are waiting for me, getting nervous, calling around to morgues and the police. I hang up the phone. By my watch, it's exactly 9:25. At 9:42 (Zhenya checked the time by his stopwatch) Raika zeroes in on us at our table at the Aragvi. The family squabble continues. The evening is ruined.

In the morning, we part friends forever and ever. The fact is that I counted, and from my house to the Aragvi it's forty-five minutes by subway or twenty minutes by cab. And after all, Raika had to dress, fix her face and catch a taxi. That means the taxi is out. There's no doubt: in nine minutes, she could only have flown in on a broom.

There's no doubt that Raika is a wonderful companion in an age of earthquakes, shipwrecks, plague epidemics, anthrax, miscarriages, and cholera. However, in our normal life. . . . And then, I couldn't marry a woman who had that kind of friskiness.

However, it wasn't ruled out that I'd still call her if, of course, some day, some certain dappled dark gray-brown someone brings me about a hundred rubles in a dark race.

THE RACES

He came up to us and breathed heavily in everyone's ear:

"Guys, drop your pants and bet it all. Kaleria's all alone in this race."

Of course, we needed to send Yurochka the Gas Man right on his motherfucking way. But Vadik, a jockey acquaintance of ours, was assigned to Kaleria. And the signal came from him.

Vadik said it just like this: "Pass it on to the guys that I'm losing them all in the third quarter."

We pressed Yurochka the Gas Man into the corner of the box. Yura stared and swore at everyone in the world.

"You gassing us, bastard?" asked the Professional.

"If I'm lying, may I burst," sobbed Yurochka. "Once in a blue moon you get a real chance. Kaleria's got the reserve— you yourself know that."

We did. Vadik had been hiding Kaleria for a long time.

"Guys, put down a tenner for Vadik and a fiver for me."

"You'll make do with a three," said the Dandy, "and that's a bit much."

Any other time, even a ruble would have been enough for Yurochka. But we were in the money. Even if Yura did have time to spread it around, all the same, going for broke looked solid. In the program, Kaleria generally looked like a nogoer. Last race nothing but a break of stride.

"Need to take a look," said the Professional, as usual, but I was already feeling a tremor of impatience.

What's there to look at? Once Vadik's riding, everything's all set. But what if we don't make it to the booth in time?

Vadik is breezing. He stretches out, opening Kaleria up right at the finish pole. He always does that when he intends to ride seriously. The Professional clicks his stopwatch, and his face darkens.

"What?" I ask impatiently and anxiously. "Bad?"

"Vadik's a fool," the Professional snarls through his teeth. "He's exposing the mare. Twenty-two seconds in the stretch. Loan me a ten."

I feverishly get out a crisp note, shove it at the Professional, and he's off at a sprint to the betting hall. I hear a plaintive whine coming from behind, saying, "You'll see. It's all true—bet a fiver for me, too, Teacher!" minces Yurka.

So that means from number seven, from Kaleria, I'm playing a ruble to everybody in the next race, to the standout—with a tenner, and to another favorite with a tenner—no, with a fiver, altogether. . . . And as usual, there's a mob at the booth. What are they, asleep at the window? I push. Yurochka helps me. From behind the shoulders of the person standing ahead of me, I see how the cashier is lazily writing out tickets. But a second line's been started from Kaleria. Why, wasn't it a dark horse? . . . You bastard, Yurochka, you managed to louse everybody up. Anyway, after such a fast dash, the racetrack's surely flogged Kaleria to death. We don't have a single stopwatch between us. Maybe it's just at our booth they're playing her? But what have I got to lose? Kaleria's a sure thing. This kind of chance doesn't come around too often. Wow, there is joy in life! My turn finally comes, and I decide to bet all of my money.

My pile of tickets is growing. The cashier's pencil briskly fills out a third line. I've never bet so much before. Behind me, they're yelling, "You fall asleep or what?" Take it easy, guys, there's still a minute to the bell.

"A fiver to number one for me," Yurochka breathes into my ear.

That means to the standout. I add it.

"But why are you tying it to nine? A no-goer!"

Go crawl up your asshole, Yurochka! My rule: if it's to all of them, then it's to all of them. All kinds of things can happen!

"Play Anton with a ruble," Yurok suddenly says with a change in his voice. "Vadik said he was only afraid of Anton."

He's gassing, the creep, he's gassing! But I won't yield to these provocations. Anton rides once a year on big holidays; Anyway, today is just that—a racing holiday. Okay, four-nine, to my bottom ruble. Close to a million.

I push my way from the booth with an armload of tickets. Yuri was already up and gone. He gassed me, the creep, and vanished.

In the box I ask the Professional: "Did you make it?" "Yeah, I made it. But Anton was breezing like all hell." Hang Yura! Smash that rip-off's mug! But how did the Professional spot Anton? The guy's got a will of iron. Come roaring thunder, he doesn't head for the booth until he's looked them over.

The Professional divines my doubts.

"Stick to your guns, Teacher—Vadik rides to the death."

The gong! And the main pack is close together. They've all rushed at once. Somebody's breaking stride. A break into a gallop. Can it be? I feel my heart beat wildly. Can it really be all over?

The break into a gallop is called on number two, the favorite. Whew, it's easier already. Vadik is first at the turn. He goes out at the break. He's going alone at the third straightaway. Anton cowers behind him, hanging two poles back.

We all four exchange victorious glances. Even Coryphaeus is smiling. And he's usually the one who's crying during the race—he's saying, "Gang, it isn't evening yet, and the horse is breaking stride, rearing back. . . ."

No, Kaleria is a speedy mare. Runs briskly, very briskly. But Anton is pulling up. Into the home stretch, Kaleria breaks into her reserve power and . . . starts to walk. Vadik has driven the mare down.

The grandstands are yelling. The grandstands are whistling. Coryphaeus pitches his tickets (accurately, by the way, into a corner so that he can pick them up, without getting them mixed up with the others).

"Hold out, Vadik," howls the Dandy, his voice unnaturally thin.

I'm praying to all the gods in this world. Hang on, Vadik! Vadik hangs on, but Anton is already alongside. He catches him. Kaleria comes to life a bit in the last meters, but Anton's stallion wins cleanly by a neck.

"Maybe they'll call it neck and neck?" the Dandy asks uncertainly.

"My dick down your neck!" the Professional answers with spite, and in turn pitches his tickets with all his might.

We try not to look at one another. It's obvious, we're all sunk.

"Well, guys, there's nothing for me to do here, today," says the Dandy after they've announced number four as the winner. "I've been stuck for a hundred fifty."

Did the Dandy wipe out all of his winnings in one shot? But I'm not any better off. I wasted forty rubles. Still, it's good I loaned that ten-spot to the Professional. But when will I get it back from him? Though. . . .

The Dandy says good-bye and walks to the exit with a heavy tread. Coryphaeus disappears too. On the quiet. He's probably stashed a three-spot somewhere in his sock; it's his nature to pull a ruble at a time out of his stash.

"Got to hang the Gas Man," I say to the Professional, and I say it just like that, just for something to say.

"The Gas Man's not to blame. Vadik drove his horse down, wasn't taking the pace into account."

"But just at the last moment, Yura told me about Anton." A shadow flashes across the Professional's eyes and I make a guess.

"But after all, you bet on Anton, too, didn't you?"

"If you think so, I did," the Professional mutters, averting his eyes. "A whole two rubles to number one. If I go up there they'll give me kopecks. And I put a twenty from Vadik."

The winnings are posted. Anton in single—seventeen rubles. That's not kopecks anymore.

"Zhenya," today for the first time, I call the Professional by name, "I've got one ticket. From four to nine. Let's go halves. I'll let you in on fifty kopecks' worth, and you let me in on number one."

The Professional snorts with contempt:

"Number nine's fit for sausage."

"Zhenya," I say in an even voice, as I normally speak to obstinate girls in my classes, "I loaned you money. It's dishonest to refuse me a share."

"Yeah, all right, that's enough begging for favors, Teacher. Of course, I'll take it, but you always find. . . ."

I don't listen to what comes next. I abruptly turn and leave. I'm sick to my stomach. If I could just get to the toilet more quickly. . . . Sometimes this kind of thing happens to me. Nerves. Emotions. Humiliation. Just what I need. After all, I'm a teacher. And they respect me at school. And I once wrote works on history. And some things of mine came out in samizdat. Just what I need. A gambler's an a. . . . It's time to sever my ties with the racetrack. I've absolutely lost my human face. I humiliate myself for fifty kopecks! And then— I always have to play to the favorite. How many times have I gotten burned on that?

The race is already in full swing when I come out of the bathroom. It's empty in the hall with the booths. But I'm in no hurry. I don't give diddlysquat. If I could, I'd hang myself. Of course, Zhenya isn't a bad guy. He snapped at me in the heat of the moment. If number one comes in, I'll turn down my half of the ticket, let him choke on it. Although from seventeen rubles in single, they ought to pay something or other. No, I'll say I don't need the money—I'll buy him 100 grams. And maybe I'll even drink a glass. This is the perfect time to get drunk.

The people are flocking to meet me. That means the race is over. I can't hear the announcer's words in the jam in the corridor. But isn't it all the same? All I'm asking is if the Professional made it.

I bump into Zhenya at the grandstands exit. He looks kind of strange—excited and embarrassed. I run my eyes over the board. Number one is posted, but at the top, above it, numbernine!

And here I am in the box, and there's an attentive, quiet half-circle around me. I pull tickets out of my pockets and discard them with shaking hands. Can I have lost it? Fournine! There it is! All in one piece. My legs are all jelly. And I hear the Professional's trembling voice:

"Old man, there isn't another ticket like that in the racetrack!"

There's an excited crowd around the pay booths, but they part for us at once. The faces of Ilyusha the Vegetable Man and the Bakunian flash past. Genochka the Bookie got up for a second, and it was as though he'd been snatched away. He disappeared. Someone's hand is being stuck out to me, and I hear the mournful squealing of the Gas Man:

"Teacher, it was me who tipped you off to Anton. Remember, I said Anton's all alone, nobody next to him!"

I'd like to retort, "But number nine? Who tried to persuade me not to play him?" But I feel that a pitiful, apologetic smile has jelled on my face. However, Yurochka's voice is immediately cut off, as though his mouth had been plugged. There are all kinds of voices, cries, but the cashier's face is pulling me in like a magnet. Her eyes are shining; she's looking at me like I was God, but her mouth is twisted in despair. What? Oh, yeah, I get it—she can't pay me my winnings, they only hand out that kind of money at central bookkeeping. I could leave her a tenner, no—a hundred at the booth, what difference does it make to me now! . . . But don't count her out in bookkeeping. . . .

The cashier walks ahead of us, carrying the pay sheet like a banner. We go through a door with a sign that reads: Do Not Enter. We go up the stairs, thread through corridors, and some people come jumping out of the side doors, cutting us off from our escorts, who forced their way after us from the betting windows. We go into a large hall, where thirty (maybe a hundred) women with beehive hairdos are cranking their adding machines and are assaulted by the smell of powder and sweat. I don't know what bursts into the hall after us. Shouting? Groaning? Rapture? A puff of wind, and the women, their mouths half-opened, freeze without completing their hand movements. One more door. Another little corridor. Another door, which separates us from the cashier.

I turn around and catch her last glance—ah, how much passion and emotion there is on that face; I have time to think that she'll remember us for a long time now, and we'll be able to bet at this booth without going through the line. (Mustn't forget to give her a twenty next time—I can get by without a twenty.) And now—now we're sitting on a sofa across from this gray, dry, severe man. He attentively and unhurriedly checks the number on the ticket against the pay sheet—and our number is circled on the register with a greasy, red pencil: then he studies the back of the ticket (as if something might be written on the back!) and picks up the phone.

"Yes," he says into the receiver. "They're here. Two of them."

He hangs up the phone. Not looking at us, he starts to look efficiently over some papers on the table. He hates us. He's a hard worker—a bookkeeper, alien to gambling and games of chance. He lives solely on his salary—and now, all at once, two bozos are supposed to get more than several years of his salary. How much did we win, anyway? Nobody's told us yet, and the sum isn't posted on the register.

I look around the room to kill time. There are portraits of Brezhnev and Budyonny on the wall. There's a small, fireproof safe in the corner. That's most likely where our fortune is.

And now my eyes meet Zhenya's. He starts to wink and smile ingratiatingly. I've long since noticed this strange metamorphosis that comes over him after the races. At the racetrack he's the iron Professional—stern, harsh—you can't get near him. After betting, he's like a child. Apparently, now he's still really scared I'll start to reproach him, or maybe even worse—I'll up and say, "What're you doing here?" I give him a wink of encouragement. And his face breaks into a smile.

The door opens. A police major is at the door. Hurriedly, in a brisk tone: "Comrades, here's what we'll have to do. Of course, I congratulate you on your success. Usually, we give the money right away and turn you loose with an escort of employees. But today's a special day; there are many visitors, the turnover is an enormous sum, and your ticket is one-of-a-kind. We can't risk it. The people have turned into animals, lots of them are drunk. They're watching for you at all the exits. For that reason, we'll take you down to the department and you'll get all that's coming to you there, in full. But for now, I've got to get some information about you, because that's the procedure." The major took a clipboard. "Last name? First? Patronymic? Year of birth? Address of registration? Place of work?"

"And do we have to indicate our nationality?" asks Zhenya.

"Note. that I've never served in the White Army and haven't taken part in any opposition groups," I say, but it's obvious right away that the joke isn't well received. After all, they take care of us, worry about us, and we stoop to taunts.

"Excuse me," I say, "it was a clumsy joke."

"That happens," the major confirms impassively. "They'll send the car soon."

It comes for us only after half an hour. Again, the winding way along the corridors, but they're empty this time. I get the impression that, unknown to the public, there's a whole labyrinth in the racetrack building. We come out somewhere in the vicinity of the twenty-kopeck grandstands, and a white Volga is parked right by the entrance, so that you can barely squeeze through the open door. The car takes off and we ride out into the street and slip into a sidestreet. The Sunday evening city is empty, and the Volga threads its way headlong from street to street, so that we're thrown from one side to the other. The tires are squealing at the turns. The driver intently turns the wheel and doesn't utter a word.

But everything's fine. We're silent. We need to concentrate and think it all over. If they're taking these kinds of precautions, we really must have won an awful lot. Maybe three, but maybe even four thousand apiece. It's great that they drove us from the racetrack. We'd have run into about a hundred people, been dragged off to a restaurant and then be left to count the change. No, once we've got the money, Zhenya and I'll celebrate somewhere in the Metropole. We'll call the Dandy and Coryphaeus. I'll invite Raika. Zhenya— whoever he wants. But maybe I don't need to ask Raika? Tomorrow I'll give her two hundred rubles for threads, but today maybe I should call that chick. Okay, let's figure it out; the main thing is not to go on too big a spree. Deposit a thousand into the savings account. Buy a suit and a sheepskin coat. Go to Sochi or the Riga Coast. Of course, everything's full up, but you can get expensive rooms in a hotel. And what if we've won so much that it's enough to buy a car? For a car, you win shit, even for a Zaporozhets, and then you've got to register for your turn and wait several years. Well, now I've stopped dreaming! A Zaporozhets! But don't you want a Moskvich? They'll give two grand to the mug in all. Already two thousand isn't good enough for you? Okay, like it was never there—half in the cachet, and I call Raika right away from the restaurant. With that kind of money in your pocket, it's best not to take chances. And I ought to hold Zhenya back, too, so that he doesn't waste his money.

I notice it seems like we're driving kind of a long way.

PART TWO

1

He continues to read:

"It has been established by the investigation that I.
M. Kholmogorov (racetrack alias 'the Teacher') and E. N.
Lomonosov (racetrack alias 'the Professional') entered into a
criminal bond with jockey second class Vadim Isakov, and
through the mediation of Y.V. Firsov (racetrack nickname 'the
Gas Man'), received the information that the fourteenth race
was 'fixed,' and only horses number five and four, that is, the
jockeys Vadim Isaakov and Anton Tabuinikov would go. It was
likewise made known to Kholmogorov and Lomonosov that the
following race, the fifteenth, would be run at a false pace, that
is, the jockeys would be letting the darkest horse in the race,
wearing number nine, pass. As a result of this, a rogue operation was promoted by Kholmogorov, I. M., culminating in the
purchase of a ticket with the numbers four-nine at booth 263,
to which major winnings fell. The ticket and the booth list
are attached. Harm was thus done to the other participants
betting through the totalizator at the Moscow Racetrack. The
cheating actions of Lomonosov and Kholmogorov are underscored by the evidence of the witness Firsov. Kholmogorov
and Lomonosov themselves disavow their criminal actions."

"Have I written it down right? Sign the protocol sheet."

"No," I say, "I won't sign. In the first place, it isn't written in Russian. What follows from the text is that the horses wearing numbers five and four are jockeys Isakov and Tabuinikov. Your own bosses will be laughing at you."

"Don't worry about me," says the very young police lieutenant, who's already been interrogating me over the course of three days. "Better think about yourself."

"But I'm a teacher; I can't go around signing ungrammatical protocols."

"A good teacher," smirks the very young lieutenant. "We'll make a report to RONO. 'Who is being entrusted with the education of our Soviet children?'"

I get a grip on myself, trying not to fly into a rage. I've been engaged in a pointless skirmish with this impudent guy for three days. Of course, there will be little joy at school when they find out I'm a regular at the racetrack. But in the end, it's no crime. Well, the principal will propose that I leave "at my own initiative." The question is, where to? In Moscow it's practically impossible to find a position for a humanities teacher in a school. Will I have to leave for the provinces, lose my Moscow registration? Why? What am I guilty of?

"Fine," I say as calmly as possible, "you write, 'criminal bond.' But everybody in the racetrack plays that way. Everybody tries to find out which horse is going and which isn't. Cheating flourishes at the racetrack."

"That's why we're trying to stop it," the lieutenant coolly parries.

"And then," I go on, "you use the aliases, 'Teacher,' 'Professional,' and 'Gas Man,' just as though we were members of some underworld gang. . . ."

"But you said yourself," the lieutenant interrupts me again, "there's an entire mafia is operating at the racetrack. And that's why we're trying to get to the heart of the matter. And then let the court decide."

There is a triumphant smile on the lieutenant's face.

I've already been through this with him over ten times; apparently, he's hoping to starve me out, but I'm not about to give in.

"Who told you the fifteenth race was run at a false pace? I didn't see anything at all. Sorry, I was sitting in the john the whole time."

"Your partner Lomonosov affirms it was a typical false pace."

"You fool, Zhenya," I think, but I continue:

"If it was a false pace, why didn't the college of judges nullify the race results?"

"It's precisely on those grounds that we're conducting the investigation. "

"I didn't know the jockeys would be letting number nine pass."

"Just why did you play him in particular?"

"I repeat, I figured it like this: None of the jockeys will turn down a dark horse in the next race. They don't ride 'for free.' That means the jockey whose horse wouldn't stand a chance in normal circumstances will try to win."

The lieutenant notes my words down in the report, and with evident satisfaction, reads over what he's written.

"We'll grant you that, but the witness Firsov indicates that he personally whispered number nine to you."

You bastard, Yurochka, I think. A sorry little nobody! They brought him to the police station and he lost his nerve, and he's ready to agree to anything just to squirm out of it. What is he, anyway? A nobody! Anyway, that's not news! Yurochka the Gas Man looks less than anyone like Alexander Matrosov. He isn't putting his puny butt on the line for anybody else.

"On the contrary," I say, "he tried to persuade me not to tie in to number nine."

"Do you have witnesses?"

"I don't have any witnesses. But if Yurochka the Gas Man knew that number four was going, knew they were letting number nine pass, then why didn't he play on that combination himself? Why was my ticket the only one in the racetrack?"

There's a thin, professional smile on the lieutenant's face.

"Because you, my dear Igor Mikhailovich, although an intelligent man, are naive, while Firsov is an old bird, and he didn't put himself under suspicion. That's why you find yourself here in the position of a suspect, while your Yurochka the Gas Man walks free, and will pass through the case as a witness. Understand, I won't embellish your case; I'm just pointing out in the report that you don't admit your criminal actions. But everything's stacked against you. Tell me honestly, who were you supposed to hand over the money to? Who were you going to share the winnings with? If you're just a front man, it would change the whole picture of the case."

"Lord!" I burst out. "I'm nobody's front man! I'm a regular guy who won at the totalizator, officially permitted by Soviet authority, and all I want is to get my winnings! Instead of that, I'm arrested, kept four days in a solitary cell. . . ."

"Do you want to be transferred to the common cell with the thugs and the drunks?" the lieutenant slips in.

"No," I change my tone, "but I don't understand why I'm being held. This isn't an investigation; it's some kind of madhouse!"

"Do you insist that your remarks about the madhouse be entered into the report?" The lieutenant slips in.

"No," I answer, having thought a bit, "perhaps there's no need."

Toward evening on that same day, they summoned me for interrogation again. But instead of the impudent, very young lieutenant, a corpulent comrade in civilian clothes was sitting at the table, and his face seemed harmless to me, but his eyes were tenacious, alive—they took hold of me in a flash; it was as though they zeroed in, took pictures, and then the man immersed himself in the readings on our affair. The folder with the papers lying on the table was already familiar to me. The main thing, however, was that Zhenechka was right there in the room, sitting hunched over in a chair. It was like they'd substituted another man for him! Hounded, confused, with a big, black and blue shiner under his left eye. When did they manage to treat him like that?

"Had it out, eh?" I ask with an intentionally hard voice, trying to cue Zhenechka to stick to his guns.

The man at the table didn't answer, but Zhenechka pulled his head even deeper into his shoulders.

We sat quietly like that, listening to the rustle of turning pages.

"Um, yes," said the man, slamming the case shut, This'll draw two years apiece. To express it in racetrack terminology, they're tying you to Ilyusha the Vegetable Man, the known speculator and gangster. Know him?"

"I've seen him in the grandstands, but we're not personally acquainted," I answered.

"That's how they," the man underscored the word "they,"
"find witnesses. The crowd at the racetrack is total riffraff
and small-timers—worthless, barely worth squeezing—
they'd put their own mamas in hock."

And such sympathy for us rang out in the voice of the
comrade in civilian clothes voice that Zhenya suddenly burst
out crying, articulating his words in a bass voice:

"We wanted to sit and relax for a while in a restaurant; big
winnings don't happen every day, but they bring us here and
throw us in a cell. They say I stole a ring from my mother.
Mama's worried. And I can't even let her know where I am."

"What ring?" I asked.

"That's ancient history," the comrade in the civilian
clothes answered for Zhenya. "Once a guy sold his mom's
ring to have enough money for the races. Who hasn't been
young once? Well, boys, are you familiar with the criminal
code? No? Too bad. Have to read this little book now and
again. The criminal and civil codes always come in handy.
Like here, they didn't have the right to keep you under arrest
for more than twenty-four hours. It's not something sanc-
tioned by the procurator's office. These obviously are illegal
methods of investigation."

Zhenya started howling even louder. The man got up
from behind the table, filled a glass with some water from a
carafe, and walked up to Zhenya.

"Yevgeny Nikolaevich, calm down, get a grip on yourself.
Who worked you over like that? Just a minute." The man
went to the light switch and turned the overhead light on in
the room. Zhenya's shiner glistened in full splendor.

"That's from when they were roughing me up in the cell," Zhenya babbled, calming down and sipping from the glass. "They promised to give me the money and they grabbed me all of a sudden, dragged us here—well, of course, I . . ."

The man clasped his hands in sorrow:

"Ah, Deryugin, Deryugin! I'm appalled at the rough job they do! And you were right, Igor Mikhailovich, when you wrote in your little article that the petty bourgeoisie had wormed its way to power. And uses that power. By the way, I'm not an admirer, however, of that little article of yours, though there's some truth to what you write. But on the other hand, the understaffed police force must accept people who haven't finished school. They do try, but it's like bears with bows and arrows. . . ."

I went cold. He'd been referring to my article. The one that's circulating in samizdat. It seems that this business has taken a more serious turn.

The comrade in civilian clothes caught the train of my thoughts.

"Excuse me, I forgot to introduce myself. Colonel of State Security Pankratov, Georgi Ivanovich. Of course I've read, 'Just Who was Victorious after the Revolution.' That's the title, isn't it? Vividly written. However, just who isn't writing these days? . . . You were understandably angry about being unable to defend your dissertation—that happens. But all this, boys, is lyricism. Let's brainstorm and see how we're going to get out of this situation."

Georgi Ivanovich took his place at the table again, and, tapping his fingers on the folder with our file, "brainstormed." I took a deep breath and plunged into it as if I were diving into water.

"Georgi Ivanovich, I'm indebted to you for your sympathy, but, as an honest man, I must advise you forthwith: personally, I'm not prepared to collaborate with the Agencies."

Zhenya cast me a frightened look, but Georgi Ivanovich smiled sadly:

"Bold and concrete. I commend you for your directness. I confess, I wasn't expecting any other answer from you. So let's speak frankly. Imagine them discussing this article of yours at the Pedagogical Council. It's horrible for you even to think, Igor Mikhailovich, about what would happen! It wouldn't be limited to expulsion from the school. They'd put you on a wagon straight to us. Why? Why, out of fear. But we read it all, and we didn't get scared. But not because we're so bold," Georgi Ivanovich paused emotionally, "but because your colleagues are afraid of the KGB, and we—the KGB itself—who are we supposed to be afraid of? I won't hide it, all kinds of people work for us, too. Not angels. But I, for example, sensed a lot of pain in your article, pain and despair. It's true—far from all revolutionary ideals have been realized. You have an excellent place there about the Petersburg workers. Bitter and just: the best cadres of the Revolution perished during the Civil War. Incidentally, my father worked at the Putilov plant. Killed in 1919 at Tsaritsyn," Georgi Mikhailovich sighed heavily. "Yes, there aren't any ideals left now. Everybody steals, everything's going to pieces. But who's going to drag the country up out of this filth? This is where you, esteemed Igor Mikhailovich, have washed your hands; you say you don't want to get them dirty. But the fact is, the racetrack isn't life for you, but an escape from life. Seems I've guessed it right. Just what are you counting on? Will someone come in from abroad on a white charger, with a cross in his hands and establish some new order?" The colonel's face grew stiff, and he didn't take his sharp eyes off me. "However, Igor Mikhailovich, as a scholar, a man of letters, a historian, you should be aware that a new order brought from without means a shock to the foundations of people's lives, blood, chaos. Is that what you want?"

"In that case," I said in answer to the colonel's gaze, "like the majority of the people in Russia, I myself would take rifle in hand and defend Soviet power, even though it has, if you'll pardon me, bored me to death."

"There," said Georgi Ivanovich, "those are the very words I expected from you. We are in agreement on this point, that we have to defend Soviet power. And a lot of things, if you'll pardon me, make me sick, too."

"But the democratic restructuring of society, perestroika, is what's needed," I began.

"Free elections, the abolition of the Agencies," Georgi Ivanovich continued in my tone, "an excellent idea, but, shall we say, not exactly fresh." The colonel became animated and clapped his hands. "Let's declare free elections. Just who will elect whom? Will the intelligentsia do the electing? It's possible. And the people? You, by the way, know very well what kind of people we've got. They stand alongside you at the 'forty' and the 'twenty.' Whom will they chose?"

"The crooks," Zhenya suddenly cut in.

"Zhenya, mind your own business," I said.

"But to be sure, Yevgeny Nikolaevich," the colonel made a wry face, "you wouldn't need . . . However, as the saying goes, the truth comes out of the mouths of babes. And if you abolished the Agencies, would you dare go out in the street after dark? In short, we don't have a different kind of people, and we're not about to engage in mass re-education in camps. We already tried. Hence, Soviet power isn't very good, but they haven't invented anything better in the meantime. However, we won't go any deeper into this political discussion. . . . Some day, another time. . . . I'm not going to flatter myself with the hope of changing your mind in a brief conversation, and don't be afraid of being recruited-wasn't that what you were expecting? I don't intend to recruit you. I've got another proposition for you. The people, no matter what kind of people, must be fed. And authority is pledged to deal with this."

"I don't get it. Just what are we doing here?" I honestly wondered.

"Oh, Igor Mikhailovich, intelligent, educated man that you are, you probably listen to foreign radio—the various Voices? Don't hide your eyes like that; who doesn't listen to the Voices these days? So you know that we buy grain and many other food products abroad. Why everything in our country is overgrown with grass is another question. You could write a new little article about it sometime. But for now, the people want to eat. What's more, they want to eat every day. And you can't feed them on promises of a 'radiant future' alone, anymore. But you need currency, hard currency, to buy grub abroad. And we're investigating various means. I stress—various. Or don't the people need to be fed?"

"But. . . ." I began.

"Grub is grub and no 'buts' about it," the colonel cut me off. "It's they," he pointed to the door, "who started the case; it's their problem. They catch crooks, and they stumbled upon you in passing. When the fisherman pulls in his net, all kinds of live ones are flapping around in it. But we've been watching you for a long time, Igor Mikhailovich, and we value your ability to find various unexpected solutions in play. In you, Yevgeny Nikolaevich," the colonel turned to Zhenya, "we value your sharp, professional eye, your calculation, your gambler's cool. Yours are precisely the qualities we need."

We became as quiet as mice, and the colonel went on in a confident tone:

"For example, you find yourselves abroad somewhere, let's say at a racetrack in one of the capitalist countries—you might win large sums—large sums of the hard currency so vital to our government? My advice to you is to forget the incident with this ticket. In essence, it's small change; it'll run right through your fingers."

"And then?" Zhenya caught on quickly.

And again, I was amazed by the striking change in his appearance. The professional rose like a phoenix from its ashes. The cold, tense poker face, his nostrils flared with excitement.

But Georgi Ivanovich made a face like he hadn't caught Zhenya's words. And he continued as though talking to himself:

"Boys, just so it's clear to everybody. We can't interfere with affairs of another department; we can't close *this*," the colonel tapped a finger on the folder. "All we can do is take this to our office. And shelve it. But don't let us down. If you're punished—that's your problem, but if we are, because we trusted you. . . ."

Silence hung in the room for about five minutes. Then

the colonel picked up the phone and dialed a number.

"Report that Colonel Pankratov wishes to speak to. . . ,"
said the colonel in something similar to his previous tone,
but we got the feeling that he was calling somewhere into
some very high spheres. A pause. And again the colonel's
voice, softened to half-tones: "Perfect! Good boys. It's the
general opinion that they can be sent. It'll be done to the letter, got it. Give corresponding instructions, prepare them and
send them to France as soon as possible. Let them tear into
the French totoshka."

The Professional's face didn't twitch; only his eyes
blazed, like during a decisive race. But I was all in a sweat,
and my head was spinning.

"Georgi Ivanovich," I uttered in a thick voice, "what
should I take 'as soon as possible' to mean? After all, doesn't
the registration alone take some time? The recommendation
from the District Committee—and with my resume!"

"You're a real joker," said Georgi Ivanovich, and he even
giggled. "You crack me up—me, an old man. Registration?
Questionnaires? Well, think a bit, esteemed Igor Mikhailovich,
what do we want with such complications? Here they are,
your external passports. All ready."

And the colonel took two new, red booklets out of the
desk.

2

—————

"MORNING PAINTS THE WALLS OF THE ANCIENT KREMLIN WITH A tender light; the whole Soviet land wakes with the dawn. . . ," a pleasant male voice sang out, and sang out rather loudly, as if it were right next to my ear. I jumped out of bed like I'd been yanked out, and the voice playfully continued: "Just what kind of pricks are you guys, that you don't you rise with the dawn?"

The half-naked and disheveled Zhenya was sitting on another bed, against the wall, probably awakened by the same voice, and he stared in amazement.

Where are we? What kind of room is this, a cell? No. Nice, clean curtains, night tables, a big cupboard in the corner. A garden outside the window. But how did we wind up here?

Recollections of yesterday, like pieces of an over-boiled potato, were disintegrating in my head. The interrogation at the police station, then the amiable Georgi Ivanovich, then all three of us had supper in a restaurant, external passports (no, he'd shown us the passports earlier), the trip out of town; Zhenya and I were apparently still putting it away here—there's an empty bottle on the table. But where did that voice come from?

"Guys, that's enough scratching your balls!" It was as if the voice came from the ceiling. "Wash up and get dressed quickly. PT in ten minutes."

Obviously there's a speaker mounted somewhere in the wall, I thought, but if the room's fixed up with a radio, they could have heard everything Zhenya and I were talking about when they left us alone and we finished the bottle. . . . Your mother! Everything's ruined! After all, we could have been gabbing about anything! . . .

As if reading my thoughts, the voice giggled:

"Yeah, guys, you really cut loose yesterday. I can't believe the amount of nonsense spoken within one square meter! A world record! And you, Igor Mikhailovich, are even being kind of a lightweight, to suspect Georgi Ivanovich of being in collusion with the police. Meanwhile, we've established who you are—made inquiries, searched the archives, and so on—the police, meanwhile, have been busy with their own case. Different departments. Okay, guys, I've forgotten everything as far as yesterday's concerned. Understood? But now I've got to go off duty. And my relief's an impressionable guy. So you should really be a little more cautious. Chatterboxes are generally a godsend for a spy. You have to get used to working carefully. *Bonne journée,* as the French say. Until we meet in the ether!"

Zhenya and I simultaneously made faces, but we'd been warned about making remarks that could be overheard. I went into the corridor first, found the toilet (next door to our room), and as I took care of my needs, I had the impression that even the toilet was listening to everything. That's why I, *pardonnez-moi,* flushed the whole time, to muffle the noises I was making.

About thirty people were standing in formation on the
lawn in front of our long, one-story house—so that's how
many neighbors we turned out to have! Wiry guys in light
athletic suits. Zhenya and I must have looked ridiculous in
our civilian pants.

PT took about fifteen minutes, but I thought I was going
to gasp my last—this was after yesterday, with a heavy head,
with palpitations! It was a good thing the instructor conducting the exercises didn't pay much attention to us.

Then a shower. Then breakfast. We ate breakfast in a spa-
cious dining hall, two or three to a small table, so that
nobody sat with us. They served rolls, butter, jam, eggs, cot-
tage cheese, and coffee for breakfast. I barely touched the
food. All I wanted was to drink.

Sizing up our neighbors, I noticed that they scarcely
spoke. We kept quiet, too.

Then, along with everybody else, we went into a class-
room located in the same building as the dining hall. The
instructor, once again in a navy-blue athletic suit, youthful,
sharp looking, announced:

"Our subject for today's study is bridges." He pressed a
button. Blinds came down over the windows; a movie projec-
tor began whirring behind us. The blackboard split and the
image of a railroad bridge appeared on the white wall, which
was like a screen. First a general view, then close-ups of the
ironwork, ties and rails. Some kind of cavities had been dug;
there were empty spaces under the rails. Farther down along
the bridge was a man walking who was always shown from
the back. The man moved unhurriedly and bent a couple of
times to tie his shoelaces.

"Task properly completed," said the instructor, and a

smallish box was shown in the screen, nestled under a rail, up against a tie. I wouldn't have noticed the box if it hadn't been for the pointer on the screen.

"Task improperly completed," the instructor announced.

The man appeared on the screen again; this time, however, he was walking hurriedly, constantly looking around (although the man's face was out of focus). At a certain point he stopped and awkwardly stuck the box under the rail, but not up against the tie, so that the box was noticeable on the track.

Then a beautiful sequence of landscapes started flashing across the screen. The instructor named: the Brooklyn Bridge in New York, Le Pont D'Alexandre III in Paris, Waterloo Bridge in London. . . . But after a general view of each bridge, the movie camera's objective slid along the parapet and rails, fixing on recesses in the wall in close-up.

"These bridges aren't guarded as a rule," the instructor commented, "but traffic on them is always heavy."

A bridge appeared with a steep arch going up to the sky. "This is the Bridge at St. Nazarre on France's Atlantic coast. St. Nazarre is an important shipbuilding center and port. The bridge has strategic significance. There are booths with barriers at the foot of the bridge. But the people in the booth aren't policemen; they don't guard the bridge, but just collect the toll from motorists. You can cross the bridge by the narrow walkway on the side without being hindered."

The objective of the movie camera began to slip along the open metal arches of the bridge again. An ocean-going ship passed far beneath the bridge. A flashing arrow on the screen jumped along the handrails of the bridge.

"It would be pointless to lay the charge there," said the instructor. "You'd only get fireworks."

The pointer on the screen showed the bridge's under-pinnings.

"You've got to lower your charges into these niches. The charge is lowered with the help of a thin steel cable and sticks by magnet to the steel crossbeam. The cable is cut with wirecutters. . . ."

When the lesson ended and everybody flooded into the hall for a smoke, I went up to the instructor, who was gathering his papers from the table.

"Excuse me, but I don't know your name and patronymic."

"Just address me as Comrade Instructor," the instructor prompted me with a tranquil smile. "Are there any questions on the subject matter?"

"No questions, Comrade Instructor," I started to hesitate, "but you see, I'm afraid this subject isn't for us. The thing is, we're horse specialists."

"Oh," the instructor whistled and looked at me with respect. "But we haven't received the racetrack photos yet. Anyway, wagering techniques is a broad subject, though it does have its own specifics. I think there'll be a special class, but for now continue this course."

In the hall the trainees stood in small groups, not mingling. I picked out Italian and German speech. But the majority of the trainees were clearly Eastern types. They were speaking a guttural language I didn't recognize.

"Why are there so many people from the Caucasian republics?" I quietly asked Zhenya. "Do you think they're Armenians or Georgians?"

"Those are Arabs. I used to wheel and deal around Lumumba University and I can make out Arabic when I hear it."

My dashing Professional had a generally sorry look. Maybe the guy still hadn't recovered from yesterday's binge?

The next hour of study was spent at the firing range. Firing from standing and kneeling positions with a pistol. In my distant youth, I used to go to the shooting club in my district Pioneer Club. Of course, my eyes and hands weren't what they used to be. For some reason I was hitting left of the bull's eye. But my shot group was tight. And the instructor, an elderly, obese man, even commended me.

But then came hand-to-hand combat. A sinewy Arab threw me and pressed me to the ground several times. I almost screamed.

"Zhenya," I said during the break, "I've see this France in the grave. Time to head for the hills."

"But how?" Zhenya whispered miserably.

How, indeed? As far as our relatives, friends, acquaintances, and generally all progressive humanity were concerned, we were in Sochi at present, resting on the seashore after our big win. In any case, that's what I explained to my brother and Zhenya to his mother. Needless to say, we were speaking on the phone as if from the main post office at Sochi, while in reality, we were calling right at the police station, naturally, in the presence of Georgi Ivanovich. I couldn't figure out where they took us after the restaurant. The car looped around a suburban highway for a long time, and we were engaged in a pleasant conversation with the comrade colonel. It seems he said we would be in some kind of athletic camp. I don't recall if the exact address was mentioned. But I distinctly recall that you couldn't phone out and that leaving the camp area was "most inadvisable." The colonel repeated this several times in such a tone that the question "why?" no longer arose. But what if we were to decide we wanted to leave the area? Out of the comer of my eye during the morning run, I caught sight of a remote concrete wall two meters high and strung with barbed wire on the top, beyond the trees.

They fed us excellently at dinner. They served us kharcho soup, Kiev cutlets, and a compote. I laid into everything with gusto, with an unexpected appetite. Things were looking up.

Having returned to our room, we fell on our beds without uttering a word, and. . . .

"Trainees Kholmogorov and Lomonosov," the voice came through like it was right over my ear, "to classes in section eight!"

I looked at my watch: I'd managed to nap about forty minutes. Zhenya hurriedly combed his hair. We silently exchanged glances. It seems we're picking up the beat of a new life.

In section eight—a tiny little room over the dining hall— the next "comrade instructor" awaited us. How was he dressed? Guess! No need to strain your brain any further; "Comrade Instructor" was dressed in a light, navy blue athletic suit with white stripes—the uniform of the Soviet Olympic Team.

"Comrade Trainees! I'll be teaching you French. Lessons every day for three hours after dinner. Kholmogorov, have you studied French? In school and at the institute? Do you read it? Write it? Forgotten it? Not too bad. Lomonosov knows English? Roughly? Not a word of French? Excellent. Starting today, we speak only French. *Comment allez-vous?*"

. . . Running ahead of myself, I'll say we spent not some

piddling number of days or weeks in this "athletic camp," but four whole months, and we devoted ourselves to French three hours a day, including Sunday. Comrade Instructor drilled us soundly in French, although, despite our requests, pleas and persuasion, not once did he utter so much as a single word of Russian. The guy's word was carved in stone!

*   *   *

Georgi Ivanovich showed up in camp a week later. By that time, I was already scoring forty-five points with five shots, while Zhenya did an excellent job of "turning the mill," that is, he'd throw his opponent to the ground. My achievements in hand-to-hand combat weren't nearly good enough, but I felt better physically, and wasn't gasping for breath at the end of the morning run. Besides that, we learned a lot of useful things, mostly in connection with blasting with a remote fuse, and it seemed to us we could tell if we were being watched on the street or in a cafe. (There was a stationary set in the camp, like in the movies, a mockup of a typical European street.)

Georgi Ivanovich, however, was horrified. He told us the seventeenth department had gotten it wrong again, and to erase anything from our minds at once.

"They mistakenly sent you," the colonel explained, "into a group for the athletic training of foreign architects and bridgebuilders. But it would be complicated to transfer you to another athletic training group immediately. The morning PT and the evening swim are good, and French is really necessary too, but as for the rest—to hell with it!

The colonel brought us a stack of last year's issues of the French newspaper, *Paris Turf*. He said this newspaper was specifically devoted to horse races and sprints. From now on, we'd be getting current issues regularly. But we needed to learn the trotters' performance from last year's results.

"What's there to learn?" Zhenya objected, "I'm used to trusting my eye. For example, I never read the information on the horses' performance in the Moscow Racetrack program. It's pure bunk."

"It's not for me to judge the Moscow Racetrack," returned Georgi Ivanovich gently, "but the French don't write bunk. And what's more, the season at the Vincennes Racetrack in Paris opens in mid-fall. And that's where they play the biggest purses in racing. I see no sense in you hanging around Paris with nothing to do."

Zhenya shut up. In order to smooth over the awkward-ness, I came out with a Young Pioneer proposal: compile a detailed card index on all the trotters over three years old that appeared at Vincennes. The colonel nodded encouragingly.

Then each of us wrote a statement to his place of work with a request to be granted a six-month leave of absence at our own expense in connection with the necessity that we take part in a remote, Far-Eastern scientific expedition. What kind, exactly? "There's no need to be specific," said the colonel. "But I'm in charge of a class," I started getting worried, "I've got tenth grade 'B' finals!" "We'll take care of everything," said the colonel. "And my graduate student record?" asked Zhenya. "Your record will be kept as it stands," answered the colonel. "Aside from that, it's been decided a salary will be put aside for you as members of an expedition— at two hundred rubles a month per person. The money'll be transferred to your savings accounts," said the colonel. "But I've never had a savings account in my life!" Zhenya exclaimed.

"Then what's this?" said the colonel, and pulled out a brand-new bankbook for him.

"Now, guys, are you satisfied with everything? The food is at public expense, free of charge, movies in the evenings, television in the lounge, newspapers and books in the library. What more could you want?"

I answered that in that regard, it never occurred to me to even dream of anything better, but Zhenya, as though bitten by a fly:

"The people want their legal one hundred grams!" Zhenya roared maliciously. "The foreigners guzzle beer in the cafe in the evening, and we, like some damn bastards, are watching *The Three Sisters* on TV. . . ."

Georgi Ivanovich frowned: "Really, that's scandalous! Why didn't they explain to you that you could relax evenings in the cafe? Let's go, guys."

Our dining room turned into a cafe after supper. We sat at our little table, and a waitress with a charming smile asked Georgi Ivanovich:

"What'll you have, boys?"

It's strange—why did she turn only to him? She knew us, not him, and how was the colonel dressed today? . . . Can you guess? In a navy-blue olympic suit with white stripes.

Zhenya ordered vodka, and I a whiskey. The colonel—a little cognac.

"How many vodkas?" the waitress asked us to specify.

"A bottle!" Zhenya snapped.

The waitress brought the colonel and me large glasses, in the bottom of which there gleamed some liquid, but for Zhenya there was a little fifty-gram rascal with a green label that read "Moscow Special."

"What's this?" asked Zhenya, stammering at the offense.

"A double portion of vodka. Get used to the European way of life. When you order a bottle of vodka in a western cafe, this is exactly how much they'll bring. Igor Mikhailovich and I can repeat our orders because we got one cognac and one whiskey, but I wouldn't recommend that you repeat yours."

"Just how do they live in the West?" was all Zhenya could utter.

"Guys, who was it that told you things were good in the West?" the colonel was amazed. "Life in the West is very hard and complex."

"I don't know how they stand it," Zhenya drawled out after some hesitation. "If I were in their place, I'd have organized two revolutions by now."

"The wave of revolutionary movement in the West is growing," Georgi Ivanovich calmly replied.

"But can't they at least get some beer?" implored Zhenya.

"You can get as much beer as you want. A whole bottle of dry wine. It's accepted in the West. The bourgeoisie is cunning; it knows how to get the proletariat unaccustomed to class struggle."

*   *   *

Compiling the card index of French trotters turned out to be an exceptionally labor-consuming affair. It was easier for Zhenya—he copied the speed posted in each race, that is, he fiddled with numbers. I was the one who studied and compared specialists' predictions and accounts of the races. But the French journalists expressed themselves in strange jargon, rarely encountered in our dictionaries, and I didn't understand the better half of it. There wasn't much use in asking our French instructor either, because naturally, he always answered my questions in French; I never squeezed so much as a word of Russian out of him. I was working so hard my face was in a sweat, like when I was writing my dissertation, and I didn't even have any free time left to sit around the cafe in the evening.

And then Zhenya started to act up. After dinner he'd drive me off to the library—said he couldn't work in the same room with me, because I bothered him.

There were black guys and Spaniards sitting in the library (the contingent of architects and builders had been replaced), but I noticed that my neighbors were studying in the library every other day, but I stuck it out at my little table every day. And I also noticed that somehow Zhenya's work had come to a standstill, and when I returned to the room, I'd find Zhenya in a playful, cheerful mood.

Finally Zhenya took pity on me.

"Okay, Teacher," he said one day after dinner, "you've been beating off long enough. Today it's my turn to go to the library, and you ask Tamara to bring you some coffee in the room. Just don't make too much noise in there."

My jaw dropped, and Zhenya grinned lasciviously. Tamara was the name of the waitress who served our table. A young girl, not beautiful, but appetizing. My head was spinning from the sight of her ass after the long abstention.

Zhenya left, and I bided my time as she drew closer to me, and with a tremor in my voice I began to speak:

"Nice weather, Tamara. I want to work in my room for a while today. Would you bring me some coffee?"

"Did you get a uniform?" Tamara inquired efficiently.

"What kind of uniform?"

"An athletic one. An olympic suit."

"But what do I want with that? We're leaving soon."

"You don't want it, but it's a gift for me. I'll sell it for a hundred in a second-hand shop. It's Romanian."

"Aha," I said. "Right away."

"The supply room is closed after dinner. But you can get it tomorrow. It's a sin to waste something decent. It's yours. But I've got to do the dishes, and I'll come in half an hour."

And here's Tamarka in my room. She's sitting on Zhenya's bed. My teeth are chattering from tension. I can't just do it straight off like that. We talk quietly about a tie match in the championship soccer tournament. Can't see Spartacus in first place. Tamara is yawning.

And suddenly, like it was over my ear, the voice. I haven't heard it for a long time:

"Tamarka. There's nothing to getting screwed. You're used to sucking the Arabs off, but here's one of your own, a Russian. Kids, why are you being so distant? Set her up doggy-style, man!"

My first impulse was to run out of the room, but Tamara was already on her knees with her skirt hiked up.

*   *   *

The leaves were falling from the maples. Summer was long gone. At morning PT formation and on the run, we stamped briskly through the puddles.

Georgi Ivanovich came to camp once every two weeks. We didn't ask him about anything; he would put us at ease, himself.

"It's okay, guys. It won't be long. Business is progressing. The papers are in the works. . . ."

As far as we could tell, the whole delay was tied to currency. But one day Zhenya couldn't stand it, and in his idiotic manner he announced that all of this bored him. He said we were being led around by the nose, and that these people had their nerve.

"And I'm not bored?" the colonel said in a changed, cold inflection.

I fell to pieces. I'd never seen Georgi Ivanovich like that. And he continued:

"I don't have nerves? Just spare me, Igor Mikhailovich, but it was simpler in the old days. Yes, I know there were various mistakes of the cult of personality, breaches of the law, and so on. But if the decision was made at the highest level, then nobody threw a monkeywrench into the works. They wouldn't have dared utter a word. And here I am, a colonel in State Security—I run up and down the stairs like a little boy, gather resolutions, settle things, coordinate, persuade. The scum begrudge us the currency. If I needed money for a *regular* action, the question would be settled in a flash, and none of these stinking pieces of paper would count. But I'm the one who has to explain that we're taking a risk. This is an original operation. You don't mix debits and credits. And they're tight, the bureaucratic bastards!"

Zhenya and I went around crestfallen for a week. I even stopped reading *Paris Turf*. But one fine day after dinner, Tamarka, usually indifferent and lazy in bed, gave me a first-class performance with youthful passion and Komsomol fervor. And then she said, "Bring me some makeup from France. You won't forget, will you?"

I realized things were on the move.

3

"THE FRENCH ARE BASTARDS!" ZHENYA KEPT REPEATING. "Scum! Parasites! You take a look at the steaks they've got, the chops! Have you ever seen anything like it in our stores?"

"Exactly," I echoed him, "crawling reptiles! I didn't know sausage like that existed."

"Look! Levis, Wranglers, John's jeans laid out in bulk and nobody's buying them. Wow, what skirts, what blouses! You could lose your fucking mind! And our girls in Moscow would screw any damn nigger in a doorway for a rag like that! Panty hose—two francs apiece! And at home they go for seven fifty, and even then you can't always get them!"

"Eight kinds of ham on one counter! Just how can they cram all that down and not choke? The whores!"

"Sony, Phillips, and Grundig stereos, cassette recorders, color TVs, stereo and quadrophonic systems! You don't need a bribe to buy them. Well, doesn't that stink? Regular whoring!"

"Grapes, strawberries, oranges, bananas, pears, plums.

The Tashkent bazaar pales! What do they have in Paris, a Central Asian climate?"

"Pineapples, Teacher, mountains of pineapples!"

"I remember last year, in the tenth-grade A class, when I was teaching Mayakovsky's "Eat pineapple, chew your grouse, your last day is coming, bourgeois louse!' and one of my students asked, 'But what's a pineapple? I've never seen one.'"

"And have you ever seen grouse? Go up to the shop window! Feast your eyes!"

"White Horse whiskey, Johnny Walker, gin, Camus cognac, Napoleon brandy, and even our own Moscow Special with the medals! You can't find hide nor hair of that stuff in the Union!"

'Tell me, Teacher, but be honest: if I had the money, would they wrap up that blue Peugeot for me without any waiting in line?"

"Look, it says right here: 'Key in hand!' That means you pay and then get behind the wheel. But you can ask them to turn the car over to you in a blue box with a pink polka dot ribbon, and they'll add something to the balance for the wrappings."

"Well, aren't they bastards!"

"Regular whores! Anyway, Zhenya, you can't dazzle a Frenchman with a car. Any monsieur, you see, drives his own handsome coupe. The city is overrun with cars. Look, there's another traffic jam!"

"Come off it. You might as well tell a starving man that malnutrition is supposed to make him lean, so a special maintenance diet's been recommended. . . ."

That's all I needed! The Professional lecturing me! After

all, we're in Paris, not the Moscow Racetrack. I'm a cultured man, an educator. . . .

"Zhenya, we're acting like savages. Like we came from a starving country!"

"So what?"

"I mean to say that Paris is the cultural center of the whole world. And on the first day one usually goes to the Louvre, to the Impressionist Museum."

"Who goes? Well, maybe some fools go, or those damn pederasts. Let them. Every family has its freak. You can make a bee-line to the Louvre, too, but pass it on to your Impressionists that I've seen them in the coffin, and in white slippers. Go, why don't you. . . ?"

"Look at that beautiful street! And the houses with the latticed balconies all around. Like the deck of a ship!"

"Street, balconies. . . . No, Teacher, you can't leave your tenth-grade class behind. What the fuck do you want with Paris, when you're looking for a moral to everything, like some theme for a composition?"

"Well, you're a fine one, too! Young guy, so deep into that display case you don't even look at the girls. And what girls they've got around here!"

"I don't give squat about them! What do I want with a girl when there's everything in Paris! Do you understand? Everything! And why, why are the French so lucky? Why do they have everything, when we have zilch! No, if I had an automatic in my hands, like the one they used to give me at military camp, I'd teach them to love freedom!"

* * *

"Well, how do you like Paris, comrades?" Eduard Ivanovich asked us when we returned to the embassy. "Get a look at the French?"

Eduard Ivanovich had met us in the morning at the airport, brought us to the embassy, and given us some instructions. He fed us in the cafeteria. Then he let us stroll around the city for a few hours. Now he was obviously interested in our reaction to our first encounter with capitalist reality. A friendly smile flickered across Eduard Ivanovich's lips, but a watchful flame shone in his eyes. He was probably waiting to hear some affected sighs out of us, like how Paris is a nothing city, and everything's better in Moscow.

"They've gotta be crushed, the creeps!" Zhenya declared with such gloomy conviction that Eduard Ivanovich burst out laughing from the bottom of his heart.

Eduard Ivanovich's Discussion on Parisian Architecture (which I cite in full)

"Well, guys, truth be told, then frankly, Paris is a beautiful little town. You can't spit anywhere without hitting some architectural monument—you can't miss. You'd wear out your tongue if you just listed a few. The first order of business is the Eiffel Tower. You can see it right away. Well, beyond that, there's the Louvre, the Palace of Chaillot, the Tower of Montparnasse—that's a new skyscraper that's visible from everywhere, too. Well, and then there're the various cathedrals to the Parisian Holy Mother, the Hotel des Invalides, the Pantheon. . . . By the way, in the Cathedral de Notre Dame de Paris, of the Holy Parisian Mother, I highly recommend you pay attention to the gargoyles—they're the

little suckers that hang down from the roof, and their mugs—
how can I describe them more accurately—well, okay, if you
swilled vodka from dawn to dusk for twelve days in a row
and then looked in the mirror—there you'd have a perfect
gargoyle! And the Hotel des Invalides is like our Mausoleum,
but more highly detailed and nicer. They keep their comrade
Napoleon there, not alive, of course, and not as a mummy,
but his remains, or a part of his remains—just which part, I
don't remember. The Hotel des Invalides is, in general, a military museum, and a hostel for the *invalides* themselves—
we'd call them 'old soldiers'—is situated in the side
annexes. No, you guys, I'm no specialist in architecture, but
I do know a thing or two about it. For instance, when I first
wound up in St. Chapelle—that's a sort of church on the
grounds of the Palace of Justice, and take note, they'll let you
in there without a pass—just like that. The stained glass windows in this St. Chappelle are so beautiful that I was moved
to tears! Anyway, you've got to have your wits about you
with these architectural monuments. One day I decided to go
to the Opera. The building is sharp, there's no saying it
isn't—the green roof, the sculpture, the balustrades. . . . But
a ticket there costs enough to take your breath away! You
could buy a pair of Levis, and they'll tear them right out of
your hands for over two hundred rubles at any Moscow second-hand store. No, I thought, better to let the French hang
themselves with their Opéra. I'd rather go to the Bolshoi
Theater in Moscow, since everybody knows our ballet is the
best in the world.

"And all the same, Paris is great. If I were an unre-
stricted tourist with a wad of currency in my pocket, I'd
want to stroll down the Champs-Élysées and the Grands

Boulevards. But you know, guys, we're here on business—
you don't just go strolling by yourself. And then we're not
authorized to hang around on our own. Officially, there's no
rule against it, but if you go out once, you'll go out twice, and
the third time, you'll be called to see the Party Organizer,
who'll politely ask, 'What's with you, Eduard Ivanovich, are
you losing touch with the collective?' It's easier to go out
with the collective, of course, but where do you get this
collective? . . . This one sits watching television, that one
watches the movies in the embassy hall, and if a troika of
guys is getting together, then by God, it's stupid to drag yourself off somewhere with a half a liter in your hand, begging,
and so pleasant to share it in warm company. . . . On Sunday
and Saturday you can go strolling wherever you please, but
they'll take you on some organized excursion or a cultural
trip—to the big department stores—to Galeries Lafayettes,
Samaritaine or Tati. Tati, by the way, has the best prices; you
can get five pairs of women's pantyhose there for ten francs.
But the people are like in our GUM—you'll never push
through them. Blacks, Arabs, Asians flee from all the developing nations, from their own Third World, and head straight
for Tati! Anyway, after Tati you can, accidentally, as though
by happenstance, rush off to Pigalle. And there on every corner, on every doorstep, at every gate, in a word—every step
of the way, stands the best-built architecture! You'll reel!
Skirts above the navel, tanned legs—they wink, they call to
you, make eyes. . . . And there are huge numbers of sex shops
as far as the eye can see, too! And they all have lit-up signs
and delicious looking chicks in photographs in such poses!
. . . And the hawkers literally drag you in by force, but we're
educated people; we know how to take care of ourselves.

You tell him, 'I am Sovietique,' and he'll jump away from you like he's been scalded. . . . All in all guys, as Vladimir Mayakovsky said, 'I'd like to live and die in Paris,' if only Moscow would give us a little more currency."

"Eduard Ivanovich," I couldn't contain myself, "excuse me, but it seems you've gotten off the subject. After all, the talk was about Parisian architecture."

"Just what is architecture? For example, there's the shop windows—you might say they were related to architecture! There aren't words to describe the shop windows, they're so enticing, but take a look at the prices, and life loses its appeal! . . . Well, but that's enough, let's get back to architecture. You know what disappointed me about Paris? They're digging it up, the creeps, like in Moscow. First one street is repaved, then there's a construction fence at another one. No, it's a grand illusion that only Moscow is being dug up. Paris, too! True, they do fill the ditches in quickly; they can't be compared to us. And then, Vladimir Mayakovsky was right again when he wrote, 'The architecture is varied: sometimes proletarian, sometimes bourgeois.' In the workingclass quarter the streets are narrow, and laundry hangs from the windows. True, the real workers live in the HLM. Those are the new special housing projects. But Asians, blacks, and Arabs are once again in the poor quarters. It's inadvisable for us to go there. Furthermore, the word is stay as far away from those French Communists as possible. They're all pure Jews . . . pardon me, I misspoke—not Jews, but Eurocommunists of questionable background."

"Eduard Ivanovich, you've gotten off the subject again. . . ."

"No, guys, I gab about architecture all the time. The architecture in Paris is the first order of business. You'd be lost without an understanding of the architecture of Paris. Let's assume you get into a quarter of solid, respectable houses with servant quarters and ornate latticework, stucco mouldings, little round balconies. My advice to you, guys, is take to your heels and fly! God forbid you should peep into a shop or a grocery store! They don't have prices, but highway robbery. But then, where the houses are a little bit more plain, without any ornate stuff, everything there—apples, tomatoes, butter— is all markedly cheaper. And if you're lucky, you might even get a sheepskin coat for next to nothing.

"But if I can speak frankly, I like the new Soviet Embassy building best of all. Good architecture—austere, restrained— just like the Kremlin Palace of Congresses. But the main thing is that our embassy is situated in an important strategic position. The Périphérique Boulevard, their ring road, is in one direction, and in the other direction is Marshall Boulevard, also a major Paris artery of transportation. If fighting breaks out, we can spray them from the windows, and we'll have the whole city bottled up in a flash!"

*   *   *

They settled us in a house I named the Soviet Trade Delegations dormitory. Only Soviet Trade Delegation firm employees and delegates lived there, and even though every family had its own separate one- or two-room apartment, order was kept as it is in a regular student or construction workers' dormitory. The front door was locked for the night, and a woman on duty, who sat 'round-the-clock and answered the phone, which was connected by switchboard to the city, kept a record of the comings and goings of all the tenants. Not once did I see a single outsider—that is, any Frenchmen—in the dormitory.

Zhenya and I found ourselves once again in the same kind of room we were used to from the "athletic camp" outside Moscow—the same two beds, the same two night tables, the dresser, the small desk, but in addition to that, we had a shower, a toilet and a kitchen with an electric range, the merits of which we would value later, when money got tight. We'd roast a chicken in the oven, or rather, the chicken would roast itself; all you had to do was push the right buttons, and it turned out really tasty.

Anyway, we didn't get to the racetrack too soon. Eduard Ivanovich explained that we had to have a "cover," that is, some proper occupation. We were considered consultants from the Ministry of Agriculture, and we were taken to tractor, combine, and cattle exhibits and invited to evening cocktail parties where we carried on stupid conversations about the weather with representatives from French firms.

The working day began when we got to the embassy or the trade delegation and made our way directly to the snack bar to drink beer. Then Eduard Ivanovich would pop in and escort us to the next office; the boss there would ask us stupid questions about anything he wanted, but not about *business!* I got the impression that either they were still *keeping an eye on us* or the final instructions still hadn't come in from home. In any case, nobody (except, naturally, Eduard Ivanovich) really wanted to know what we'd come for.

One time, in the embassy First Secretary's office, Zhenya couldn't stand it; he changed the subject to the racetrack. The First Secretary made a wry face like he had a toothache, and Eduard Ivanovich gave us a terrifying look. Zhenya shut up.

Evenings, like the majority of Soviet comrades, we watched French and American films in the embassy movie theater, free of charge. And we went walking along the streets of Paris less and less. Store windows, the lights of restaurants and cafes burned alluringly, but we very quickly came to understand that we couldn't afford the merchandise, and we kept as far away from the cafes as possible. We had the misfortune to eat dinner there on one of the first days, and the bill they gave us sobered us up for a long time.

Of course we drank, but late in the evening, with the door of our room locked.

"Just how can you live in Paris with such prices?" I asked Eduard Ivanovich.

"Just who told you it was easy to live in Paris?" answered Eduard Ivanovich.

I couldn't tell whether Eduard Ivanovich was pretending to be a fool on purpose or whether he really was one.

*   *   *

But if there was one guy who really wasn't a fool, it was Boris Borisovich. Even physically he was the complete opposite of Eduard Ivanovich. Eduard Ivanovich—the round, sweet-natured Russian mug, a round loaf adorned in a French suit. Boris Borisovich—the Western businessman with a bank director's authoritative manner. It was just as though he'd been born in a Pierre Cardin shirt. Sharp, elegant, somehow reminiscent of the instructors from the "athletic camp."

"Well, what is it," asked Boris Borisovich, as soon as we appeared at his office door, "are you guzzling vodka on the sly?"

"What else is there for us to do?" I answered. "Just how do you live in Paris with these prices?"

"You can live in Paris," grinned Boris Borisovich, "and in clover. These French creeps—is that what you call them?" (Zhenya and I looked at each other.) "Anyway, the French receive an annual 'amendment for lousiness'—that means a pay supplement equivalent to the rate of inflation. It's been quite a few years since we got that supplement. Either in the embassy or at the trade delegation. Things're bad with currency in our country. Just try not to pay it to the French—they'll call a strike at once. They've got very fierce trade unions. But our trade union's neither fish nor fowl. Right, Eduard Ivanovich?"

"In return we have complete freedom," answered Eduard Ivanovich. "If you're not satisfied, you can go back to Moscow and try to find a somewhat better job."

I looked askance at Eduard Ivanovich. Something different could now be divined behind the round loaf mask. Maybe he's a complete fool or no fool at all.

"But I've never heard," Boris Borisovich went on, "that anybody from the embassy staff ever fled from Paris to his native birches on his own initiative."

I sensed from the tone of the conversation that some kind of game was going on between them—one I'd rather not have been participating in. And Zhenya (you've got to give him his due) also caught wind of some kind of trick or hustle. He didn't say anything.

Our silence was evaluated on I don't know what scale, but they adduced some kind of appraisal for us.

"Edik," said Boris Borisovich, changing his tone, "let these guys get boiled in the tent. Take them to our retail shop. And then their money will sprout wings."

"Who's their sponsor?" Eduard Ivanovich asked dispas-
sionately. "After all, they aren't *staff*. They aren't authorized."

"They can mention my name," said Boris Borisovich,
"we won't be watering down our tea if the guys acquire some
whiskey and cigarettes at cut rates. And afterwards, come
back; I'll be waiting for you."

"What kind of tent is it?" Zhenya asked Eduard Ivanovich
when we found ourselves in the corridor.

"Tent?" Eduard Ivanovich hemmed significantly. "Borya
calls the embassy 'the tent.' You have to go up to the second
floor to get to the retail store."

*   *   *

However, we didn't get back to Boris Borisovich for two
and a half hours. The problem was that a bunch of people
were crowded into this special retail store, most of them
dames—embassy workers and embassy workers' wives as we
ascertained from conversations. (They let us in the door, but
that was it.) Eduard Ivanovich whispered something at length to
the stern comrade guarding the door until he finally relented,
but we were afraid to go back out. Eduard Ivanovich had
slipped off, and who would let us in without him? Bottles of
whiskey, vodka, and cognac, cartons of American Marlboros,
Winstons, and French perfume, sparkled on the shelves
behind the counter, but the dames were buying panties, bras,
nightgowns—and buying them by the bundle. We tried to get
through without waiting in line, explaining (it was a blessing
that all around us were our own Russians) that we didn't
need that junk, we only wanted whiskey and cigarettes, but
the dames raised such a cry! It was so like being in Moscow

at some vegetable stand that we thought, "Now they're going to throw us out." We had to honestly wait our turn. And they only allowed one carton of cigarettes and one bottle of whiskey to the mug. But the discount was double.

"Where did you get held up so long?" Boris Borisovich asked with irritation, and, after looking us over, he added:

"You wouldn't be coming from the bathhouse, would you?"

We dumped ourselves exhaustedly into the chairs.

"Yes, from the bathhouse—the women's."

Boris Borisovich always caught our drift.

"What were they offering today?"

"Ladies underwear," answered Zhenya.

"Apparently there's a shortage of panties and bras in Paris," I added.

Boris Borisovich cheered up: "Yes, our little honeys have disgraced themselves before our Moscow guests." (In another, sharp tone): "Filthy, scavenging stringbaggers! The Tishinsky market weeps for them." (In the former, cheerful tone): "Guys, they got some currency stuff from brand-name stores. By the way, the French ladies line up like that too when cheap goods are advertised." (In the other, sharp tone): "But they clear at least a hundred for these, and ours—kopecks. They'll hang themselves for a franc!" (In the former, cheerful tone): "We'll never build communism with people like that!"

We harkened to this one-actor theater with astonishment. After a final, profound pause, Boris Borisovich changed to a calm, businesslike tone:

"Okay, comrades, like they say, 'a bit closer to the vest.' At present, your stay in Paris seems like idiocy to you. But even real (the word was emphasized) people on missions don't spend their time here any better. The benefits of their excursions don't amount to a hill of sand. Except, of course, for gifts for your near and dear ones. An official junket abroad to a capitalist country, in a majority of cases, is a reward for exemplary conduct. We know that, and the French know it, too. That's why you have to look like everybody else. Your business activity might alert someone. And I don't want you to attract any attention."

"Boris Borisovich," Zhenya interrupted him, "I learned my lessons well in the athletic camp. Maybe I'm wrong, but I swear I haven't once detected a tail on us."

. . . Look at that! Zhenya's outdone himself! While I, to tell the truth, had actually forgotten about such fine points!

Boris Borisovich heard us out, thought for a bit, and went on, not changing his voice:

"If you believe the mercenary French press (it goes without saying that I don't), according to the experts' calculations, in Paris on this very day, there are four and a half thousand intelligence agents from the USSR and the countries of the socialist camp. They all have various official covers, but for the French DST, the nature of their activities presents no mystery. Thus, the number of people suspected by French intelligence exceeds the personnel of the French security service. Besides that, Paris is the playground for an enormous number of Libyan, Palestinian, Israeli, Latin American and other agents. Add to them the Corsican and Basque terrorists as well. All these cause the French DST a bigger headache than so called spies from Eastern European countries. I don't envy our French 'comrades.' With such a shortage of cadres, the main thing is to find time to follow each other to make sure none of their colleagues have been recruited. It would be a great honor for you to be favored with a personal tail. For that to happen, you'd at least have to announce in French in a loud voice in a cafe that you were preparing to make an attempt on the life of the president of the republic. And they might not check that. They'll call and ask me if the gentlemen aren't insane and whether it wouldn't be better if you went quietly back to our nation's capital. To make it short, walk freely in Paris, guys, and don't go tying your shoelaces in plate-glass windows. But. . . ." (A thirty second pause!) "By some kind of miracle, they do find out a lot. It's not like the intelligence service had anything to do with it, but some yellow journal, like *France soir* or *Libération* will suddenly write about your exploits, with close-up photos. Nothing terrible will happen, but it'll be uncomfortable for me. Sunday is your first working day at the Vincennes Racetrack. Study the papers. I'll give you a thousand francs for a trial run. A purely personal question—you don't have to answer—do you yourselves believe in your impending exploits?"

"Why would we have come here otherwise?" muttered Zhenya.

Boris Borisovich looked at Zhenya, then at me. No emotion whatever could be read on his face.

"Personally, I don't believe in you. That is, I absolutely don't believe in the success of this totally hopeless business. The French aren't such fools that they wouldn't pick up money if it was lying around. However, I'm only expressing my personal opinion. Another department got into this mess with you. Let them get out of it themselves. My business is to provide you with a cover. I'm always at your service."

4

IT'S LIKE THIS: THE VINCENNES RACETRACK, OF COURSE, IS BIGGER than ours—it's quite nice, but somehow it's uncomfortable.

We got there over an hour before the first race and ran from floor to floor for a long time, checking the labyrinths of the racetrack. It was important to study them and learn which windows were where beforehand, but there were a lot of them, and they were all different. At some of them they only play express or pairs; in others, you can bet on a horse that takes one of the first places or wins the race. There's one more booth where they take bets on the three first horses; it's called *trio,* but trio isn't played in every race.

We bought a pack of special tickets and a pair of metal tongs. They explained to us that you punch out the numbers of the horses you've chosen with the tongs, and then you hand the tickets in to the booth. Bets in pair, express, and trio aren't accepted any other way. Each bet costs ten francs. So, translated into our customary language, we had a hundred bets for every hundred rubles. I'd never played with such an enormous sum at the track.

There were eight races in all. That's twelve bets a race. It seemed that soon all the money in the banks of France would be transferred into my pocket. But do I have enough pockets? Should I send Eduard Ivanovich for a sack? However, there's time enough for that; Eduard Ivanovich is over there, following us like a tail, snuffling respectfully. He understands that the professionals have come to do "business!"

A cold wind was blowing in from the field. The Frenchmen scarcely showed themselves in the grandstands; they were standing in the halls around the booths, studying the newspapers. We had studied the same newspapers this morning. Of course, some interesting details in the newspapers had changed, and the fool Frenchmen are going to be following the printed predictions. Anyway, we figured that the jockeys had read the newspapers, too, and that they knew beforehand who the crowd would be betting on. And if the crowd hits the horse to death, is it going to be worth the jockey's while to touch it? Go on the favorite for a franc and a half? In short, we decided to stay with our well-tested Moscow system—to play against the favorites! The public has faith in the printed word, but we—in our eyes. We'll see everything at the warm-ups.

The only strange thing was that the horses didn't come out for warm-ups. Several harnesses wove slowly past without numbers. (Who? Which race? Just try and guess!) And some machines slowly moved along the track, discing the cinder surface flat. Zhenya was, as always before a play, cool and concentrated, but something secret flashed and merrily danced in his eyes. I myself felt a joyful excitement and was finding it hard not to shake with excitement.

"Old man," I said, "Hemingway was right when he called Paris a moveable feast."

"Hemingway had the racetrack in mind," Zhenya gave me a wink.

"They say Hemingway won at the races, too," Eduard Ivanovich grew bold enough to add.

I snorted. In this phrase, I liked "too" most of all. But Zhenya sternly straightened Eduard Ivanovich out:

"Run down to the booths and see who they're hitting!"

And now Eduard Ivanovich struck us with how well informed he was.

"Boys," our companion peaceably answered, "see those numbered dials with the pointers over there on the far side of the track? Over every one is the number of the horse. The lower the figure the pointer shows, the more people are playing the horse. It's automatic here—they've got it all figured out."

We quickly got out the binoculars. The pointer on dials three and eight had gone almost full-circle and frozen at the number "two." The pointers for numbers eleven and thirteen were showing ten-to-one. The pointers on the other dials had barely moved. It immediately became apparent how the betting was going. They've beaten down the troika and the eighter (two-to-one); they're playing up eleven and thirteen. They aren't touching the rest.

"French creeps!" Zhenya whistled. "They make life easy for themselves."

I even got a little upset. Really, if the play is laid out for you, if you can select any variant of wager—a pair, express, the winners, if bets on dark horses are indicated right away (the pointer will show them), then the question arises: come on, just how do people manage to lose at the Vincennes Racetrack? And if nobody loses, then just who wins?

But we were in for a blow. We were in the dark. At last
the participants of the first race came out, and . . . they calmly
pranced over to the other side of the track. Nobody warmed
up in front of the grandstands. There was no chance at all
of your speed being timed at that distance. We stopped our
stopwatches. Our main weapon had been struck from our
hands. Strictly speaking, as honest men, we should have left
the track immediately and flown to Moscow that very
evening.

But. . . .

We can let this race go by and get ready for the next one.
What if somebody stands out right away?

But.

What if the racetrack's right and only these four horses
stand a real chance? If the prediction specialists who hang
around the stable for days on end, sewing things up, know
exactly who is going to win? In the end, what do they pay
them money for? After all, it isn't for the deception of the
esteemed public!

I glanced at my watch and tore off to the booth in a hurry. If
only I can make it! Three minutes to the start. For some reason,
half of the booths aren't working. There are lines at the other
windows. I brazenly screw myself into the middle of a line. I
work feverishly with the tongs. Tie four horses in pair—that's
six tickets, and repeat the favorite play—three-eight—four
times. In all, a hundred francs. Even in the event the favorites
come in, I'll be left with some pretty good winnings. They'll
pay at least thirty francs a ticket for three-eight, won't they?

It astonishes me how lazily and unhurriedly the line
moves. I manage to stick the tickets into the booth right
before the bell. (And here's what's interesting: the monsieur

I cut in front of, who, because of me, just like that, didn't get to bet, this monsieur, instead of punching me out or telling me off, excused himself when I accidentally shoved him, as I pushed my way from the window!)

When I showed up upstairs, the horses were walking past the grandstands in a pack, descending into the depths of Tartarus, into the netherworld of the Vincennes Racetrack, into "the spaces of a wonderful homeland" . . . the enormous field of Vincennes! And the view opens out onto the distant suburbs of Paris. And two balloons hovered over the forest, navy blue and green.

Zhenya stood morose and immobile as a cliff along the Volga. I wanted to touch him to see if he was grown over with moss.

'Take the plunge?" he snarled, not turning his eyes in my direction.

"Aha, and you?"

"Zhenya passed on the race!" Eduard Ivanovich announced almost solemnly.

I couldn't understand what the announcer was jabbering over the loudspeaker. For that matter, I hadn't memorized the names of the horses I bet on. Now a race was picking up on the track on the other side of the racetrack. I couldn't even make out the numbers with binoculars. Somebody picked up the pace and took the lead, a jockey in red silks. And what colors are my jockeys wearing? I don't even know that. Whoever was in the lead taxied out onto the home stretch first. His pace was faltering. Five harnesses were just about to catch him. Whoever was in the lead was wearing number eight! (I could see them at the very end.) Numbers three and thirteen were pulling up alongside.

Well!

Some gray scum darted in along the inside!

Eight held on to first place, thirteen came in third, and the gray scum (second place) turned out to be number ten.

Eight-ten was posted in pair.

A hundred of my francs gone as though I'd never had them. A hundred francs! That's two men's sweaters. Three blouses for Raika—if, of course, you buy them at Tati, but in Moscow, even they would pass for an expensive gift. Once at a cafe I spent twenty-five france and went around like a sick man for a whole day. A hundred francs—all at once—under a mare's tail! Got to come to my senses! I can't play like this!

But how?

If I'd bet on eight to win, I'd have gotten fifteen francs for ten. If I'd played him as one of the first three—twelve francs. And here number ten pulled two hundred francs worth! And in pair, they pay five hundred! And after all, it was easy to guess—tie number eight to the whole race—thirteen bets—you bet one hundred and thirty francs; you get five hundred. Is that really so bad? And just why in my old age did I start chasing the favorites?

The second race was run over a shorter distance. The jockeys were saddled up. (You almost never see saddle races in our country.) They warmed up somewhat closer to the grandstands. Number five turned at the finish pole. He stretched out really fast several times. There really wasn't anybody to compare him to. The rest went to a walk as they approached the finish pole. I opened up the newspaper. According to the prediction specialists (. . . their mothers!), number five had a chance. The dials were showing that the racetrack was beating two and seven down. But the pointer for number five was halfway around, too.

There are twelve horses in the race. I tie five to all of them and add two more tickets to two and seven. The booth has relieved me of 150 francs.

As before, Zhenya was playing the role of the cliff from the Russian folk song.

"Take the plunge?" "Uh-huh. Did you?"

"I'm passing."

". . . nothing grows on top of him." It seemed to me that Eduard Ivanovich looked upon me with disapproval, as on a potential plunderer of the people's property.

And after all, I guessed, I'd almost guessed! If number five hadn't gotten jumpy in the home stretch and gone past the finish pole at a gallop. . . .

Seven and fourteen came in. I'd have recouped on seven, but for five-fourteen, I'd have made a modest million. . . .

"Who's going to win the parliamentary elections?" the mare Alissa asked the stallion Archibald, "they maintain that the opposition has a good chance."

In reality, Alissa didn't give diddlysquat about politics; however, she'd long been giving Archibald friendly, sidelong glances, and now fate had brought them together in the third race, and she couldn't let the opportunity to make his acquaintance slip by. Rumor in the stable had it that he was an ardent supporter of the Socialists.

"It's a complex situation," Archibald shook his head, "let's run to the finish pole and I'll explain the circumstances to you."

Eleven and twelve stretched out fast. And what's more, Alissa (number eleven) was outstripping twelve by a neck the whole time and merrily twisting her little tail as well. I put down 150 francs on Alissa, besides having tied her to all of them in pair, plus a supplementary ticket each to the favorites and to Archibald. The track wasn't touching either number eleven or number twelve; the pointers were barely moving in their dials, but all my previous experience was advising me that they wouldn't playact for no reason at the finish pole. The racetrack smelled of a mob scene. Alissa was supposed to be bringing me a fortune.

"You understand," Archibald went on, "the Socialists' real opponents aren't the Gaullists, but the Communists. The public referendum will give preference to the Socialists and in the event of a victory, we'll have a parliamentary majority. If that happens, the Communists will have to sniff Mitterand's tail. The voter will desert to the Socialists. . . ."

"Might we pick up the pace?" Alissa timidly suggested. "We're flagging along in last; there'll be other conversations. . . ."

"Nonsense!" Archibald began to neigh. "Master is sparing me for the Prix Bretagne. If I take a paying spot now, they'd have to give twenty-five meter odds. Let's go for the Prix Bretagne. Stay right behind me. I'll lead you through the people. By the way, how do you like my stride?"

After the fourth race (my horses, naturally, dragged themselves in in the second echelon.) Zhenya took me aside:

"How much have you blown?"

"Five hundred."

". . . Your mother! You've lost your mind, Teacher! You're all through playing for today."

"But they gave us a thousand each, didn't they?"

"For betting, yes, but not for losing. Eduard Ivanovich advised me to stop you. He's been watching you, and he realizes you're getting burned. If we blow all the money right away, Boris Borisovich'll send us to Moscow. We're just one more headache for the embassy personnel. Losing two thousand on the very first day will just give them grounds for getting rid of us. That kind of sum will make an impression on anybody you want. If we save even five hundred francs apiece and explain that we weren't having any luck today, it's not our day—we'll have a chance to come here next Sunday. Eduard Ivanovich talks sense; he doesn't mean us any harm.

"And why don't you step forward?"

"I don't see anybody," and having become silent, Zhenya, with undisguised malice, added, "Fourteen—twelve horses to a race. They don't show anything at the warm-ups. You could sink millions here."

The thrill of play abandoned me. It was replaced by the horror of the realization of the amount lost. My throat was dry. I tried not to look at the track or the winnings board, nor at the French creeps who unhurriedly and with pleasure squandered their own currency so vital to the Nation of Victorious Socialism.

Then I suggested to Eduard Ivanovich that we have some beer. We went down to the snack bar, and I paid, having, moreover, stressed that it was out of my own personal money.

Passions were boiling all around us; thousands of feet stampeded along the stairs and corridors; lines were snaking around the booths; the grandstands exploded into a mighty roar. We were drinking beer. And we watched the fifth race in the bar on the television.

Eduard Ivanovich no longer regarded me as a class

enemy. Maybe he liked the fact that I had found the strength in myself to quit playing or that I was generous with the beer. (Needless to say, we ordered another bottle each.) He became more open and carefully, with half-hints, sketched me another, different picture—a diagram of the game that was going on around Zhenya and me.

The embassy was categorically opposed to this whole undertaking. The Agencies in Moscow insisted. However, the locals—the embassy KGB men, that is—weren't delighted either. All the more, since we were being supported by the Paris Embassy. They gave us a thousand francs apiece out of the embassy's own budget. So, we were an unnecessary expense. Money for us from Moscow still hadn't been forthcoming. If we blew it all, the embassy would wash its hands of us and promptly shut down our mission. It was in our interest to hold out a little longer, that is, to make practically no plays at the track. Scores of reasons not to play (to be present, but not to play, that is) could be found. They'd be obliged to put up with us until the two thousand was all gone.

Just what kind of curve had that most intelligent Boris Borisovich thrown us, giving us the whole sum right away?

"You're nice guys," concluded Eduard Ivanovich, finishing off his beer. "And I enjoy your company, too. After all, Sunday at the track counts as a working day for me. Then I'll get a day off. And the track isn't the same as the 'tent' for me—this is paradise! Breathe fresh air, drink beer—look, it's just that I'm worried about you. Tell Zhenya not to bet so much as a centime."

We went down to the grandstands in a complacent frame of mind. Zhenya's prickly stare greeted us.

"Go to the booth and get in line!"

"Zhenya, we'd better not play," I started to mutter.

"Yeah, and the booths are packed with people," Eduard Ivanovich backed me up.

"Go to the booth!" roared Zhenya, and we submitted as timidly as rabbits.

The booths were turning into a nightmare. There were huge lines everywhere. The crowd had grown to monstrous proportions for the sixth race. Leaving Eduard Ivanovich in his place, I decided to shove through to the window. A group of black guys formed a wall, and they wouldn't let me through.

Zhenya put in an appearance. Appraising the situation at once, he started trying to shove me into the line. According to my watch it was time for the race to start.

A black man in a white fur coat started growling.

"Go . . . yourself!" Zhenya said to him, smiling.

"You go . . . yourself!" the black man answered in perfect Russian.

"Where do you know Russian from, buddy?" I yelled at the guy in delight.

"I studied at Lumumba in Moscow."

"Fellow countryman," I implored, "Let us through. It's our last chance to recoup our losses. We're getting burned."

"Well," said the black guy, which apparently meant, "Okay"

But where's Zhenya? He'd vanished.

The bell sounded. The black guy, giving me a puzzled look, stuck his tickets into the booth. But what was I supposed to bet with—and the main thing—on who?

"Did Zhenya play?" Eduard Ivanovich asked me when the mob at the booths had dispersed.

"No, he didn't have time."

"That's good," Eduard Ivanovich breathed a sigh of relief.

We found Zhenya in the grandstands, in the pose of the cliff—true, the cliff smelled like a cigarette.

"Did you make it?"

"Yeah," Zhenya said through his teeth. "Pray for number four."

"How much?"

"Everything. To win."

A sharp pain pierced me through the heart. Our Paris was finished!

Just then the horses were going by below us. Number four (Jockey in brown silks) took the lead straight off.

It was a hard-run race. They almost caught up to number four, even tried to get around him on the rise, but he didn't give up the inside. Three horses went down the home stretch, neck and neck. And right at the finish pole (it seemed. . !?) number four stuck his nose out.

The winner, determined by photofinish, was number four.

I clutched at my heart. Eduard Ivanovich, who'd dropped his jaw (when he heard Zhenya'd bet everything), still couldn't shut it.

After spitting out his cigarette butt, Zhenya pulled a thick pack of tickets out of his side pocket—a hundred tickets. From his pants pocket—a fifty franc note.

"There's this one booth—I noticed it right off," Zhenya explained efficiently, "that only takes hundred franc bets, and only on the winner. And they give you back five francs on every hundred. That is, ten tickets cost ninety-five francs. I saved fifty francs. Keep it in mind; there aren't going to be any lines at that booth."

Zhenya smiled nervously, and I saw how, out from under the cliff-face mask, an exhausted, human face was showing through.

The winnings were posted. Number four pulled seventy-five francs per ticket.

A thunderous snap resounded throughout the track— Eduard Ivanovich had managed to shut his lower jaw.

*   *   *

On Monday we made our report to Boris Borisovich.

Zhenya solemnly laid two thousand francs on the table: "Here's what you gave us to bet. We're returning it. We've got another five and a half thousand to play."

The expected response was not forthcoming.

"That's silly, boys," Boris Borisovich shrugged. "You can't imagine how hard it is to beat money out of our book-keeper. I took out a sum like that for you straight off to make life easier for myself as well. After all, there's so much paper-work! So many signatures to collect! The accounts depart-ment will be happy to snap this money up, but next time, we'll have to start from the beginning."

I'd tried to persuade Zhenya the night before not to return that two thousand, too. And Eduard Ivanovich sup-ported me. But Zhenya was immovable: if you want to gam-ble, then gamble; he said we had to wipe Boris Borisovich's nose for him.

"There won't be a next time," Zhenya snapped back. "We came here to make currency for the government. It's enough that we're paid a travel allowance."

I looked at Eduard Ivanovich. Eduard Ivanovich, sprawled

in an easy chair, was studying the ceiling with an indifferent look. Nevertheless, the self-control of these embassy comrades is amazing! Yesterday evening, when Eduard Ivanovich took us to the striptease after the restaurant, and we were drinking champagne there, mixing it, to the waiters' horror, with whiskey and beer, as naked dames threw their tanned thighs around to the beat of the music and twirled their naked asses, but this didn't sway us, as they say—we were busy with our conversation. Last night Eduard Ivanovich, who'd guzzled more alcohol than Zhenya (which wasn't easy), swore his eternal friendship and love to the grave for us—and today our heads are splitting, but Eduard Ivanovich is fresh as a daisy; he's sitting there with all his buttons buttoned, and we're as alien as Martians to him.

By the way, we squandered five hundred francs with the dear comrade yesterday evening! My stack! But Zhenya promised he'd indulge me two thousand for future exploits, and that, knowing his character, was sheer nobility.

Somehow Boris Borisovich guessed where my thoughts were wandering, because he asked:

"Did you get a good buzz yesterday?"

"What buzz?" I winced (the whiskey was kicking me again). "All I bought was a bottle of vodka. . . ."

". . . and herring tails," Boris Borisovich went on in the same tone.

I realized Eduard Ivanovich was working both sides.

"Would you like a little cognac?"

We wanted a little cognac. The office boss hid the money in the safe, exchanging it for an already opened bottle and glasses. The cognac went down famously. And an angel of peace glided down from the ceiling.

"One thing isn't clear to me," said Boris Borisovich, "You maintain that they don't identify the horses warming up, and it's impossible to get a fix on the fast moves. Just exactly how did Zhenya guess number four? Let the hero tell his secret."

I'd already heard this story three times in the evening, but I was ready to hear it over and over again.

"I noticed the jockey in the brown silks working that little chestnut long and patiently. He did four laps at a walk and then sent him fast several times. That doesn't just happen." Zhenya was quiet for a moment. "In Moscow, it would have meant something. But the hard part is that the exercising is done without numbers, and the main thing was to determine which race the stallion was from. He turned up in the sixth race and made straight for the track to hide. I looked in the newspaper—the press had written him up, the racetrack played up to him. Of course, I wouldn't have decided to play him to win, but the black guys had taken the booth where the Teacher was standing, and I simply wasn't left with any choice other than to put it all down 'to win' at the only accessible booth. In principle, we got lucky. It would have been more judicious to win in show, that is on anyone of the money places. Then it's a sure thing."

"Uh-huh," said Boris Borisovich, and I felt as though he were giving us some kind of grade again.

5

WE STARTED GOING TO THE VINCENNES RACETRACK LIKE IT WAS a job—every day, weekdays and holidays, whenever there were races being held.

We lived modestly. The stake money was sacred to us. Not only didn't we touch it for threads or food, but we also added a trifle to it from our modest travel allowances. Our primary objective was to hold out in Paris as long as possible. The stake money was gradually dwindling. (Miracles, like the one with number four, weren't happening any more.) We tried to cut back on our daily bets. Neither Zhenya nor I once guessed it in pair, but sometimes Zhenya would win on a horse in show.

The money still hadn't come from Moscow for *the big play,* and I, frankly speaking, personally was glad. There was no way we were ready for a big play.

Some things at the track were cleared up for us. For example, the warm-ups before the race depended not on the jockey's fancy, but on the distance. They honestly warmed up where the start was given. For the usual distance—2600 meters, the start was given at the turn. You couldn't see shit. But now a 2200-meter heat on the big track was almost acceptable to us because the harnesses stretched out in front of the grandstands. It's too bad the short races were run so seldom. We had to take into account the head start that the strong horses would give to the weak ones. The head start, as a rule, was twenty-five meters. And here, not two or three horses (at the most!), like in Moscow, but five to eight harnesses fight the battle at the finish. And the ride was run hard, severely; nobody was giving anyone any gifts (like we do). Nonetheless, the favorites seldom came in. What couldn't be ruled out was that the jockeys might sometimes hold them back. Anyway, when they run seven horses in a Moscow race, and it's hard for the favorite to hide, the jockey goes at an obviously false pace. But here, there're ten participants with roughly equal chances in the race. It's enough to barely stop short in the distance, like "the train is gone," and some mare gets two hundred francs per for first place at the totalizator. Needless to say, the mare doesn't get it, but the gambler who bet on her. The jockey and the owner get extremely decent winnings in readily converted French currency. I don't know what the mare gets (maybe a lump of sugar, maybe a pat on the head). However, the French horses didn't show any signs of dystrophy, which means they'd been getting enough carrots and hay. And speeds, in spite of the long distances, were considerably faster than at the Central Moscow Racetrack.

. . . What dull racing trivia we have here. Excuse me.

One weekday, we'd arrived at Vincennes, and we're about to pay for our admission tickets, but they aren't taking any money. "Why?" "It's free, today." "Why?" "They're on strike." "Who?" "Is it the jockeys, the grooms, or the horses that don't want to run?" The totalizator cashiers are walking out. But are the races themselves going to take place? Please move along. And people move. But what's there for us to do?

"Here, Lomonosov and Kholmogorov, feast your eyes on the grimaces of capitalism. An outrage like this couldn't happen in the Soviet Union."

We'd noticed a long time ago that whenever something wasn't quite right, Eduard Ivanovich would switch to an official tone with us. And here's what's upsetting our embassy comrade: if there are no races, they won't count today as a work day for him, and Edik will have to pull duty on Saturday in "the tent."

"An outrage like this couldn't happen in our country," confirms Zhenya. "The totoshniks would set fire to the stadium and tear it to pieces."

"Comrades, we can do without the political allusions!" Eduard Ivanovich protests.

"Yeah, right, Edik, I say. "We'll use today as a training day. Then, who knows, what if after a couple of races they open the booths? Races like this are a loss to the management. You'll see, they'll give in and meet the lawful demands of the working class. And that just amounts to a couple of tickets on account for us, since we decided to hold back on the major bets."

Eduard Ivanovich cheered up. Zhenya, it's true, expressed himself gloomily on the point that the races without betting are just like watching a sex scene at the movies and not screwing a dame yourself.

But where else is there to go? Don't turn back! All the

more, since the weather's turned out to be beautiful: the sun's shining, it's warm—the fierce Parisian winter. . . .

The first three races were run without the totalizator. And the curious thing was that the press's favorites won. What's more, they won easily, all alone.

"Just our luck," Zhenya was irritated. "Today would have been just the day for playing the favorites—drop your pants and bet it all!"

They announced over the loudspeaker that several total-izator booths had been opened in the first floor hall. The track began to bill and coo. And someone in the stadium let out a howl of joy: "Unemployed—to the windows!"

We thought it over fast—throw a hundred on a standout! We ran into the hall and took Eduard Ivanovich with us. But it was a nightmare in the hall! The Battle of Borodino was taking place around the open windows! The three of us led the attack by the rules of the Moscow Racetrack. We wedge ourselves into the center. Buttons fly, bones are snapping, Frenchmen are falling out like they'd been shot. A mixed group of Arabs and blacks are slashing away at each other at the booth windows. As the poet said, "May you never see such battles!" Eduard Ivanovich whines, but we're strict with him: "Enough, Edik, no more sitting like a lump in the grandstands—your turn has come to work by the sweat of your brow!" Ah, where haven't Russians fallen? We forced our way through and pushed the money and the tickets in, but the bell's rung and the booth's closed. It shuts down automatically. The cashier shrugs and turns up his palms. He'd be glad to help, but he can't.

Cursing, we go down to the grandstands. We watch the track. But there's a metamorphosis: the favorites are flagging along in the rear; a dark horse is straining along in the lead. In

short, some creep butted in that hadn't been written up in any
of the newspapers, while our favorite came in like a fifth wheel
in seventh place. In a word, we saved ourselves a hundred!

And likewise, all the rest of the races went awry.
Somewhere we contrived to play two tickets, just for the
record, but we didn't stick our noses in any further. We realized that while the local crooks were trying to make up for
lost time, it was best we got out of the way.

In the course of six weeks, all I got was a pair for thirty
francs. My finances were singing sad songs in harmony. Zhenya
played bigger and, correspondingly, he went through more.
Neither stopwatches nor science nor God were helping us!

We should go hat-in-hand to Comrade Devil, shouldn't we?

* * *

You can't get bored in Paris. Everyday somewhere in the
city a new exhibit opens: Japanese stones, Arabic ceramics,
English graphics, Belgian weapons, African masks and
Soviet painting. The devil himself would break a leg running
around to see it all. Apparently to save their own skin, the
devils got together and organized an exhibit called "Demonic
Art from Its Inception to our Time" beneath a skyscraper. It's
rather modest and tasteful! And if you've heard the aria from
the opera *Faust* ("Satan holds his ball there") and are interested in where it's going on now, here's the address: Paris,
Palais Royale Square, the Louvre, antiquities, second floor.

It's not at all necessary to sell your soul to the devil for
admission. It's enough to pay six francs to a charming young
"witch." However, those whose souls are in pain can follow

the instructions on the wall of one of the halls. They aren't really instructions at all, but a letter, an example for imitation, written in the thirteenth century by a young individual: "I, the sorceress Didim, surrender my body and soul to Thee for time eternal; I renounce God and all the angels and holy apostles for time eternal. I will be obedient and faithful to Thee while I live on the Earth. I sign my name in blood."

True, it didn't say what a soul was worth in the thirteenth century. Prices have gone up since then—inflation—so it makes some sense to haggle if you want to.

Satan presides over his ball in a half-darkened place, where visitors walk in a circle (one of the circles of Hell!) and scrutinize the spotlighted artifacts of black magic. Fortune telling cards, enchanted statuettes, knives with skulls and bones on the handles, demonic dolls, secret volumes of *The Red Dragon* and *The Black Chicken* with cabalistic signs, and there, under glass, is the petrified heart of a ram, stuck through with hundreds of pins. However, it seems to me that it isn't these marvels that draw the inquisitive crowd, but the antiquarian objects connected with the cult of Satan: carved walking sticks, round inlaid tables, painting and sculpture. It's not for nothing this exhibit's called "Demonic Art." There's also a bust of Mephistopheles done by a wellknown master. I'm sure the client was satisfied. Mephistopheles is sculpted as a tragic, significant person with a cunning grin on his lips and goodness in his look. It brings to mind Goethe: "A part of that Power which wills forever evil, yet does forever good."

Alas, history hasn't been very kind to this creator of good and his followers. The pictures and drawings on the walls attest to that—here Satan is expelled—he flies head over heels from the heavenly heights; here three plump warlocks swing from the gallows. The curious can touch the instruments of torture of the Holy Inquisition. Brrrrr. . . .

Nonetheless, interest in forces from the beyond hasn't abated. The occult sciences flourished both in the last century and at the beginning of the present one. For example, an extravagant easy chair on little goat legs stands at the center of the exhibit; the arms are buffalo horn and a perfidious little face crowns the back. "Yuck," spits the respectable visitor, "and for what obscurantist was this done?" Don't jump to conclusions. The easy chair belonged to the esteemed writer, Anatole France, whom *The Soviet Encyclopedia* calls "a progressive man of culture." France liked to cavort with unclean powers in moments free of progress!

And nonetheless, in my opinion, all this occult science has lagged far behind contemporary life. Can black magic really compete with scientific progress? Childish prattle! The demonic laughter that peals invitingly from the speakers in the halls of the exhibit seems like the whispers of people in love compared to the roar of Japanese motorcycles on the streets of Paris. And such dazzling little witches glide along the streets that even Mephistopheles himself would most likely be ready to give himself up for immolation. . . .

And next to "Demonic Art" there are hundreds of the usual little shops, but there's so much antiquarian deviltry in them, and at such devilish prices, that you can't help but think whether people have ceased to fear God?

* * *

They were supposed to start a tierce tournament at the Vincennes Racetrack. All of France plays tierce, placing their bets in cafes. The principle of tierce is simple—you need to guess the first horses in the race. Every tierce ticket costs five francs. But if you manage to guess the horses "in order," that is, the ones in first, second and third places respectively, then you'll receive, as the sports commentators put it, "a most attractive sum," sometimes getting as much as thirty to forty thousand francs. (In the first case, they pay a hundred francs minimum to the ticket.)

We weren't interested when they were playing tierce at the other racetracks, where the thoroughbreds ran, because we don't know anything about thoroughbred racing or the steeplechase. But now that it was a question of trotters, which we'd studied to some extent, tierce seemed very attractive to me.

Zhenya categorically stated that tierce was folly. You've got to see the horses before the race. The horse could go lame in the morning, and you, unaware of anything, would already have taken the plunge on it at dinner at the cafe.

Boris Borisovich, on the contrary, took to tierce with enthusiasm. The possible sum of winnings apparently impressed him. He advised me to check the back issues of the newspaper *France Soir Tierce*. My work piled right up, so there was no more time for walks around Paris and visiting exhibits. But I liked this work. It was as though I mentally suffered through the problems of play in every purse. On the eve of the tierce, *France Soir* would do an in-depth study of all the race participants' chances and gave the predictions of five of their own journalists and ten jockeys, as well as opinions from thirty other newspapers, radio and television. In the next issue of *France Soir Tierce*, I would find the results of the race, the amount of the winnings, and an account of the battle.

Just how many of the predictions came true?

Here are my (tentative) conclusions:

1. You couldn't trust any of the journalists or the jockeys blindly. Everyone of them would make a great guess on the tierce twice a year. (I repeat, it was a question only of the Vincennes Racetrack.)

2. If the jockey himself considered his horse to be in the running, then you had to consider it.

3. The bigger the purse, the more exact the predictions of the press.

4. If the press, as a whole, guessed the results, they paid kopecks.

5. An unimportant purse, run in the rain, snow, or a strong wind often led to a mob scene at the Racetrack, and, accordingly, to a big payoff.

6. Whenever journalists wrote that horses stood reasonable chances, you could boldly throw them out of play in the majority of cases.

7. Horses' record times posted in previous races had little significance.

8. The overall list of horses compiled by a newspaper on the basis of journalists' predictions sometimes (extremely rarely) were justified.

9. Combinations of four horses recommended by the newspaper as the most hopeful have never won.

* * *

Pushkin's miserly knight, who'd gone down to his treasures, was greedily fingering the gold ducats, heraldic French gold and silver pieces, chains, and rings. Shut up in the evening in our room, we'd also pulled the French change from our pockets and sadly count it over. We left the paper money for betting and lived on the pocket change.

We already knew that Prisunic (the big store) had the cheapest coffee, tea, macaroni, and sugar. We bought potatoes, tomatoes, and lettuce at the market. A chicken and pork ends for grilling could be had for cheap at our friendly butcher's. Vodka and cigarettes—from the "tent" through Eduard Ivanovich by coupon. In a word, we conjured up what we could, but somehow our pocket change didn't propagate itself and didn't breed.

We treated five franc coins with great respect.

And we'd still often recall how on our first day at the track, after the win, we went on a spree in the restaurant, and then at the striptease, and we cursed ourselves for getting drunk right away for no reason that time; we didn't sensibly taste our dishes at the restaurant and didn't watch the girls like we should have, but kept harping on about number four: how he came in, how he might not have come in. . . . No, we'd dream, next time we'll win big, keep the money for ourselves and let Moscow send us the "lettuce" to play. Next time we'll load up on sale goods at Galeries Lafayettes—we'll buy sheepskin coats, jeans, blazers, slacks, brand-name shirts, ties, socks, shoes, Seiko watches, Sony radios, Phillips tape recorders, blouses and sweaters for the Moscow chicks—we'll pack it all in suitcases (leather, brand-name!) and take it off to our room in the Trade Delegation dormitory; and then we'll saunter to the restaurant! We'll order a bottle of burgundy, a bottle of Beaujolais. You can't drink too much wine—we'll polish off the blanquettes, shashlik, escargots, oysters, well, and then off to the night beauties at St. Denis.

The French ma'amselles are getting tired of waiting for us, and besides, Moscow society will never forgive us if we don't give the French girls a try. With a big win, we figured, there ought to be enough for us, and we won't go throwing money left and right like idiots! Enough, we knew the price of a pound of evil.

We'd learned a few things lately!

True, one day we had it good (in the sense of grub), when Boris Borisovich took us to a reception for some French manufacturers on their way to Moscow with a trade delegation. The tables were groaning with caviar, salmon, and crab dishes tenderly crowded up against the ice-cold Stolichnaya, but the French capitalists (blanquette sons-of-bitches! Oyster prostitutes! Escargot scumbags!) looked askance indifferently at the hors d'oeuvres, as they smeared their bread with a thin layer of caviar, drank vodka by the thimble and discussed the development of international relations, favorable credit and mutually beneficial trade the whole time.

We'd have taught them how to drink vodka, how to make short work of the crab, the creeps. We'd have shown them where crabs spend the winter, but Edward Ivanovich latched on to us with a death grip and whispered into our ears. "Don't get carried away with the salmon, guys! Pass that toast! That's enough—lay off the caviar! Maintain the dignity of a Soviet—you can stuff yourself when you go to Moscow!"

But where in Moscow can you get caviar now? No, screw inviting him to the bar if we win. Let Edik lick his lips. To hell with him!

Then Boris Borisovich glided down from somewhere and dragged us over to introduce us to a certain French gentleman, a sort of modest horsebreeder—all in all, he had two stables at Vincennes. At first, we spoke about peace and friendship, and Eduard Ivanovich was about to drag us off by the lapels, but the conversation turned to the Sunday races, and we began to discuss the favorites' chances; Boris Borisovich pricked up his ears, and Edik faded at once.

One word after another, balls to the wall, Zhenya and the French millionaire flew into a rage—they're arguing, grabbing each other by the shirt. We stand there and take all this in, as though every word were familiar to us, but we don't understand what they're talking about.

"The stallion has a gliding gait and a short neck," reiterates the Frenchman.

"His hind legs are green, his belly drags, and he throws his head back," answered Zhenya.

They haggled like that for half an hour (what's more, Zhenya dropped all the articles to his nouns, and the man he was talking to endured it), but then the Frenchman, almost with a tear in his voice, proclaimed:

"As many of your Ministry of Agriculture workers as I've met, this is the first time I've met a man who really understands horses! Let's drink, gentlemen, to the health of Mr. Lomonosov! A true professional!"

Well, once the French capitalist invites us to drink, who's to stop us? Boris Borisovich has flushed at the praises directed toward Zhenya, while Eduard Ivanovich, the damn chameleon, fixes us sandwiches himself and babbles in our ears, "Come on, come on, you guys, have at it, vodka loves an appetizer!"

We, of course, ate ravenously.

*   *   *

The stallion that played the deciding role in our Paris epoch was called Alyosha. Actually, he had another name, made up of two words with the article "le" in the middle, but Eduard Ivanovich read it wrong. It came out "Alyosha." We laughed a bit, but the new name pleased us, so we started calling the stallion Alyosha.

We had already noted Alyosha in the "athletic camp," when we were studying the French newspapers. Alyosha was the champion for his age group, and last year, admitted for the first time to the Prix America, the unofficial world championship, he'd unexpectedly taken second place.

Even now, they were writing a lot about Alyosha in the press. In the spring, he knew no defeat. In the summer, he trained on a fixed schedule in Normandy. He wasn't taking part in any prize races. He was supposed to come out Sunday at Vincennes for the Grand Prix, the first time since his rest. The press was predicting a victory for him. The approximate odds in the totalizator for Alyosha were two to one.

All week Zhenya had been racking his brain over the problem of Alyosha. At night, through my sleep, I'd hear him getting up and going into the kitchen. In the morning I'd discover an ashtray full of butts. I understood why Zhenya was so nervous. After the reception at the embassy, Boris Borisovich hinted that something had come from Moscow, and that if we had a sure horse. . . .

As for me, I'd retired from major plays. I was racking my brain over the problem of the tierce. I'd already played tierce at Vincennes several times, but it'd brought me no joy. I'd guess two horses to the ticket, maximum. I noticed, by the way, that I was falling under the hypnosis of the newspaper predictions. The specialists really demonstrated their choices' chances very convincingly.

On Friday we requested a meeting with Boris Borisovich. Zhenya was in an antagonistic mood. He said:

1. The track would beat Alyosha down to kopecks.

2. Alyosha wouldn't go for first place because the jockey was getting him ready for the Prix America.

3. Even if the jockey decided he wanted to, Alyosha wouldn't manage to take first place—the purse was big, and his competitors were strong.

4. After a lengthy break in appearances, no horse was in condition to win a major heat—things like that don't really happen.

5. Our task was to play against Alyosha. Any horse (except Alyosha) would bring a big payoff.

Zhenya's plan struck me as brilliant. Eduard Ivanovich said you couldn't think of a better one. Boris Borisovich sighed heavily and took five thousand francs out of the safe.

On Saturday evening, I was conjuring my tierce. I decided to play all the money I had left. The tierce was running after the Grand Prix in which Alyosha would appear. Zhenya was going to make his millions on the Grand Prix—and I trusted Zhenya—so that I could romp around in my tierce. I combined the press's favorites. I combined the dark horses that weren't mentioned in the press. On the last ticket, I marked three numbers: 19-18-11. Nineteen was the big favorite; the press didn't even bother with eighteen or eleven—out-of-towners from provincial racetracks. Vincennes was too tough for them. But there, in the provinces, they'd been taking first place, and something Zhenya'd said came to mind—he said that horses needed to race and be in the habit of winning victories.

We were probably the first ones in the Vincennes grand-stands that morning. We spotted Alyosha at his preliminary warm-up. He was going at a walk. "Looking good," Zhenya said through his teeth. "Basically, looking good!" A jockey in green silks was for a long time persistently drove the hell out of another jet black stallion on the back stretch. "There's the one that'll win the race," said Zhenya, "Make a note of that stallion!"

When the participants of the Grand Prix rode out onto the track, we recognized the black stallion. It was Archibald, wearing number four.

"Four's our lucky number!" said Zhenya, and he gave the order, "To the booths, men!"

They were paying through the nose for Alyosha—number nine—at the booths. Zhenya put two hundred tickets on Archibald to win, and Edward Ivanovich and I—a hundred fifty each.

Archibald took the inside with a rush and was leading the race. He was doing everything right; he didn't step on the brakes and he didn't go roaring up the bank, so as not to get winded; he wasn't letting anybody by on the inside, but forced his pursuers back outside, making them go the extra meters. And the speed was stupendous. Archibald was going easy and even, like a machine.

"Class!" muttered Zhenya. "That's the way to win!"

Archibald quickly slipped out onto the home stretch from the final turn, but now there was a rising roar in the stadium. Out of the turn, just about the tenth wheel, having taken an inconceivable detour (an extra fifty meters), a harness flew out and literally, in a few seconds, tore away from the base group of leaders by about twenty meters. That was no horse—that was a rocket! From the stadium's triumphant roar I could tell who won—Alyosha, of course!

It seemed as though Alyosha went the last meters of the distance at a walk. Needless to say, it only seemed that way. After the stunning send out at the turn, it seemed as though everything was standing stock still, and the jockey dropped the reins.

And really, what did he have to be afraid of? His competitors were on horses—he was on a rocket!

I'd never seen anything like it in my life.

I think Archibald even lost second place, but that didn't interest us anymore.

"What a race!" Zhenya was raptly repeating. "Now that I've seen that, I can die."

"Are we out of our misery?" asked Eduard Ivanovich.

"Shut up, Edik," Zhenya silenced him, "You don't understand anything about art!"

And strange as it may be, Edik shut up.

I begged the guys not to leave, but to stay for the next race and watch the the tierce. We continued to talk about Alyosha and didn't pay attention to the warm-ups, and we continued to talk about Alyosha during the race, saying that we'd never seen anything like him. We didn't give a damn about our losses. We were going to Moscow. Once you've seen Alyosha, you can die. . . . Zhenya and I were talking, but Eduard Ivanovich was silent; having been shut up, he was squeezing the pack of losing tickets in his palms. Then, when the crowd started yelling, I looked at the home stretch and shut up myself.

Zhenya kept talking: "What a race! Now that I've seen that, I can die. Alyosha is God, I don't give a damn about anything, let's go to Moscow. . . ."

"We aren't going to Moscow," I said and pointed to the board. On the board, the numbers 19-18-11 were lit up.

"I guessed the tierce. In order."

Now Zhenya shut up, and Eduard Ivanovich sobbed:

"You guys are unsinkable!"

* * *

Naturally, at the "briefing" on Monday at Boris Borisovich's we announced that we were taking the entire three and a half thousand francs I won for betting. We were going to fight to the last centime.

"And if I were in the Minister of Finance's place, I'd put all the Soviet government's currency on Alyosha in the Prix America. Alyosha can't lose!"

It seemed to me that Boris Borisovich reacted to my tierce with some indifference, but Zhenya's obviously made an impression.

6

SOMETIME I'LL TELL YOU ABOUT THE GREEN PARIS WINTER. The leaves in the Bois de Vincennes had long since fallen, but the trees were green with some kind of fine moss that covered the trunks. I only saw snow in Paris one time, and that was mainly on the roofs of the houses. It happened around New Year's, when the temperature dropped suddenly and sharply from eleven above to five below, Celsius. The panic in the city was terrible. The radio and TV announcers kept repeating a weather bulletin for the capital and around the country every single God-damned hour, stressing: "Watch out for icy conditions! Use public transportation!" And really, almost no one was driving their cars—the streets were empty. We were riding around in Eduard Ivanovich's Zhiguli, dying of laughter. The weakling French were afraid of a little chill!

Radio Moscow broadcast that right now in Moscow it was twenty-five below Celsius in the afternoon and thirty-two below at night. That meant the Central Moscow Racetrack was open. The races in Moscow weren't cancelled until the daytime temperature dropped under twenty-nine below.

It's good to play the races in a hard freeze. You just have to dress real warm and wrap your feet in newspaper before you put your socks on. If a jockey hopes to win, he should warm his horse up and work him carefully. That kind of a breezing gets spotted from the grandstands right away; that's why really big winnings just don't happen in freezing weather. You can't fool totoshka.

Sometimes I'd dream I was standing in our box at the Moscow Racetrack and was surrounded by familiar faces: The Professional, Coryphaeus, Dandy, Ilyusha the Vegetable Man, Bakunian, Yurochka the Gas Man, Lard Lardych, Fat Fatych, Paunch Paunchich—the dear faces of the Moscow crooks. And the Professional and I'd think up a fantastic combination, run to the booths, push ourselves into line, and . . . we wouldn't make it in time to bet. I always woke up at the very same point.

We always had time to bet at the Vincennes Racetrack, but our wonderful combinations weren't realized. True, we were playing a risky game for big payoffs. There were big payoffs at Vincennes, but we weren't the ones who got them.

And not once in Paris did I dream of the Vincennes Racetrack.

Once Zhenya sat with me all evening, observing the way I prepared for the tierce, by what theory I picked out the horses and combined them. And then he said:

"This is all nonsense; you're not playing tierce; you're playing Sportlotto. For you, the combinations of numbers are more important than the horses' class."

He was right, by the way. For example, I loved the numbers five, seven, fifteen, and eighteen, and then to connect thirteen with twelve and fourteen. My hand wouldn't take

another course no matter how illogical this combination
seemed in light of the press's predictions.

We lived as before, economizing on matchsticks and
keeping about two hundred francs apiece for the races. Plus,
each tierce cost me fifty francs. Our playing money was melt-
ing right away, although this didn't alarm us much. We knew
we'd recoup in the Prix America, that Alyosha would bring
us three times more than we put down on him, and, see,
how much we put down wasn't our worry—that's Boris
Borisovich's headache; that's what he gets a salary for.

And right then, after Sunday, we'd really go on a spree in
Galeries Lafayettes, dance around there with the Seikos,
Sonys, jeans!

Boris Borisovich had involved negotiations with
Moscow. Once a week, he'd call us to an emergency meeting
and ask us to "substantiate" and "toss out facts" and "corroborate arguments. . . ."

"And why should we substantiate and corroborate. . . ?"

Zhenya was indignant. "Have them bring us a boxcar of
currency from Moscow! We'll send them three boxcars
back!"

The conversation went around in the usual circle:

"And if Alyosha loses?"

"Alyosha can't lose!"

"You yourself used to say, 'Any horse can break stride,
stumble, go into a gallop. . . .'"

"Any horse, but not Alyosha. Alyosha's a space rocket."

"But what if everybody at the racetrack just plays
Alyosha? They'll give franc for franc—no winnings at all."

"They never just play one horse at the racetrack. The crowd is a fool—it hunts in the dark. Moreover, they bring the best trotters from Germany, Italy, Sweden, Belgium, and the USA to the Prix America. They'll definitely get played. We checked out the newspapers' files for the last ten years. We looked at the results. Not once has the winner of the Prix America been worth less than three francs to one! Of course, the majority is going to be betting on Alyosha, but only to show. That's kopecks. But Alyosha's going to take first place—that's where our winnings are."

"Do you give a full guarantee?"

"They only give full guarantees at savings banks. Put the currency in a French savings bank, and then you'll get five percent annually."

"You guys've got to understand, the Ministry of Finance of the USSR never ventures to risk a large sum in hard currency. No responsible official would underwrite that kind of amount."

"Then what the hell did they send us to Paris for? Why are we torturing ourselves, not sleeping at night and gagging ourselves on boiled chicken? We suggest the most advantageous combination: three hundred percent return on the sum invested. "

"Now you suggest we risk a thousand and win a million! . . . There is such a thing as a theory of probability. You remember the classic example, how they bet you couldn't meet a hundred men on the street without meeting a single woman, but a military regiment went by. . . ."

"That's enough, I'm tired of this," howled Zhenya, "Personally, I'm flying back to Moscow!"

"Yevgeny Nikolaevich," protested Boris Borisovich, "you

have no right to leave! The Prix America is just around the corner. What if Alyosha goes lame in the warm-ups? Just who could catch that besides you?"

"Then bring me a sack full of currency from Moscow!"

. . . Things had come full circle.

It ended when Boris Borisovich pushed a shot of cognac at each of us and began to compose the next message to Moscow himself.

*   *   *

On Saturday we saw Alyosha on television—they were showing him on the news on Channel 1. We listened to the racing predictions of all the radio stations of France. We bought all the French newspapers, including *Humanité,* and attentively studied the pages devoted to the Prix America. All the commentators agreed that Alyosha was in excellent shape. His competitors were considered to be the American mare Gloria, the Swedish stallion Swensen, the French horses Archibald and Alissa, as well as the racing veteran Infection (not, moreover, a winner in the last two, but in one of the purse positions). Gloria had posted the best time in the world that year, and Swensen hadn't known a single rival in his last seven appearances—he always took first place.

"Great," Zhenya was glad, "six press favorites! And the crowd is still going to be hunting in the dark. You'll see. They'll give thirty-five francs at least for Alyosha to win!"

At eleven at night, Boris Borisovich called:

"Is Alyosha all right?"

"Alyosha's all right," answered Zhenya, "but what's keeping you awake?"

"I was listening to the BBC. The English bookmakers are backing Alyosha to win."

"The English bookmakers're no fools. Swensen's only beaten Finns and Danes! Even ours in the Moscow Racetrack beat them! Gloria's really fast, it's true, but the Vincennes track's high grade will be too tough for her. You have to get used to Vincennes, and this is Gloria's first time in France. Get the sack of currency ready and sleep tight, dear comrade."

Zhenya hung up the phone.

"The management's getting worried, Teacher. I'll give you four free horses for your tierce. First—Alyosha, second—Archibald, third or fourth place—Gloria or Swensen. Let's play two tickets for twenty francs—four horses in each, and consider the tierce in our pocket."

"Maybe we should play on Alissa and Infection?"

'Teacher, this is the last of our money! The slaughter will be horrible. After all, they're running for a million-franc purse! Just who is going to let Alissa stick her head out? And the French are off their rockers over Infection! The stallion is ten years old and hasn't made first place in two years! Time to put Infection out to pasture for his labors. They'll be paying kopecks for the tierce, but that's better than nothing for us. You can buy Raika some undies."

*   *   *

Eduard Ivanovich picked us up in the morning and handed us two thousand francs apiece.

"Is that all?" Zhenya was astonished.

"Well, I've still got a little something," the embassy comrade modestly lowered his eyes.

We saw all the participants in the Prix America in the preliminary warm-ups. You couldn't confuse them with the horses from the other races—they stood out by their class.

"Is Alyosha all right?" Eduard Ivanovich would periodically bother us with the question.

I just happened to look around. Right behind us stood four guys in identical dark-brown sheepskin coats. I didn't hear them exchange so much as a word, but I can spot a Soviet mug a kilometer away. . . .

And here's the Prix America. The horses, covered with multi-colored blankets, solemnly pass in review.

"Alyosha's all right—he isn't limping?" Eduard Ivanovich won't quit.

"Alyosha's all right," Zhenya brushes him off.

"Alyosha's all right," Eduard Ivanovich loudly repeats.

I turn around. The four characters in the dark brown sheepskin coats have scattered like leaves in the wind. Even Eduard Ivanovich had disappeared.

"Zhenya, we're not the only ones backing Alyosha," I said. "I've known that for a long time," Zhenya grinned, "the embassy is playing big time."

Honestly, we took all our money to Zhenya's favorite booth, where they take bets of not less than a hundred francs, or, more precisely, ninety-five francs for ten tickets, and only on the winner. That way, we bought four hundred tickets and each of us saved a hundred—bread on the table. . . .

. . . In general, you should show that kind of race in a close up, in slow motion, but at the track it all flies by in an instant, in a fevered heartbeat.

Archibald dashed ahead right out of the gate. Alyosha managed to take second position behind him. They took over the race together, tore away, and the terrible swordplay began.

"Alyosha's running right," I hear Zhenya's words, "he doesn't want to risk it."

Archibald and Alyosha were completely occupied with each other, leading alternately, setting a giddy pace, and, it seemed, not paying attention to their competitors.

The competitors pulled up on the high grade, on the back stretch. Alyosha came out of the turn onto the home stretch. But where is Alyosha's crowning sprint? And the harnesses flooded down from the outside, took Alyosha by surprise, and he threw his front legs into the air (like a man who throws up his hands in despair), broke into a gallop, and Infection went to the finish handsomely.

That's it. They're in.

Infection had won the Prix America. Second and third went to Alissa and Gloria.

Zhenya was in hysterics. He was howling and tearing up the tickets.

Eduard Ivanovich had vanished.

It cost me no small effort to calm Zhenya down and get him out of the racetrack. We returned home on public transportation.

While we were still in the elevator, we could hear the telephone ringing in our room.

It was Boris Borisovich calling. He said he'd be over in fifteen minutes.

*   *   *

Since Zhenya was in hysterics, I spoke the accused's final words. I said that Alyosha couldn't have lost. It was the jockey who lost. You can't lead the whole race from start to finish all-out with that class of competition without even giving the stallion a second's breather and that this had turned out to be a different kind of race for Alyosha. Infection didn't get around Alyosha; he tricked him. He sat it out behind the other horses' backs, the creep. Alyosha fought like a trooper, but the jockey was a coward and a no-count. They ought to hang the jockey by the balls.

"You, too," said Boris Borisovich.

After that we sat quiet.

Boris Borisovich got up and walked over to where his coat was hanging—we thought for a moment he was going to leave—but Boris Borisovich took a bottle of Stolichnaya from one coat pocket and a package of sausage from the other. It was so unexpected, so like home, so like Moscow, that even Zhenya roused himself.

"Let's shake it out a little, you guys," said Boris Borisovich.

I hastily got wineglasses and a knife. We "shook" a round "out" right there, cut the sausage on the bare table, and had another glass each.

"That's how they lived," Boris Borisovich said.

"Slept apart and still had kids," I continued the well-known joke.

"They talked on the phone," Zhenya glumly concluded.

But contact was reestablished. We drained our third glass with conspiratorial winks.

"We won't consider how much we've dropped," Boris Borisovich began, "although I commend myself because I played correctly and didn't give in to the persuasion of our Professional. Isn't it clear? I only gave you half of the money Moscow sent. So, we still have a little something left. Now we have only one mission—to win it back. If we win it back with some extra, we won't be criticized. But win it back we must, come hell or high water! What do you suggest?"

"Drop your britches and bet it all on Alyosha in the Prix de France next Sunday!" Zhenya responded promptly.

"We had our fill of Alyosha today," Boris Borisovich cut him off. "Our britches were crammed full. The conversation is over with Alyosha. It would behoove us to hear what Igor Mikhailovich, our specialist in tierce, has to say. What if we put it into tierce?"

I realized that Boris Borisovich hadn't forgotten my win. Okay, if you need to figure, then you figure. I went and got my bookkeeping.

"So the same eighteen horses'll be in the Prix de France. As before, six have realistic chances: Alyosha, Infection, Gloria, Swensen, Archibald, and Alissa. We can tie all six together, but that's senseless, since the payoff in tierce (not in order) would be less than the money you put in. Need to pick four and play tierce in order (a hundred twenty francs to the ticket), and then there's hope of making a little something, because the smallest payoff for tierce in order will draw two hundred francs. I propose to play Alyosha, Infection, Archibald, and Gloria."

"I've seen Infection in the grave," Zhenya interrupted, "There won't be any more gifts for him. Archibald exhausted himself in the battle with Alyosha. If we pick four as a basis, then only Alyosha, Gloria, Swensen, and Alissa."

Boris Borisovich's pen scratched away in his notepad, which he then decisively slammed shut.

"We're getting nowhere, guys. If we want to play big—let's say a hundred tickets—then we've got to risk twelve thousand francs to clear eight thousand. Moreover, you can't pick four from six favorites. And what if some dark horse stomps into third place?"

"Be better to bet twelve thousand on Alyosha in single," said Zhenya. "His breaking stride scared the track. They'll pay four to one to win."

"And if Infection comes in again?"

"Alyosha can't lose," Zhenya asserted.

"Who lost the Prix America?" Boris Borisovich was outraged. "Alexander Sergeevich Pushkin? No, guys, we're at a dead end. Tell me, is there a theoretical situation in which none of the favorites would come in?"

"Like what?" Zhenya was astonished. "How could they not come in?"

"Like this! Before the start of the race—a hurricane, an earthquake, a flood, and airborne invasion by Chinese volunteers. In general, anything supernatural."

"I've got it," said Zhenya. "Bring Soviet tanks into Paris. That'll work."

"Tanks—that's an idea!" Boris Borisovich began to chuckle. "All kidding aside, guys. The question is purely academic: how would the horses behave, let's say, during a natural disaster? During, let's say, an extreme situation?"

Zhenya picked up a racing form and started to think.

"Okay, then, take it case by case: if we bring in the tank guards' Kantemirovsky Division. . . ."

"Yevgeny Nikolaevich!" Boris Borisovich made a wry face, "It isn't funny anymore. Besides, the walls have ears. . . ."

"Are there microphones in the Soviet Trade Delegation dormitory?" Zhenya was amazed. "Thanks for the warning. Okay, I'm kidding. Pass that around, too. In short, at the time of natural disaster, write: Alyosha will break into a gallop; Alissa's got bad nerves. Swensen's a fickle stallion; he'll break stride; Archibald'll spook; Gloria isn't used to that kind of fun. The Italian wearing number five can't even hold out in a normal battle. Those French mares were raised under hothouse conditions. . . . Just who's left? That damn Infection is left; even the Chinese volunteers don't scare him. That leaves Jean, because he's deaf—he couldn't hear a nuclear blast; Valjean won last year in a raging blizzard, and May Day is a stupid stallion, but a powerful one; tractors shy away from him."

"Infection, Jean, Valjean, and May Day," I summed it up. "A wonderful combination. Any combination of those in tierce would pullover a million francs."

"But if they notice that you're playing that combination in the cafe, they'll call emergency medical assistance and cart you off to a psychiatric nursing home."

We all three laughed for a long time. Boris Borisovich took us to dinner in an inexpensive Chinese restaurant.

*   *   *

Eduard Ivanovich didn't surface the whole next week. But Boris Borisovich would call from time to time and express an interest in what shape Alyosha was in.

"Alyosha's the only one," Zhenya answered him.

I was the one who, in my turn, insisted that we needed to play the tierce, and only my foursome: Alyosha, Infection, Archibald and Gloria.

Anyway, there was nothing original about my proposal. It was in complete agreement with the press's predictions. The press, naturally, added Swensen and Alissa.

On Saturday, though, I opened *L'Humanité* and gasped:

"Zhenya, just look at this—they've gone insane at *L'Humanité*. Guess who they picked as winners of the Prix de France—Alyosha, Gloria, Infection. . . ."

"Well, so what?"

"Keep listening! . . . Jean, Valjean and May Day!"

"So who told you that French Communists were noted for their brains?" Zhenya blurted out.

Then we stopped talking at the same time and looked askance at the walls.

Anyway, other things were bothering us that day. Our phone was silent; they weren't answering the phone in the embassy. We didn't know if they were going to give us any money for wagering or how much.

On Sunday, by around twelve noon, we realized the embassy was ignoring us. Apparently Boris Borisovich had received corresponding instructions from Moscow. "That has its own logic, too," I thought bitterly. "After all, we didn't propose anything interesting. . . ."

We had a hundred francs apiece left. I managed to run by the cafe and bet twenty francs' worth on my favorite four horses in tierce, not in order, and we set off for Vincennes.

Getting off the bus, we walked through the woods a bit. The sun was shining like springtime; a warm breeze was blowing. There wasn't a trace of any natural disaster in the air at all.

We spotted Alyosha at the preliminary warm-ups. He was invincible.

I rushed to the booth as soon as the participants for the Prix de France started to pass in review, I had to shove my way into the general line with my eighty francs, and the lines at the Vincennes Racetrack when there's a grand prix are in no way inferior to the ones in Moscow.

Finally I put my eight tickets down on Alyosha. My last chance, but a real one. Sufficient to buy some stuff for Moscow.

I went up into the grandstands, and didn't recognize the racetrack field when I saw it. There were some people with red banners running around the track. At the turn, where they should have been exercising the trotters, a mob was forming. The thin line of policemen was having trouble restraining them.

"What's going on?" I asked Zhenya.

"A demonstration by the Communist Trade Unions, the CTU," Zhenya growled. "The creeps, they're wrecking the races."

Reporters with cameras were circling the crowd. A helicopter, which also probably belonged to the press, was thundering low over the field.

"They'll spook all the horses like that!" the people next to us raged.

"Everyone has the right to demonstrate and strike," another group answered them.

A rank of guys with long hair was marching along the grandstands. They were carrying huge placards with slogans: "A Thirty-Hour Work Day for Grooms!"; "Legalize the Rights of Temporary Workers!"; "Bourgeois Money Is Not for Horses —But for Children's Day Care Centers!"

"Look what they're doing!" Zhenya was aghast.

Several of the harnesses were still trying to continue warming up on the back stretch, but the demonstrators shoved their signs into the horses' muzzles, and the trotters were rearing up. . . .

A group of potbellied men came down out of the grandstands to the field and dashed into the mass of demonstrators.

The grandstands whistled their contempt.

Only after half an hour did the police manage to quiet the demonstrators down and clean off the track.

I was so nervous I didn't even find the sun pleasant any more.

Now the horses wanted nothing to do with lining up. There was always one jostling and pushing the one next to him.

They barely managed to get off. Half the horses got off to a bad start—the jockeys were throwing their weight back, pulling the reins to the limit to keep their horses from breaking into a gallop. Infection and Gloria went out in front with a gap. Alyosha was running behind the pack; his jockey was almost lying on his back, while Alyosha still fooled around with his gait. Swensen broke into a gallop in the turn. Infection and Gloria tore away by about fifty meters. But Alyosha fixed his gait and walked by the rest of the group.

"Come on, Alyosha," whispered Zhenya. "It ain't over yet!" At the final turn, there, where half an hour ago the demonstration had been raging, Gloria suddenly got up and went into a fatal gallop. But having broken into a gallop, she made Alyosha brake sharply.

Infection was already out of reach. Three harnesses were trotting briskly along behind him. Alyosha bolted forward, passed by one harness like a shot, and flew into . . . fourth place!

The board showed the numbers: 18-2-3.

Number eighteen was Infection. And who were the nags wedged in behind him? I took a look at the program. Number two was entered as Valjean. Wearing number three—May Day.

We saw the TV evening news at eight. After the international and French stories, they showed the racetrack and, of course, started with the CTU demonstration. Then they covered the race (all its misfortunes) and noted (I quote): "The magnificent victory of the remarkable native trotter, Infection" and announced the payoff in tierce:

Tierce in order—37 thousand francs

Tierce not in order—9,500 francs.

"So where are your millions?" asked Zhenya. "Look how little they're paying."

* * *

In the morning I ran down to the kiosk and bought four Paris newspapers with the last of my money. The commentators in *Aurore* and *Parisienne Libérée* commended Infection overall and regretted Alyosha's failure. *Figaro* said that the play for the Prix de France was practically ruined by the CTU demonstration, and out of fairness, the results should have been nullified. *L'Humanité* noted with pride that its prediction for tierce was the only right one, and, needless to say, it will create an opening for dissatisfaction with the bourgeois press, but just let the workers read and subscribe as they had before to their own newspaper, which guards the interests of laborers.

"Well, what's up, you guys, going to Moscow tomorrow?" Eduard Ivanovich, with a dazzling smile, asked us in the embassy corridor. "Lucky you!"

And he darted through the door.

"Go to the cashier and get your Aeroflot tickets and the additional seventy-five francs travel allowance that you each have coming," Boris Borisovich uttered in a businesslike fashion, and as though incidentally, he added: "I hope you played the tierce? After all, you named the combination yourselves. . . ."

He squinted an eye and fixed it on the looks on our faces: "Oh, Lord! What dickheads!"

I decided to go to Tati. I wanted to buy a sweater and socks, and pantyhose and a blouse for Raika with the seventy-five francs.

Zhenya glanced nervously at his watch and declined to go with me.

"Don't Zhenya," I said, guessing his intentions, "take at least something back to Moscow!"

Zhenya started to hiss and ran to the subway.

I knew that today was a racing day at the suburban race-track at Enghien.

Zhenya came back late in the evening as full of hate as the devil. I didn't bother to ask him about anything.

Boris Borisovich called from the dormitory lobby at ten in the morning.

"Ready? Take your stuff out to my car."

He skeptically observed the way we loaded our old suit-cases from Moscow into the car.

And now we were in the car. A last tour of the streets of Paris.

"I suppose you headed for Enghien yesterday, Zhenya?" Boris Borisovich asked.

We didn't say anything.

"You're at least taking some presents for your honeys?"

I had a hard time restraining myself from telling him to go to hell. In the end, this sounded like mockery.

"You guys are a hassle," said Boris Borisovich. "You're like little children. Okay, we've still got half an hour. Let's go to the 'tent,' and I'll get you some coupons for sheepskin coats, cigarettes, whiskey, and ladies' cosmetics. Let off some steam in our store. But be quick about it."

At the cafeteria at Orly Airport, we split two bottles of champagne with Boris Borisovich, vowed eternal friendship and love, hugged and kissed each other.

The plane went through thick cloud cover. Zhenya was asleep, snoring softly, burrowed into the collar of his brand new sheepskin coat. I lazily looked through the headlines of the day's French newspapers. My thoughts had already touched down in Moscow. I was looking forward to calling Raika, to how she'd come tearing along, how I'd hand her the perfume, the blouse, the pantyhose, how. . . .

A short note in *L'Humanité* under the headline "Routine Harassment" attracted my attention:

"On Monday afternoon in the Café Rotonde," said *L'Humanité,* "agents of the DST (French counterintelligence) arrested two Communist workers from the Renault factory, who were peaceably drinking beer with a fellow worker from the Soviet Embassy, diplomat E. I. Dicksky. The sum of three million seven hundred thousand francs was discovered in the Soviet diplomat's briefcase. Under different circumstances, the DST would have taken the opportunity to charge the Soviet government with bribing the French Communist Party, but complications with the witnesses' testimony have now arisen. Witnesses have maintained that it wasn't the Soviet diplomat who gave the small suitcase to the French workers, but, they say, the French workers who handed the briefcase with the astronomical sum to E. I. Dicksky. The absurdity of similar statements forced the DST agents to apologize to the Soviet diplomat and return the briefcase with the embassy's money to him. Even the right-wing press, fond of this kind of sensation, has thrown this red herring back. However, this incident shows that there are still people in the ranks of the French Special Services capable of anti-Soviet action. . . ."

I mentally divided that sum by a hundred. . . .

INSTEAD OF A EPILOGUE

THE WAN YELLOW LIGHT OF THE ELECTRIC LAMPS, THE FLOOR strewn with torn programs and losing cardboard tickets, and a couple of people standing around the booth windows. The races are over, and we're waiting for our payoffs on the single for the last race. For some reason, you always have to wait a long time for the last payoff. Zhenya reeled in a fiver on Epilogue, who was pulling Anton, but they came in neck-and-neck with Give the Finger. The results of the photofinish still haven't been announced. And Epilogue and Give the Finger are both pretty dark horses. The crowd, having basically played the favorites—Hope and Berenday—from the start, have gone home anyway.

"Hey, Frenchman, did you go with Epilogue?" Yurochka the Gas Man is asking me.

I shake my head, no.

"I knew Anton would come in all alone," says Yurochka the Gas Man.

He's lying, of course. If he'd known, he'd have told me beforehand. By the way, it's been a long time since they called me the Frenchman at the racetrack; my old name—the Teacher—has come back. Only Yurochka, apparently, still remembers the times when, after France, the Professional and I rolled high and even sewed the races up. Yeah, we had money then, saved up in the savings bank, plus we caught several big doubles. Alas, all things come to end. I still have my threadbare sheepskin coat as a memento of Paris, but Zhenya sold his for a hundred rubles right here at the race-track when we really started going bankrupt and got into debt.

All things pass. All things change. And the Professional isn't the same handsome man—he's gone flabby and bald; and Yurochka the Gas Man looks every bit of fifty, and his face is pale, edematic, like the old men's—my neighbors from when I was in the hospital not long ago, where that same kind of dim yellow light was burning in the hallway as here, in the betting hall.

Sometimes I ask myself a question: was France really mine? She vanished so precipitously, and she was forgotten immediately. True, roughly a month after our return, Georgi Ivanovich called me and said that he was terribly busy, but, of course, we ought to get together, that our "business" with the OKhBSS still wasn't finished, but as long as he was with the Agencies, we didn't have anything to worry about, but we should understand. . . . We understood what the colonel was hinting at. For this reason, we told all our friends and acquaintances we were sent to Paris on assignment to improve our proficiency, to master the language. Well, we ran off to the racetrack on the sly a couple of times. At first our friends would ask about the Paris stores, about the Vincennes Racetrack, and then they stopped asking, and somehow we even got bored telling our stories. It came, and it went. And the comrade colonel didn't surface anymore.

About ten years have gone by since then. Coryphaeus and the Bakunian died. The Dandy quit the races; they threw Lard Lardych in jail; Ilyusha the Vegetable Man emigrated to America, and there, rumor has it, he opened a Russian restau-

rant in Brighton Beach. Raika and I kept splitting up and getting back together.

Only at night, and then not often, do I dream of the lilac
Parisian streets, the "Demonic Art" exhibit in the Louvre's
Antiquities, and Alyosha's hellish send, but Alyosha somehow always finishes in the Moscow Racetrack, and I don't
make it in time to bet on him. And with that, I wake up.

The excitement of those days seems funny to me now. It
would have been good to go to the Russian bookstores in
Paris. You know, I never glanced into any of them, not even
once. There wasn't time. And then there was big trouble—
we'd squandered a pile of public money! By the way, that
French money isn't what it used to be; it's been devaluated
twice. The fact is, there's raging inflation in those damned
capitalist countries. . . . And they've probably built a second
column at the entrance to The Races Restaurant on the money
I've parted with at the Moscow Racetrack these past ten years.

And in general, boys, I've noticed one thing: Health is
more important!

"Hey, Teacher!" Zhenya's pestering me, "come and get
your nine rubles."

Well, thank God, they've got the winnings.

Oh, yeah, I forgot to tell you the most important thing:
after the photofinish, the panel of judges recognized Shiesh-
with-Butter instead of Epilogue as the winner! I played him,
in spite of the Professional's opinion, with two tickets. I've
won nine rubles. That's four and a half to the ticket. Not bad.
Zhenya and I have every right to stop in at the carryout and
order pelmeni and a bottle of "ink."

Moscow—Saint-Blaise—Paris
1976-1981